PRAISE FOR PRIS

"Oliveras has perfected the second chance romance trope with Alejandro and Anamaría. Their anguish is so real that the book should come with tissues. The Key West setting is vibrant, adding a blessed touch of armchair travel to the current global circumstances. Wonderfully soapy, this is a romance to read in one sitting. A stunning romance of first love found again."

—*Kirkus Reviews* (starred review), *Anchored Hearts*

"The Florida island setting is only part of the appeal of this character-driven, second-chance romance between smart and badass Anamaría and sexy and artistic Alejandro as they slowly realize that successful relationships have room for both partners' professions and dreams. Another draw: Oliveras's portrayal of family and social media ties are reminiscent of Alisha Rai's romances."

—*Booklist* (starred review), *Anchored Hearts*

"A bighearted, beautiful book about first love, second chances, and finding one's place in the world. Oliveras writes with a rare warmth that not only brings her characters to life but also lets her readers sink into the gorgeous Key West sunrises she so lovingly describes. An exceptional getaway of a book!"

—Emily Henry, *New York Times* bestselling author of *Beach Read*

"Oliveras has been steadily growing her presence as a romance author, one with a knack for heartwarming family ensembles and a cozy sense of home. But *Island Affair* is her strongest work yet, perfectly calibrating its inviting family scenes with a sweet, heart-melting romance."

—*Entertainment Weekly*

"I finished *Island Affair* with a big smile on my face. I can't decide what I adored more: Luis and Sara's love story; their relationships with their complicated and difficult and loving families; or the setting of Key West, which sounded so beautiful I wanted to jump on a plane. I can't wait to read more by Priscilla Oliveras!"

—Jasmine Guillory, *New York Times* bestselling author

"Oliveras's outstanding debut tangles romance into family life . . . The realistic, multifaceted characters have interesting nuances, and Oliveras never stoops to employing contrived misunderstandings, instead creating real obstacles with meaning and depth. Moving familial relationships and splashes of Puerto Rican culture round out this splendid contemporary and bode well for the future of the series."

—*Publishers Weekly* (starred review), *His Perfect Partner*

"Warm, sweet, and spicy in just the right amounts . . . A delicious read!"

—Kristan Higgins, *New York Times* bestselling author, *His Perfect Partner*

"Oliveras tops her excellent debut, *His Perfect Partner*, with this revelatory, realistic second romance set among the Puerto Rican community in contemporary Chicago . . . [Her] integration of cultural and class differences, familial expectations, and career objectives into the couple's romantic decision-making immeasurably enriches a moving plot about good people making difficult choices."

—*Publishers Weekly* (starred review), *Her Perfect Affair*

"Rising author Oliveras continues her excellent contemporary Matched to Perfection series featuring three Latina sisters, following the acclaimed *His Perfect Partner* (2017) . . . Oliveras infuses warmth, intelligence, and emotion into this refreshing read."

—*Booklist* (starred review), *Her Perfect Affair*

"The word I use the most often for Ms. Oliveras's writing is *warm*. I feel comfortable in whatever world she's created for me, and I usually love spending time with her people. You know those houses you walk into and there is something delicious-smelling in the kitchen, and you are welcomed with hugs and told to take your shoes off and within seconds you completely belong? That's Ms. Oliveras's writing . . . If you're a fan of second chances, I cannot recommend this enough. Warning, though, the descriptions of the warm breezes of the Florida Keys may just have you booking a flight!"

—All About Romance, *Island Affair*

"Delightful romance author Priscilla Oliveras offers an amuse-bouche of a holiday treat with this novella . . . Oliveras's own love for her family and passion for the great American pastime shines through as bright as a Christmas light."

—*Entertainment Weekly*, *Holiday Home Run*

"Priscilla Oliveras comes through with a sweet novella filled with charm and spirit, *Holiday Home Run*. *Holiday Home Run* gives us a beautiful peek into the vibrant lives of Puerto Ricans celebrating the holiday season, a memorably strong and smart heroine, and a hero who is charming and sexy."

—All About Romance, *Holiday Home Run*

"Such a sweet treat to get you in the upcoming holiday mood. Author Priscilla Oliveras has a hit to add to your Christmas reading list this year."

—*Mid-life Goddess Books*, *Holiday Home Run*

"Oliveras's marvelous third Matched to Perfection contemporary (after *Her Perfect Affair*) tackles domestic violence and policing in Chicago's Puerto Rican community with superb nuance . . . Oliveras's tangled, topical conflicts between multidimensional characters blend with lovingly portrayed family life and an intricate, realistic plot, enmeshing the reader in her created world."

—*Publishers Weekly* (starred review), *Their Perfect Melody*

"Readers will feel utterly carried away . . . Whether you're well versed in Puerto Rican culture or completely new to it, Oliveras welcomes readers into a space that feels both familiar and new and exciting . . . A romantic, diverting melody."

—*Entertainment Weekly*, *Their Perfect Melody*

"Sexy, sassy, and overflowing with music, complex emotions, and family-loving Latinx American and Puerto Rican characters, this romance is a compelling, often joyful read and perfectly wraps up the Perfection trilogy."

—*Library Journal*, *Their Perfect Melody*

KISS ME,
CATALINA

OTHER TITLES BY PRISCILLA OLIVERAS

Queens of Mariachi series

West Side Love Story

Keys to Love series

Island Affair
Anchored Hearts

Matched to Perfection series

His Perfect Partner
Her Perfect Affair
Their Perfect Melody

Paradise Key series

Resort to Love

Novella

Holiday Home Run, digital only

Anthologies

Summer in the City, "Lights Out"
A Season to Celebrate, "Holiday Home Run"
Amor Actually, "Meet Me Under the Mistletoe"

KISS ME, CATALINA

PRISCILLA OLIVERAS

Montlake

Published by Montlake, Seattle

www.apub.com

Amazon, the Amazon logo, and Montlake are trademarks of Amazon.com, Inc., or its affiliates.

ISBN-13: 9781542034425 (paperback)
ISBN-13: 9781542034432 (digital)

Cover design by Faceout Studio, Jeff Miller
Cover illustration by Lucia Picerno
Cover images: © Ashas0612 / Shutterstock; © Brumarina / Shutterstock; © Cienpies Design / Alamy

Printed in the United States of America

For those fierce mujeres pushing the envelope,
shattering the glass ceiling,
breaking barriers, and paving the way.
Sí se puede, mis amigas.

Chapter One

This was *huge*!

Like, cue the trumpet section in her mariachi band and let out a celebratory grito.

Call her mamá to share that all the candle lighting at the Basilica had finally paid off.

Buy the bar a round of margaritas because this chica had finally done it!

Hot damn!

Satisfaction swelled in Catalina Capuleta's chest like churro dough plopped into a pan of hot oil. Only this satisfaction was *much* sweeter than the cinnamon sugar sprinkled over the delectable pastry.

Her heart racing, Cat stared down at the contract George Garcia, an executive producer with Padua Records—sí, *the* Padua Records— had presented her with a week ago.

She had read over it countless times since then. Discussed the offer with her parents and sisters, hyperaware of a barely-there undercurrent of hesitation no one in her familia dared to mention. To be safe, she had asked Señor Porras, the aging lawyer who offered free guidance for parishioners, to review the document. The old man hadn't found anything worrisome in the contract, and even though he'd recommended she seek out an entertainment lawyer for confirmation, she'd decided his thumbs-up would have to be good enough.

The clock was ticking here. Padua couldn't—wouldn't—wait for her if she took too long.

Eyes on the printed words—words that would effectively change her life—she twirled the well-known producer's fancy pen through her fingers like a mini baton. The teen inside her, the one who'd sung her heart out into her round brush while standing on the double bed she shared with one of her sisters, screamed with excitement.

Flipping through the multiple pages, Cat pretended to scan the document riddled with legalese one last time. A stall tactic to give the teenager she'd once been, filled with dreams and raw talent, a few seconds for a celebratory, hip-shimmying cumbia before shushing her and getting back to business.

She had to keep her cool. Act like the consummate professional she prided herself on being. This was a major move. One that required her to bring her A game. All week she'd been channeling her older sister, aiming for Mariana's calm focus instead of her own typical rash, storm-the-castle-and-pummel-the-patriarchal-system-that-had-long-ruled-the-mariachi-industry behavior.

"Is there . . . something else you'd care to discuss?" the executive producer asked. "I recognize that this is a big decision for you. Coming on tour to write new music for Patricio's next album means leaving Mariachi Las Nubes. After having just won the Battle of the Mariachi Bands with your sisters, I'm betting you ladies are in high demand now. You pulled off quite a feat."

Cat didn't bother curbing her self-satisfied smirk at George's praise. Pride for her sisters fed her confidence. The eight of them, who together comprised Mariachi Las Nubes, had worked hard, put in the long hours of rehearsal, and ultimately overcome the odds and naysayers, kicking ass on their way to being crowned the first all-female Battle of the Mariachi Bands champions.

"Gracias. You're right. We definitely pulled off a feat," she answered, her chin jutting at a haughty angle. "Though I never doubted we would."

"Pfft." The sarcastic huff came from the man lazily sprawled in the dining chair next to George.

The same man Cat was trying hard to ignore, determined not to let herself be intimidated by the internationally acclaimed mariachi singer, whose stellar career she idolized.

The same opinionated, too-sexy-for-his-or-Cat's-own-good heart-throb she had spent a sizable chunk of the Battle rehearsals butting heads with.

"Patricio, por favor," George grumbled under his breath.

Patricio Galán gave no indication that he heard or cared about his record producer's plea.

Her interest piqued, Cat watched the silent interplay between the middle-aged man who occupied a place of authority within the singer's record label and the multi-Grammy-winning megastar who also happened to be the only son of mariachi royalty.

Despite their differing personalities—one sharp-minded while gentle with encouragement, the other sharp-tongued and demanding—the two men had worked well as band mentors during Battle rehearsals. But today, and when she had met with them a week ago, here at Patricio Galán's rental home in San Antonio, Cat sensed an undercurrent of . . . displeasure? Frustration?

It wasn't necessarily directed at her, yet the air of discord tinted her euphoria. Had the tiny hairs on the back of her neck rising with suspicion over what might be going on behind the scenes. Most importantly, how it might somehow spill over onto her.

George cleared his throat and pointedly shifted in his seat to face Cat. Stretching forward, he splayed a hand on the table in front of the contract. "This affects everyone in Mariachi Las Nubes. Your entire familia, really. So, it's understandable if you or they have questions. If there's something you need clarified before signing."

"Sí, I'd like—"

"*I'd* like to have this finalized sooner rather than later. Definitely before my tour kicks off after our concert here in San Antonio in two weeks." A bored expression blanketing his angular features, Galán crossed his arms and leaned back in his chair. His broad shoulders and tall frame dwarfed the high-backed seat with intricately carved wood edges and bone-colored upholstery.

The insolent oaf didn't even bother to apologize for interrupting her. Ha, he probably didn't know how to apologize. More used to snapping his fingers and having his minions jump up, ready to do his bidding.

Bueno, she was not his minion.

If he hadn't figured that out already, a reckoning was headed his way.

"Obviously, it only makes sense to have everything decided by then," she agreed.

"At least we're on the same—"

"But I won't be rushed into signing something that impacts my career. No matter who's involved." Mimicking his arms-crossed stance, she didn't bother hiding the challenge in her equally rude interruption. Two could play this chess game.

A sardonic brow arched. His chin tucked and he shot her that provocative "oh, you know you want this" stare that graced the cover of one of his many platinum albums.

Silencio, she ordered the fangirl swooning in her heart.

She had to approach this conversation as if they were industry peers. That meant her days of fangirling when it came to Patricio Galán were behind her.

So, too, were her days of managing her fledgling career along with gigs, promos, and musical direction for Mariachi Las Nubes. Going on tour with Galán meant her sisters would have to pick up the slack her absence created within the band. Plus, she wouldn't be around to teach music classes at her familia's community center on the west side. Not for the next few months anyway. Longer if things went as well as she hoped.

This contract with Padua Records and Patricio Galán put her on the fast track. The idea both intimidated and energized her.

She'd die biting her lips closed before admitting to the first emotion. And use the second as fuel in her bid to—as Beyoncé suggested—run the world.

"The last thing we want is for you to feel pressured or rushed, Cat." George slid Patricio a side-eyed warning.

Once again, suspicion tiptoed across Cat's shoulders in a goose bump–inducing trail.

The arrogant megastar ignored his producer. Instead, Galán's penetrating stare remained glued on her. "You *are* aware that this is a huge opportunity for you, Catalina."

A statement, not a question.

An impassive mask skimmed the angles of Galán's straight nose, square jaw, and sharp cheekbones, but the piercing gleam in his black-coffee eyes snared her with its challenge.

Her stomach muscles clenched, squelching the nervous jitters intent on knocking her off balance.

Feigning nonchalance, she relaxed against her cushioned chair back. The plush leather creaked in protest, as if calling bullshit on her tough-girl charade. The spurt of uncertainty inside her threatened to morph into a fire hose, and she fought to tamp it down.

She knew what this was: the age-old fear of not being good enough that plagued many in their rejection-filled industry. Typically, she had no trouble silencing self-doubt.

But from the moment she had parked her used sedan, with its leaky moonroof and temperamental AC, in front of the posh residence Padua had rented for Galán during his stay through the Battle and his concert, squelching her awe had proven more difficult than normal. How could it not, when faced with the air of wealth and stature that permeated every room in the place—a mansion that probably cost more than the entire Casa Capuleta property that housed her familia's community center; the two floors of apartments above it, where her parents and younger sisters lived; and the large courtyard in the back.

Sitting at this ostentatious dining set, which boasted thick glass atop oversize claw feet ornately carved and brushed with a gold patina, she faced two of the biggest names in the mariachi industry. As if that wasn't nerve-racking enough, the insidious voice from her childhood, the one that harped in her head that she wasn't enough, had managed to grab a bullhorn to blast its deflating message at an earsplitting volume.

Rather than cower, Cat met Galán's challenging stare and channeled the negative energy churning through her into fuel, feeding her desire to prove everyone who had ever doubted her, or any female mariachi, wrong.

"This is an opportunity most singer-songwriters would grab with both hands," Galán pressed when she didn't respond to his earlier taunt. "Without hesitation."

"It's safe to say that I am not like *most* singer-songwriters. If I was, I doubt we'd be having this conversation. Nor would Padua be offering me this contract."

"Confidence. Arrogance. There's a fine line between the two."

"I'm walking that line along with one of the best," she countered, tipping her head toward him.

"Much of this arrogance is hard-earned."

"And the rest?"

George sputter-laughed, quickly turning it into a cough he covered with a fist. His gold wedding ring winked under the chandelier's light, as if it, too, found Cat's cheeky retort humorous.

Again Galán arched a dark brow in that smoldering expression he had mastered. Those mesmerizing bedroom eyes, combined with his angular jaw and full lips, sun-kissed bronze skin and wavy black hair itching to be finger-combed, had been the impetus for so many of her adolescent and young-adult dreams. Tingles of awareness quickened her pulse. Cat ignored them, eyeing him expectantly.

"Lucky gene pool," he finally answered. "Yours?"

"Blood, sweat, and tears. And a long-lasting red lip stain."

A corner of Galán's full mouth twitched with amusement. "Lip stain, huh? Who knew it was the key to greatness."

Ay, the infuriating man and his propensity for toying with her.

It spoke of his Texas-wide ego. Backed up by his array of awards, number-one hits, packed stadiums, and countless endorsements.

But as hardheaded as he might be, he'd been a fair—if pushy— mentor to her and her sisters during the competition. Working with him, learning from him . . . she had hoped doing well in the Battle would get her boot in the door she'd been banging her head against for years now. But actually getting her songs on Patricio Galán's next album would kick the freaking door down.

And yet she knew—to the marrow of her bones, she *knew*—if she didn't stand up to him, go toe to toe without flinching, he wouldn't respect her.

Worse, she wouldn't respect herself.

Tapping a finger on the edge of the contract sandwiched between them, Cat sat up straight. "Look, I'm not going to bullshit you. Either of you."

She looked from Galán to George, then back to the famed singer. Even though the record producer had wielded the contract on behalf of Padua, something told her that Galán had been the one to decide whether the document had been typed with her name or someone else's.

He'd been the one to first approach her about writing songs for his next album, initially asking for "No Me Olvides," the angsty, don't-for- get-me love song she had written for the competition.

A request she had turned down. Partly out of spite after his bald claim that her song would benefit from a few tweaks he had in mind. And partly because she'd been savvy enough to recognize a potential opening to something bigger. If he wanted one song, why not more?

Gracias a Dios her hunch had paid off.

"Call me arrogant or . . . carajo, even bitchy." She swiped a hand in the air as if swatting at a bothersome fly. "That word gets thrown out far too often when a strong woman mariachi pushes back against patriarchal thinking. My own sisters teasingly call me the familia shrew because I refuse to pander to foolish machismo. I do whatever it takes to ensure Las Nubes is shown the respect we deserve. And while they might complain because I extend our rehearsals when we don't have a song, transition, or the choreography exactly right, my sisters understand why. Because I want us to be the best. *I* want to be the best."

Long-held dreams and desires and fears coalesced inside Cat like turbulent tornado winds, forcing the words from her in a rush of uncensored truth. Her heart pounding madly in her chest, she slid the contract closer, swiftly thumbed to the last page, then signed her name with a scrawling flourish and a triumphant grin.

"I want this. I've worked my ass off for this. You better believe I'll give it my all. But I also expect anyone partnering with me to do the same. That blood, sweat, and tears I mentioned earlier will go into every note, every lyric I write. They have to. Because I want my work to resonate. To move people. To stand the test of time. And now that I'm working with you—no, now that *you're* working with *me*—I expect the same in return." She waggled the fancy pen at Galán, maintaining their game-of-chicken stare. "Sí, yo lo sé—actually, not just me . . . *All* of us know this is a major career boost for me. But I come to this table confident that having my musical talent and skills contributing to your album makes you equally as lucky."

George's bushy eyebrows rose with obvious surprise at her bold claim.

In an instant, the tornado wind that had whipped Cat into a frenzy suddenly died down, leaving her spent and on edge. Slightly dazed by how unceremoniously she had signed the contract. Worse, had she really just told El Príncipe . . . mariachi royalty . . . that he'd be lucky to work with her?

The potential ramifications of her brash actions settled over her like a prickly wool blanket. Itchy and uncomfortable.

If she had overstepped, Galán wouldn't hesitate to call her on it. She'd lost track of the number of times he'd done exactly that during the Battle. To her annoyance, more often than not with good cause.

Galán's bland poker face gave nothing away.

Too late, Cat's older sister's often-issued warning whispered in her ear: *Think before blasting a verbal zinger you can't rescind.*

A weighty silence filled the room, broken only by the insistent thrum of Galán's fingers on the glass table. Lips pressed in a thin line, eyes narrowed, he studied her.

Cat bit her tongue to keep from speaking first. She had said enough already.

"Great!" George clapped his hands, punctuating his announcement. Then, an overly animated grin widening his mouth, he reached for the signed document. "Sounds to me like this will be a match made in heaven."

"Maybe," Galán murmured. "Be prepared, Catalina. I have high standards of my own. This is my album. I call the shots."

Yes, but if she had correctly read the subtext of their earlier conversations and Padua's thinly veiled explanation for bringing her on board, he'd been experiencing a bit of a writing slump.

George cleared his throat and shot Galán a reproachful frown. "Teamwork, remember."

Galán released a moody sigh but didn't argue with his producer.

A giddy exhilaration bubbled up inside Cat.

Well, well, well. Looked like she was right. The great Patricio Galán needed her as much as she needed him.

Chapter Two

"This is definitely cause for celebration!"

George's exuberant announcement had Patricio pausing midpour, barely a finger of his favorite añejo tequila filling his tulip-shaped copita. Cutting a glance over his shoulder, he eyed the man who had been more like an older brother than a record executive since Patricio had signed his first contract with Padua Records as a teen.

Their personal relationship made the ruse Patricio had put into play prick his conscience like a spike from the blue agave succulents grown at the craft tequila distillery he'd recently invested in.

"Who says I'm celebrating?" he countered.

More like girding his loins for the farce he embarked upon. By necessity.

"I like her."

The unwanted announcement came from his assistant, Alberto, who sauntered in from the grand hall and entry after seeing Catalina Capuleta out.

Not that the headstrong woman needed an escort.

Madre de Dios, she was fire and brimstone and pure determination. Her passion reminded Patricio of a different time in his life. Back when the tight shackles of expectation hadn't pinched and strangled . . .

Ay, enough! Stubbornly he stomped out the useless thoughts.

Stressing over them did nothing to assuage his current predicament. The same one he initially had sought to get himself out of with Catalina's unknowing help. Only, now that she had signed the damn contract, he prayed the woman wouldn't exacerbate his secret problem. Or, worse, figure out his charade.

The potential threat of his plan coming back to bite him in the ass was the reason behind his current "it's five o'clock somewhere" mentality on a Monday at one in the afternoon.

Not bothering to respond to either of the men, Patricio finished pouring two fingers of the limited-release tequila into the copita, his mind replaying the last few moments of their meeting.

After dropping a cheeky "See you at rehearsal," her cherry-red lips quirked in a satisfied smirk he found annoying and tempting as hell—which annoyed him all over again—Catalina had spun away. The waves of her long, satiny hair danced across her shoulder blades, the tips brushing her lower back like a lover's caress. A tight black sweater hugged her petite figure, and slim-fitting dress slacks drew an appreciative eye to her delectable curves. Her vibe was chic and professional and far too enticing for his peace of mind.

Alberto's suit jacket had flapped in the wind as he hurried to catch up with Catalina and usher her to the front door. She never broke stride. Her stilettos tap-tap-tapped down the dusky rust-colored tile with purpose. A woman on a mission. Intent on conquering an industry that had been less than fair to most women, even those with her level of talent and skill.

Under different circumstances, Patricio would champion her goal. Do what he could to assist with her trailblazing. Growing up in the industry under the larger-than-life shadow of his father, a man who believed his nickname, El Rey del Mariachi, warranted royalty treatment and status, Patricio had been inspired by and lucky enough to collaborate with numerous female mariachis who hadn't been given their due because of antiquated patriarchal traditions. The younger generations were pushing back, making inroads. But they needed others in the industry to stand with them.

And he planned to do that for Catalina. Only, not in the way she and George had anticipated.

"Catalina Capuleta is exactly what you need," Alberto added. "Maybe *she* can shake some sense into you, ha, jefe?"

Patricio rolled his eyes at Alberto's subtext-riddled jab and shameless needling by referring to him as "boss." A tongue-in-cheek moniker at best. Over their nearly two decades together, Alberto's role had gone from the chaperone of a gangly fifteen-year-old to, officially, executive assistant. Unofficially, the voice of reason and counsel—albeit one who often suffered from a severe case of selective listening that had gotten worse over the years. The old man had no qualms about breaking out his raised-brow disapproval.

Like now. The viejo was still peeved by Patricio's decision to pursue his current course, despite the number of times Alberto had tried to "talk some sense into" him. To no avail.

The only potential fly in his cajeta—a fly Patricio was determined to shoo away from his favorite goat milk and sugar dessert—was pint-size Catalina Capuleta with her rapier-sharp tongue and bulldozer personality. Keeping her in the dark might not be as easy as he'd thought.

Arms crossed over his burly chest and a-few-enchiladas-too-many, expanding paunch, Alberto leaned a shoulder against the archway. His parental glare telegraphed his uncanny ability to read Patricio's thoughts.

"I agree. Having Catalina on board is a real coup." George swiped the drink Patricio had just finished pouring for himself. The wise guy raised the copita to his face and breathed in the rich scent of the caramel-tinted añejo. "Good stuff, güey."

"I only invest in the best."

George paused before taking a sip, his crafty eyes glinting with zeal. "Same with me. Which is why I'm betting on Catalina Capuleta to pull you out of this slump or whatever it is you're not calling it. She's smart, wickedly talented, and not afraid to speak her mind."

"Eso es lo que me preocupa," Patricio grumbled under his breath.

"What worries you?" George asked, catching Patricio's complaint with his keen hearing, lauded for discovering diamonds in the rough from only a short music clip and grooming and polishing them to star status.

"Is it the fact that she's smart enough to know her worth?" George continued. "Talented enough to run circles around any of the other songwriters we considered? Or that she's feisty enough to call your bluff like she did today? *And* during the Battle."

Patricio scowled and grabbed a fresh copita from the wrought-iron rack mounted on the wall above the left side of the fully stocked bar. "Maybe I was wrong to suggest her. She's too wet behind the ears."

In the inkblot-shaped mirror hanging beside the rack, he caught Alberto's slow shake of his head. Patricio's gut clenched with unease. Worse than the old man's nagging was the idea of disappointing him. The one person Patricio could count on to always have his back, no matter what.

"Maybe we moved too quickly. Going on tour is stressful enough without bringing along a first-timer," he complained. "I need to write in my off time. Not babysit."

"I call bullshit," George fired back.

"Meaning?"

"Meaning there have been plenty of first-timers on the tour before. You're going to have to come up with a better excuse. Especially since working with her was your idea in the first place." George raised his copita to point at Patricio, his round face creased with a mix of worry and stress, proof of his difficult rock-and-a-hard-place position between brotherhood and business. "I can't hold off the other executives much longer, güey. You've vetoed every other person we suggested. All of them. Pero you haven't produced anything on your own. For months now."

Frustration and a sensation he refused to acknowledge as fear clawed Patricio's chest, as if the eagle perched in the center of the Mexican flag that was tattooed over his heart had bared its talons. "I've been writing," he hedged.

"Show me," George demanded.

Patricio's jaw muscles tightened as he bit down on a curse.

"C'mon, let me hear it."

"Nothing's ready to—"

"Bullshit," George repeated. He took a swig of the añejo, sucking in a sharp breath as the barrel-aged alcohol burned a path down his throat.

"So we bump the release date a bit," Patricio pushed back. "No big deal."

"What?"

"¿Qué?"

George's and Alberto's twin outbursts hit Patricio in a unified barrage. One man pushed away from the wall; the other flinched on the sofa like he'd been poked with a hot branding iron. Both gaped at him, slack-jawed and bug-eyed over Patricio's unacceptable answer to the problem.

"You have *never* delayed an album, Patricio." George's confused glance skittered from Patricio to Alberto, who still loomed in the archway. Only now the old man stood with his hands stuffed in his suit pants' pockets, mouth turned down in a serious frown.

"¿Qué te pasa?" George asked.

What was wrong with him? If that wasn't the damn question of the hour. The past year. Longer, if Patricio were being truthful. But he wasn't being truthful. Not to anyone but Alberto, and even the viejo didn't know how screwed up Patricio felt inside.

For a while now, discontent had been chipping away at the facade he showed the world. The one hiding his struggle with the personality fans had come to know, the performer his father expected him to be, and his own dreams.

But George Garcia the record executive didn't want to hear about his star's existential crisis. Hell, Patricio didn't want to hear about it. Refused to talk about it and risk breathing life into the maldita morass of confusion messing with his head. And now there was the added risk of Catalina figuring out how bad things really were.

Irritated, he strode to the bay window overlooking the front of the rental property. A circular brick-and-concrete driveway and parking slab cut a swath through the lush grass, flowering bushes, and shaped hedges. The house and grounds were majestic and ostentatious. Exactly what his father would have expected. Patricio didn't need a ten-thousand-square-foot mansion with six bedrooms and an equal number of full baths for him and Alberto during their two-month stay in San Antonio. But the place came with a soundproof music room in the left wing. Complete with a piano, keyboard, and recording system that Padua Records had assumed Patricio would put to good use.

Ha! He'd spent more time in the saltwater pool and Jacuzzi out back. Staring up at the night sky. Thinking.

Brooding, as Alberto preferred to call it. A facetious remark Patricio chose to ignore.

Behind him, a phone vibrated. A welcome interruption.

"Ching—" George cut off his grumbled curse at the same time the vibrating stopped.

Patricio assumed his good friend—and boss—had declined the call, which had probably been from another executive at Padua. Checking in. Again. Stressed about what was wrong with El Príncipe. Hell-bent on keeping the problem out of the news and off social media.

At least they all agreed on that point.

Outside, a stiff late-April breeze shuddered through a towering live oak. Brownish-yellow leaves, decaying after winter's chill, clung to the tree or floated toward the ground. Much like him, clinging to the belief that he could resolve this mental block on his own. Small green buds dotted the tree's gnarly branches, getting ready to bloom and flourish.

Much like Catalina Capuleta, anxious to burst onto a larger concert stage in all her glory.

The woman certainly knew how to own the stage. She was magnificent. Unfiltered and real. Pure, raw talent that intrigued him in a way little else had lately.

"Look, I can't keep dodging their calls," George said, exasperation weighing his words. "Whatever's going on, if you won't level with me, then, madre de Dios, I hope like hell that you're at least talking to Alberto."

"He's not," Alberto grumbled. The traitor.

"I'm fine."

The words sounded hollow even to Patricio's ears.

George's scoff said he heard the lie as well. "You know the deal, güey. We have concert dates set for the next two years. With a new album promised in there. Fans are clamoring for it. The industry expects it. Top brass and your contract demand it."

"And I'll deliver." Patricio pivoted to face the others, pointedly ignoring the oversize elephant squatting in the center of the room. Somehow its weight still managed to press on his chest, suffocating him. And his muse. Rendering him unable to write.

George's eyes narrowed. His bushy black brows angled together with his dubious scowl.

Ire sparked, fiery flames licking at Patricio's pride.

"When in all these years have I *not* delivered on whatever's been asked of me, George? ¡Dime!" he demanded when the executive didn't answer.

"Never."

"Exactamente. So you have nothing to worry about." Patricio took a swig of his añejo, relishing the liquid's burn, the warmth that seeped down his throat, into his chest. Grateful to feel something other than the emptiness.

"Pero dime esto . . ." George scooted to the edge of the leather sofa cushion, his tone sharpening as he repeated, "Tell me this: Which was the last album that you didn't spend months sending me random texts about at all hours of the day or night? Recordings of chords or lyrics you couldn't get out of your head, ha?"

Patricio hitched a shoulder in an irritated shrug. They all knew the answer.

"None," George supplied unnecessarily, pouring salt in the wound Patricio hid from those closest to him. "With every album since the first one, we couldn't shut you up about it. ¿Pero con este?" Rolling his lips between his teeth, he slowly shook his head. "With this one, silencio."

Because the music inside Patricio had gone silent. Ominously so.

"If you won't let Alberto or me help you, who then? I'd suggest talking to your father—"

"No!" The denial burst from Patricio like a cannonball fired across a ship's bow in warning.

He refused to show any sign of weakness to his father. With Vicente Galán there was always a risk of you becoming a punch line in one of his interviews or while he made small talk in the middle of a performance. Especially if it made him look good. Patricio hadn't gone to his father for counsel or praise or comfort—or anything parental—in years. Their relationship consisted solely of making appearances together. Another facade for the media and the record company's benefit.

The closest he had to a real father figure still hovered in the archway, one beefy hand stuffed in his pants pocket, the other now resting on his paunch. Alberto's light-brown eyes brimmed with understanding and worry.

"I figured as much," George murmured. He stared down at the glass cradled in his right hand, swirling the caramel-colored liquid. "You know that for me, this is about more than Padua. Or the damn album. I'm worried about you, güey. So, whatever it takes to get you feeling back on track, do it."

"I will," Patricio promised.

He had to. If not, this hollowness inside might consume him.

George's cell phone started vibrating again, rattling against the surface of the rustic wood-and–burnished metal coffee table. Ignoring the call, he drained his glass, then thunked it down next to his cell. He pushed to a stand as he sucked in a breath through his teeth. "Hijole, that stuff's good."

"At two hundred and fifty a bottle, it damn well better be."

They shared a chuckle, the tension between executive producer and talent dissipating under the warmth of their nearly twenty-year brotherhood. Relieved, Patricio crossed the living room, his boots scuffing on the dusky tile. They shook hands and leaned closer to bump shoulders.

"Gracias, compadre," Patricio said.

"Look, güey, you gotta help me help you." George cupped Patricio's shoulder in a tight grip, giving it a good shake. "So temper this grumpy, overbearing attitude and play nice with Cat. I'm convinced that the two of you will be brilliant together. If you don't kill each other first."

Chapter Three

As her sisters busied themselves packing up their instruments after band practice, a wave of bittersweet nostalgia washed over Cat. Warm and salty like the ocean water that tumbled onto the shore at Padre Island.

Moments ago, the strains of the last song in their set had filled the large music room at Casa Capuleta. In two weeks, they would take the stage as the opening act for Patricio Galán's concert here in San Antonio and kick off the thirteen-city, seven-week West Coast leg of his tour. The one she would join him . . . bueno, *his band*, not only the singer himself . . . on now that she had signed the contract with Padua Records.

A strange jitteriness buzzed inside her—a mix of euphoria, madre-de-Dios disbelief, and revenge-inspired satisfaction.

She had been pushing herself and encouraging her sisters for years, dreaming of an opportunity exactly like the one Padua presented. Pero—that jittery sensation hummed louder—grabbing at this chance meant letting go of something else. Stepping out of the safe, secure world her parents had provided when she and Blanca had landed on their doorstep at the ages of ten and eight, wards of the Texas Department of Family and Protective Services. It meant fully venturing into a world she had cursed as a child.

Not anymore, though.

Now she was intent on proving her sinvergüenza of a birth father wrong.

Ha! "Shameless" didn't even *begin* to describe the cabrón who had walked out on her, Blanca, and their birth mom all those years ago, intent on making it big as a mariachi—and obviously failing miserably, seeing as how she'd never heard of him again.

If Cat played her cards wisely, soon she'd be on her way to filling stadiums and amphitheaters. Bringing any of her sisters who wanted to come along with her. Providing financially for her familia.

They would see who "made it." Who understood the responsibility of caring for loved ones. Those by blood, like her younger sister, Blanca, and those by choice, like Arturo and Berta, who had officially made her a Capuleta when they adopted her and Blanca, gifting her with six, soon to be seven, more sisters. She and Blanca weren't alone anymore, thanks to the Capuletas.

The familia who believed in her. Who stood by her. The people she was determined to make proud.

Cat might be leaving Mariachi Las Nubes, her sisters, and her parents to pursue her dreams, but they would always be in her heart. Casa Capuleta would always be home. And she vowed to always take care of them.

Rather than slip her vihuela into the padded backpack she used to carry the small guitar-like instrument, she hugged it to her chest and sank back against the plastic chair, watching the others. The usual post-rehearsal chatter bounced off walls adorned with posters of famed musicians and inspirational messages in Spanish and English.

Off to one side, the three teens had gathered in a circle as Claudia shared something on her cell phone. At sixteen, she was the oldest of the "next generation" of Capuleta girls, a group that also included Nina, the newest Casa Capuleta resident, who hadn't joined the band . . . yet . . . and was upstairs doing homework. Claudia and her two younger sisters jabbered away about the goings-on at school—so-and-so had said this and so-and-so had posted that. This papi chulo had been caught cheating on his girlfriend, leaving the poor girl heartbroken. An unfortunate reminder that being hot didn't necessarily make a guy Prince Charming.

Cat shook her head, lamenting the drama of high school.

Her gaze shifted to the twins over in the far corner of the room. Sabrina put away her guitarron while Violeta snapped her guitar case closed as they bandied fast-food options to pick up on the way to their shared apartment. In their midtwenties already and those two were still joined at the hip. Probably always would be, in part because of the trauma they had experienced before coming here—a reality all the girls identified with.

Blanca sat in a nearby chair, her violin resting on her lap, goofy smiling at whatever she was busy reading on her cell screen. Her tan cheeks darkened with a blush at the same time her mauve-stained lips tipped in a secretive smile. She darted a furtive glance to the right and left as if making sure none of the other girls were peeking over her shoulder.

Interesting. If Cat didn't know her shy sister better, she'd think the chica was sexting with someone. But fat chance of that happening, not with her straitlaced sis. Blanca hadn't mentioned anything about a new guy lately. Plus, they'd been up-to-their-eyeballs busy with the Battle and some other familia concerns—when would Blanca have had time to meet someone anyway?

Blanca giggled, her blush deepening as she slipped her cell into her purse, then cupped her cheek and let out a besotted sigh. Cat frowned. Her big-sister intuition perked up like a prairie dog poking its head out of a hole, sensing trouble, and she made a mental note to do a little investigating. Her sister's soft heart was easily broken, and if that happened again this time, Cat wouldn't be around to help pick up the pieces and give her typical that-man's-a-pendejo-if-he-can't-see-what-a-prize-you-are speech.

Guilt over her impending departure churned in her belly. Doggedly, she reminded herself that this situation was not the same. She was nothing like the man who had abandoned her as a child. Still, leaving to prove it was possible to achieve your dreams without sacrificing those who loved you meant walking away from familia responsibilities here at home. Like making sure that whatever Blanca was hiding on her cell didn't crush her sweet spirit if it blew up.

Biting back a sigh, Cat realized she would need to give Mariana a heads-up about her Blanca hunch. As the oldest, and because of her slight control-freak, though levelheaded, nature—useful with her job as an ER nurse—Mariana usually took on the role of problem solver among the sisters. She soothingly discussed and advised. Cat bulldozed and harangued.

Across the room, dressed in soft green scrubs after coming straight from a day shift at the hospital, Mariana hunkered down in front of her trumpet case. Probably already reviewing her long list of to-dos for the next day. The responsibility gene was strong in that one.

Closing her eyes, Cat listened to the familiar sounds around her.

Usually, she'd be rushing them out the door. Nagging at her sisters to hurry up and head home—to their own places for the older girls, upstairs to the familia's apartment for the teens. Reminding them to get some rest. They had another late rehearsal tomorrow. Every night until their debut on the big stage at the AT&T Center before Galán's concert.

She wasn't rushing tonight, though.

No, tonight she felt a need to soak in mundane, everyday moments like this—to record the sights and sounds of her sisters enjoying life. Imprint them in her memory so she could call up the mental video later, when she yearned for a touch of home.

Meanwhile, inside her satchel, the Padua contract thumped like Poe's telltale heart. Proof of her decision to leave her familia behind in pursuit of her own dreams. Exactly like her birth father.

A chorus of teen giggles and a moaned "¡No me digas!" interrupted her sliding-into-melancholy mood. The shocked "you don't say" was a common phrase in a house with nine sisters prone to chisme and the drama such gossip brought with it.

As much as she didn't miss the highs and lows of teen angst, she was going to miss this. Making music and laughter with her hermanas.

"A penny for your thoughts." Mariana nudged Cat's knee with her trumpet case.

"Girl, my thoughts cost way more than that." Holding out a hand, Cat wiggled her fingers in a *gimme* motion. "Pony up."

Mariana chuckled, the laughter softening the striking features of her high cheekbones, angular chin, and almost hawklike nose. She dragged a chair closer with the toe of the rubber-soled granny shoes she swore made long ER shifts more bearable. "Did you get your official copy of the signed contract?"

"It's tucked safely in my bag. But I have to admit, part of me thinks I should have made Galán stew a little. Hold off as long as I could before signing."

Mariana's long black braid swung over her shoulder as she shook her head. A knowing smirk curved the corners of her mouth. "Ay, chica, why do you insist on making things harder for yourself?"

"What I'm doing is trying to level the playing field. The power balance is tilted heavily in his favor. And his big ego knows it."

"That big ego has a track record backing it up."

"Pfffft." Cat slid her older sister a side-eyed scowl.

"Patricio's not the bad guy, Cat. You and I both know who is." Mariana clasped Cat's knee, giving it a tight squeeze through her Levi's.

"Galán's smug attitude bugs me. Especially because he's usually right. It . . . I don't know . . . it—" Her hands moved in a circular motion in front of her as she sought the right words to describe the admiration-irritation Galán evoked within her.

Emphasis on "irritation" when it came to his "constructive criticism" of her songwriting skills.

"Personally, I think it's good for you to have someone who'll challenge you. Very few people aren't intimidated by your waspish ways. He's one of them."

"Waspish wa—chica, please!" Cat blew out a harsh scoff, the sound morphing into a laugh when Mariana grinned.

"I say that with all the love," her sister teased.

"Yeah, well, this wasp has a stinger, and I'm not averse to using it. Patricio Galán needs to know that I'm not a pushover. No man, especially no mariachi, will ever get the better of me. I'm not like—"

She broke off when Mariana's cool palm covered the fist Cat had tightened on her thigh.

"Remember what Mamá has always told us: Our birth parents do not define us. We do." Mariana's grip squeezed on the last two words. She ducked closer, her steady gaze ensnaring Cat's. "I know Mamá and Papo have some concerns about you leaving. Parental prerogative, that's all. And, sure, the teens are nervous about the hole you're leaving in the band."

Cat swallowed the guilt-induced bile creeping up her throat at the thought of anyone in her familia feeling the abandonment she had struggled with as a child.

"But we'll all be fine," Mariana continued in her calm I've-got-it-under-control tone. "Las Nubes will be fine. This is *your* time, Cat. You've proven yourself here. Now's your chance to get out there and show the world what we already know. That Cat Capuleta is a force to be reckoned with. In the best way possible."

Tears burned the back of Cat's throat at her sister's unwavering belief in her. Her eyes stung and she blinked quickly, willing away the moisture.

"Gracias," she murmured, tugging Mariana in for a tight hug. "You know I plan to give 'em hell and make you proud."

"Hey!"

"¡Oye! We want in on the lovefest!"

"Wait for me!"

The chorus of cries from the rest of their sisters greeted Catalina seconds before she and Mariana were engulfed in a Mariachi Las Nubes group hug.

As they showered her with messages of support and love, and a grumbled "ay, watch your elbow" from someone, a whispered promise to attain her dreams *and* take care of her loved ones ribboned through Cat's head.

Whoever said you couldn't have it all obviously hadn't met her.

The strains of an acoustic guitar drifted down the long, tiled hallway of the East Wing at La Hacienda, Cat's secret nickname for Patricio Galán's sprawling rental estate.

The moniker seemed appropriate given the autocratic patrón vibe the man often exuded. His commanding voice, regal bearing, and know-it-all smirk—not to mention his usual all-black ensemble, from his custom-made boots to the cowboy hat he often wore—reminded her of the wealthy-landowner alpha heroes in the telenovelas that kept her mamá glued to the TV.

Too bad for him, Cat could never fill the role of the needy, helpless heroine waiting for the hero to save her.

Galán had yet to play the role of a romantic hero in a telenovela or film, but his music videos were guaranteed instant hits, liked and shared and saved on streaming services and social media platforms worldwide. Her accounts included. The number of times she and her sisters had swooned and mooned over the passionate videos featuring the hunky heartthrob was actually embarrassing.

Not that she would feed his ego by admitting such a weakness to him.

The instrumental music grew louder as she continued down the hallway. Alberto had said that she'd find Galán in the music room. It must be him playing the guitar.

Ignoring the collection of landscape paintings with ornate gold frames on her right and the wall of windows overlooking the pool and estate grounds on her left, she lightened her footsteps, straining her ears to better hear the tune she didn't recognize.

She glanced over her shoulder, checking to make sure Galán's assistant wasn't still watching her from the foyer. No sense embarrassing herself by getting caught eavesdropping on the famous mariachi. But she couldn't help wondering if the piece was something new he was working on. And, if so, whether he would share it with her.

The few times during the meetings that George Garcia had mentioned Galán's search for a writing partner, she had caught a flash of frustration in the superstar's obsidian eyes. Quickly snuffed, but not fast enough for a girl who had learned at an early age how to read people out of necessity, seeking the signs of her birth mother's depressive bouts, usually triggered by a call or postcard or an unkept promise from the selfish man who hadn't deserved her devotion.

That instinct, honed during Cat's time in the foster system, warned her that Galán might not be as thrilled about partnering with her as George or Alberto let on. Even though it had supposedly been Galán's idea in the first place.

George had been effusive with his praise when he called Cat to confirm whether her official copy of the contract had arrived via courier. He had even relayed a "thrilled to have you join the label" message similar to the ones she'd heard from several other Padua executives. But she hadn't heard a peep from Galán, the person she'd be working closely with.

Bueno, if they intended to do this right, they'd be working closely. And when the hell had she done anything involving her career half-assed?

Now certainly wasn't the time to start.

Reaching the music room's threshold, she paused just shy of the open double doors. Eyes closed, she listened to the ballad, letting the chords strum through her as potential words and lyrics slowly took shape in her mind.

"How long do you plan on hovering out there?"

She flinched at Galán's gruff question. Her cheeks warmed, but she leaned against the doorjamb and sent him a disapproving scowl. "I am not hovering. It's called 'not interrupting in the middle of a song.' My parents taught me good manners."

His raised brow said he might think otherwise. The louse.

"Bueno, pues . . . Bienvenida to the tour, Catalina Capuleta. Buckle up. You made a smart choice accepting Padua's offer, but life on the road isn't all champagne and roses like you might think."

Rather than turn her off, his taunt-laced welcome had Cat stepping into the room with a proud toss of her head. She strode across the carpeted floor, past a wooden coffee table with sheet music scattered over the surface and a cushiony leaf-green sofa, heading toward a shiny black baby grand piano along the far wall.

"I'll accept your welcome," she told him. "As for smart choices, I'd say Padua made one by recognizing the right person for the job. Me."

His husky chuckle and murmured "touché" had her lips twitching with a smile of their own. Funny how the man could both annoy and amuse her.

She eased onto the piano's wooden bench and set her purse by her side. Leaning her left elbow on the closed keyboard cover, she eyed Galán, who was seated on a short rolling stool by an electric keyboard.

"Whether or not this partnership is a smart choice . . ." she said, tacking on a shoulder hitch. "Bueno, that remains to be seen. Depends on a few factors."

"Such as?" Relaxing his broad shoulders, he released his grip on the acoustic guitar's neck and draped his right forearm across the top of the instrument's curvy body. His palm cupped the rounded edge, the pads of his long fingers gently brushing the wood. Unbidden, her mind flashed to a scene from one of his recent music videos . . . him lying on a bed with crisp white linens, locked in a passionate embrace with a dark-haired woman wearing a lacy, red negligee, his black shirt unbuttoned to reveal a light dusting of dark hair over his muscular pecs, his large hand skimming the curve of her hip, the dip at her waistline, higher. That rich baritone voice of his crooning words of love and desire and . . .

Lust-filled heat oozed through Cat like warm honey on a sopapilla fresh out of the fryer.

"Catalina?"

"Hmm?" she murmured, her name on his lips initiating a mental tug-of-war between the erotic daydream of her lying beside him and the reality of their uncertain working relationship.

"I said, I'm intrigued by what those factors determining the success our new partnership might be."

"Factors? Uhhh . . ." She blinked several times, clearing away the delicious, if also dangerous, daydream. The expectant look on his face told her this wasn't the first time he had posed this question.

Crap!

So much for leaving the fangirl side of her back at her apartment, safely locked in her bedroom. Five minutes into their first rehearsal together and she'd let wild meanderings drag her into forbidden thought territory.

Forbidden in part because she had made a promise to herself years ago that she would *never* be like her birth mother, falling prey to a mariachi who continually cast her aside for his true love—music.

Forbidden also because she needed this opportunity with Galán to catapult the trajectory of her career. She couldn't risk mucking it up by allowing fickle lust to get in the way.

Get your shit together, girl!

Buying herself some time, Cat leaned forward and craned her neck to peer down the empty hallway. George had said he might not be here today, but Alberto had mentioned bringing them some water and the cup of hot herbal tea she had requested.

"Are you expecting someone?" Galán asked.

"No. Just checking for witnesses before I answer."

"For wit—" He broke off on a cough.

His wide-eyed surprise softened the angles of his chiseled face, reminding her of the photograph on his first album cover. Back then, baby-faced, seventeen-year-old Patricio had stolen hearts with his boyish charm and hesitant smile. Then the album released and he blew everyone away with his stellar vocals on the tracks. Twelve-year-old Cat had been at Casa Capuleta for two years by then, finally allowing herself to believe that life with Arturo, Berta, and Mariana, who had arrived a year before Blanca and Cat, could be her new normal. A preteen in braces, experiencing her first celebrity crush, she'd hung a copy of his album cover on her shared bedroom wall. Then she'd spent countless hours gazing up at it and spinning dreams.

Back then, Casa Capuleta had offered the beginning of a new life for her. Today, this contract and the chance to be a part of Galán's next album represented a new chapter.

If she didn't screw it up. That meant never giving the exasperating mariachi the upper hand.

"What exactly are you implying, Catalina Capuleta?" Humor laced the skepticism in Galán's tone.

"Do I have you worried? Maybe you should be. You have no idea what I'm capable of." She winked, pleased by the puff of breathy laughter he let out as he shook his head. Straightening on the bench, she swiveled to face him. "Look, there are two lessons I've learned from the rift between my papo and his childhood best friend. The genesis of the decades-long feud between the Capuletas and Monteros that nearly sabotaged our chances in the Battle of the Mariachi Bands."

Galán nodded, having been a front-row witness to the bickering between the two familias and their bands during the competition. Worse, there'd been Cat's miscalculation in taking the feud to social media in the heat of her anger. Not exactly her finest hour.

"Business relationships will fail if emotions get in the way or if either party isn't on the up-and-up with the other," she shared.

Galán shifted on the rolling stool. His jaw muscles tightened, but he didn't refute her claim.

Encouraged, also hoping her grab-the-bull-by-the-horns tactic didn't come back to spear her in the ass, she continued. "For the sake of starting things off on the right note, I'm going to level with you, okay?"

"Something tells me you would even if I said no, not okay."

For once his know-it-all smirk had her biting back a grin instead of a snarl.

"Am I that transparent?" she asked.

"No, you're that much of a fighter. Someone who knows what she wants and goes for it."

"Gracias."

"Even if in sometimes foolhardy ways."

"¡Oye, qué malo!" She swatted at his knee, the seam of his black jeans scraping against her palm.

His rich laughter filled the room. "Mean? Ha! What happened to being truthful? You weren't exactly patience personified during a few key moments in the Battle."

She shot him a playful scowl.

"Fine, I will admit, grudgingly, that my temper can get the best of me sometimes. It's a work in progress. But my heart." She pressed a palm to her chest, covering the crucifix that hung from a gold chain around her neck, a Confirmation gift from Mamá and Papo. The reminder of her familia, of their sacrifices for her dreams, sobered Cat. "My heart and soul are one hundred percent into making our partnership successful. Which brings us back to one of those factors that plays into whether or not this was a wise decision."

Galán swallowed, his expression turning serious as he waited for her to go on.

"Sure, my contract is with Padua, but it's no industry secret that when it comes to even the smallest detail on your album, the buck stops with you. Not any record producer or executive. Not even George, who's been with you since the beginning."

When she paused, allowing him time to deny or chime in, Galán answered with a haughty arch of a brow in a silent "And?"

"Aaand . . ." Cat rubbed her hands up and down the tops of her thighs in a bid to chase away the strange nervousness attempting to creep in. The heat generated by the friction between her palms and the jean material sparked a sense of urgency that galvanized her admission. "I keep getting a distinct not-interested-in-playing-with-others vibe from you."

"Oh, I like playing with others."

Mischief sparked in his black-coffee eyes. His lips tipped in a secret smile that had Cat imagining all kinds of secret pleasures those lips, that mouth, could treat her to.

Desire curlicued over her breasts, down her torso, and lower. Seeping into private places she should not be thinking about this man pleasuring.

The wheels on Galán's rolling stool squeaked as he leaned toward her. Not invading her personal space but definitely hanging out on its fringes. Close enough that she noticed the tiny red line, a nick from his razor blade, marring his chiseled jaw. Near enough that her next inhale teased her with hints of his earthy, ginger-scented cologne. Tempting enough that her gaze slid to his irresistible lips.

"What do you say, Cat? Interested?"

The intimacy lacing his husky voice had her body screaming *hell yeah*.

But acting on the lust lighting her insides with delicious flames that licked and aroused would definitely *not* be a smart choice.

He certainly had to know that, too. So, what game was he trying to play here?

More importantly, if he thought she couldn't beat him at whatever he was up to, or at least give him a run for his money, he had another think coming.

Matching Galán's move and upping the ante, she invaded *his* personal space by cupping his cheek. The warmth of his bronze skin against her palm was almost as satisfying as the surprise that flashed in his eyes. Leaning closer, she brought her lips mere inches away from his mouth, her intent gaze never leaving his.

"Ay, papito, I am definitely interested."

His pupils dilated, desire turning them into dark pools that beckoned in the seconds before she planted her hands on his shoulders and gave him a hard shove, sending his stool wobbling backward.

"In writing some chart-topping songs and bringing concert crowds to their feet."

"What the f—!" Galán bit off the curse as he nearly dropped the guitar. His right arm flailing, he teetered on the small round seat until he planted a boot on the cream-and-brown-flecked carpet to halt the stool's momentum.

"Did you already forget the first lesson I learned from the Capuleta and Montero feud?" she threw at him, fists balled on her hips. "Business partnerships and personal relationships do not mix. Plus, I don't get involved with musicians."

Lips pressed in a thin, unreadable line, his face a stern mask of harsh angles and planes, Galán studied her through narrowed eyes.

For a hot nanosecond Cat worried she *might* have been a bit over-zealous in making her point. The machismo was strong in this one, and she'd given him a pretty good shove. But if there was a line in the sand she had to draw with him, it was this one.

"Look, I know that all of this"—she motioned from her head down her torso—"is hard to resist. And you—" She huffed out a breath as she jabbed an open palm at him. "Bueno, we both know you've perfected that swoony Latin-lover charm your fans adore. But it's wasted on me. Are we clear?"

As clear as Texas oil spewing from the ground, considering her body's hyperaware reaction whenever he was near. An annoying response she was determined to ignore.

Galán stretched to lean the guitar against one of the keyboard legs. With a heavy sigh, he rose to stand, his six-foot-plus height towering over her from her perch on the piano bench.

"Swoony Latin lover, huh? Is that how you think of me?" A corner of his mouth quirked at his playful teasing.

"You wish." A breathy, relief-tinged chuckle accompanied her retort as she stood. At barely five foot two, she was still dwarfed by him, but now her pugnacious chin jut wasn't at quite such an awkward angle.

Galán stepped toward her and held out a hand to shake. An unexpected move given her recent back-off shove.

Cat stared up at him, searching for any sign of subterfuge or gamesmanship, relieved when she found only respect and sincerity.

Trusting her instincts, she clasped his hand. His long fingers enveloped hers, sealing her palm against his. A dangerous electric current shot up her arm.

"I have a similar no-performers dating rule. No one on tour, actually, whatever role they play," he admitted.

"Muy bien. Then we're on the same page."

"With this, sí." His mouth curled in a sexy smirk again, and the fiery lust his touch ignited inside her flared.

Their hands still firmly clasped, a comfortable yet charged silence hung between them.

"Catalina Capuleta, you are a force to be reckoned with."

"Are you just now figuring that out?" she joked, pleased by the laughter that crinkled the edges of his eyes. "Only, don't go talking to my familia. Too many of my sisters have big mouths. No telling what they'd share that could tarnish my image."

"Hmm. Now I am intrigued." Head tilted, he squinted, his forehead wrinkling as if he pondered a difficult question. "Which of your sisters do you think would spill first?"

"Oh, you're gonna be like that, huh? Maybe I should go have a chat with Alberto," she challenged, Galán's playful teasing egging her on. "He's been saddled with you since you were a pimply-faced teen. I'm sure he's got some good dirt I wouldn't mind getting under my nails for fun."

She released her grip and moved to step around him, but Galán's hand tightened over hers, drawing her to a halt. Cat shot him a coy look out of the corner of her eye.

He grinned. Not the practiced, camera-ready smile he flashed the paparazzi but a natural, relaxed, eyes-alight-with-pleasure grin she hadn't seen before but found herself hoping she would more often.

"I have a better idea instead. Why don't we focus on the songs I've selected for our set during the concert?" He tipped his head toward the coffee table and the sheet music strewn across its surface.

Our set.

Ay, how she relished the sound of that phrase.

"You mean the songs you'd like us both to consider, seeing as how this entails our mutual approval," she corrected, pointedly not making it a question.

"I'm open to suggestions. But as you are well aware, I've got strong opinions, usually correct ones, about every detail that goes into my shows. Just like my albums."

"Hello, pot. I'm kettle."

Galán tipped his head back on a bark of laughter that should not have sent delicious thrills swirling through her. But it did.

34

Her palm glided over his as she wiggled her hand free and made herself step away from him.

He followed her to the coffee table, stopping alongside her, close enough that his arm lightly brushed hers before he edged to his right.

Tucking her loose hair behind her ears, she bent to riffle through the sheet music. All duets: two old classics; several of his own hits; and an original of hers, "No Me Olvides," the sentimental, aptly titled don't-forget-me duet she had written for the Battle.

It would be the first of her songs ever performed by anyone other than her and her sisters. This time, by one of her biggest idols, onstage, in front of a crowd of thousands in her hometown. With *her* accompanying him at the mic.

Talk about a sueño come true!

Goose bumps chased each other up her forearms beneath the sleeves of her light-pink, open-front tweed jacket. Her shoulders shimmied as an excited chill tiptoed across them.

Of course, "No Me Olvides" was also a song she and Galán had butted heads over during Battle rehearsals. Given the short time frame her sisters and the other band they had been paired with were given to learn and perfect the new piece, Cat had deliberately kept the musical arrangement simple.

Galán's "some sections are rudimentary" comment when he first heard her song still rankled. His unsolicited advice that she learn the difference between criticism and a helpful critique, delivered in his brusque tone, had bugged her even more.

"Let's start with this one." She scooped up the pages for her ballad, then straightened. No use putting off the first potential disagreement of their partnership. "I'll never forget how it brought the house down in the second round of the competition. Exactly as I predicted."

Galán took the pages she held out to him, a dubious expression drawing up his dark brows.

"And it will do the same at the AT&T Center when the two of us perform it," she claimed. Closing her eyes, she envisioned the crowd rising to their feet with boisterous cheers. Their chants for more bouncing off the rafters. Rapturous wonder at the very real possibility of her long-held dream coming true welled in her chest. Excitement crescendoed, spewing out in a rush of pride for her work. "Your fans are gonna love it! 'No Me Olvides' has the perfect 'I burn, I pine, I perish' angst that people—"

"The 'I' qué?"

The octave-raising "what" at the end of his question barely registered and she blinked up at him, her thoughts busy careening down the path leading to her song becoming a number-one hit.

"Uhhhh, you know. That I-burn-for-you, I-pine-for-you, I'll-die-without-you feel?" His confused frown deepened, and she rushed on, fed by her enthusiasm. "The kind that has fans clutching their chests. Overcome by emotion as they relive their own lost love. That first crush who broke their heart. The one that got away. The soul mate they haven't met yet."

"Mira pa'llá." Patricio slowly stretched out the words like an "aha" and shook the sheet music at her with a cheesy, full-of-himself smirk.

"Look at what?"

"Who would have guessed that underneath that ambitious, rebellious, kiss-my-ass attitude, you're secretly hiding a mushy romantic. Burning, pining, and perishing for true love to sweep her off her feet and ride off with her into the sunset."

"¡Por favor!" She scoffed and snatched the sheet music from him. "I can ride my own horse, thank you very much. But you tell me, why is being a romantic a bad thing? Why is it that so many men and their machismo criticize women for being too emotional?"

"Hold on, that's not what I meant." Galán held his palms out as if to ward off the verbal barrage he sensed was imminent.

"Like feeling is a bad thing and it somehow makes us the weaker sex?"

"Catalina, you don't—"

"I've spent years studying my craft and the industry. I'm good at what I do because *emotion*—anger, heartache, over-the-moon love, knee-buckling fear, and everything in between—bleeds from me onto the page."

Outrage surged through her, spawned by years of dealing with those who sought to silence or dismiss her, her sisters, and other female mariachis.

"That's what has people humming my songs long after Mariachi Las Nubes has played them at a gig. It's what will make your album go platinum. And eventually, it'll win me a Grammy."

Her ire at full-steam-ahead level, Cat spun on her bootheel and stomped to the piano. Sinking onto the bench, she plunked the sheets of paper onto the piano's music shelf.

Galán's nostrils flared with a heavy exhalation.

Cat shot him a pointed let's-get-to-work glare, then lifted the fallboard and placed her fingers on the piano keys.

"This business isn't always fair, Catalina, especially to women."

"Tell me something I don't already know," she muttered.

"Like you, I have high expectations. For myself and those I collaborate with. I don't give in or give up easily. Many rely on me and my career for their livelihood. That's a responsibility I don't take lightly. My success is theirs, too. So, in this partnership of ours, I will question and critique and push you to do better. Even when you think it's unfair."

He stalked closer, and her spine stiffened.

Men constantly beat their chest, crowed their own praises, or demanded their due. They were cheered for doing so. But when a woman did the same, she was labeled brash, aggressive, or worse. If Galán was annoyed by her outburst, too bad. He'd simply have to get used to her speaking her mind.

Frustration boiled in her belly. Along with a trickle of *oh shit*. After all, she *had* just spewed one of her infamous injustice rants at the mariachi who could make or break her career.

Regardless, she straightened her shoulders, unwilling to back down.

Galán reached her side. She held her breath, fully expecting a stern rebuke.

"But I can assure you," he told her, "I am in your corner. I have no doubt that, one day, you will be holding your Grammy high."

Startled by his unexpected praise, she swung her gaze up to meet his.

Unequivocal certainty stared back at her.

Her pulse tripped, then bumped into triple time. Cat rarely doubted herself. And her familia's belief in her talent and passion had always buoyed her. But Galán's confidence . . . it filled her with a burning desire to prove him right. So different from the driving need to prove her birth father wrong.

"Of course"—arms crossed, Galán leaned a hip against the baby grand—"I'm guessing that you'll be telling the patriarchy what they can kiss in your acceptance speech."

A loud cackle-laugh burst from her before she could stop it.

His sexy grin flashed.

"Probably," she conceded.

"Ay, pero that temper of yours," he lamented. "Quick to light and rapier sharp."

"It's part of my charm. Best thing to do is realize that I'm always right, so there's no use arguing with me."

His husky chuckle washed over her, warming her in places it really shouldn't. One in particular: her heart. Something many men had labeled hard or cold because she stood up to them. Pushed back. Didn't take their patronizing crap.

In hindsight, if she had heeded her older sister's advice and paused before letting her indignation take the reins, she would have remembered that as a mentor and host of this year's Battle of the Mariachi

Bands, Galán had proven himself different. Cocky and self-assured but never condescending.

Even now, his smirk was a playful tilt at the corners of his mouth, teasing a similar response from her.

Relieved they had moved past the uncomfortableness her outburst had precipitated, she offered an olive branch he deserved. "I don't trust easily, but I am willing to admit that you're probably not the enemy I should be railing against. The fairness you showed my sisters and me during the Battle—it meant a lot to me. Bueno, to all of us, including my parents. Who, while worried about me going on the road for the first time, are so freaking proud that you and I are collaborating on your album."

Galán flinched and pushed off the piano. A strange expression flitted over his face, but he ducked down to grab the guitar before she could decipher it. He slung the shoulder strap over his head and settled the instrument in his arms.

Moments later, she was counting out the song's tempo, and any thoughts about his odd reaction were brushed aside. Instead, her complete focus turned to the unbelievable reality of Patricio Galán's rich baritone giving voice to her lyrics, his guitar accompanying her on the piano.

The twelve-year-old fan with an all-consuming crush on the young mariachi sighed and batted her lashes in a knee-wobbly swoon.

The twenty-eight-year-old professional warned her to keep her eyes on the prize—success and financial security for her and her familia, vengeance against the desgraciado who had abandoned her to chase a dream that had never materialized.

A dream she would be closer to achieving if she ignored her niggling doubts and allowed herself to trust her enigmatic new partner.

Chapter Four

¿Qué estás haciendo, güey?

Patricio tightened his grip on his rental car's steering wheel, the "what are you doing, man?" echoing in his head like a howl bouncing off the dusty walls of a deserted canyon.

An hour ago Alberto had rapid-blinked in shock at Patricio's idea, the viejo's brows raised high on his wrinkled forehead. A sure sign the old man agreed this was a pendejada of an idea.

Gracias a Dios George didn't know what Patricio was up to.

Ha! If so, his description of Patricio's idea would have been peppered with much more colorful words than "idiotic."

And yet here Patricio was, seated in his rental car, the dark, tinted windows of the Escalade rolled up tight against the cool late-April weather and prying eyes. Parked in the lot in front of the run-down strip mall next to Casa Capuleta.

There was no good reason for his compelling need to allay Arturo and Berta's concerns about their daughter packing her bags to live on a bus and in a string of hotels from Texas to California with a group of strangers. Catalina was an adult. She could make her own decisions.

Sure, he always felt a measure of responsibility for everyone on his tour. With Catalina, though, the responsibility felt different. Bigger.

Maybe it came from getting to know her entire familia so well during the Battle. Hearing the Capuletas' Lifetime-movie-worthy story.

Witnessing the tight bond among the sisters despite their varying personalities and backgrounds.

There'd been a time when he had hoped for the same type of connection with his papá. Ever since his father first brought him onstage during a concert in Mexico City and thrust a microphone in his hands. Patricio had been barely five, but he remembered that moment as if it had happened yesterday. Nervous sweat coating his face. His red tie choking him. The weight of his papá's beefy hand on his shoulder, both comfort and pressure. The gleam of pride in Vicente Galán's eyes as he introduced "*mi* hijo."

Patricio hadn't realized it then, but years later, his father's emphasis on "my" proved telling.

Ultimately, music had driven a wedge between them. Unlike the Capuletas, whose love of music bonded them tighter than superglue. What happened to one affected them all. Assuming responsibility for Catalina as part of his team meant doing so for her entire familia.

The certainty of that fact had Patricio reaching for his cowboy hat and sunglasses, despite the overcast day, to exit his vehicle.

He scanned the area in front of the strip mall where he'd parked. Late Sunday afternoon meant most of the shops were closed. Good. The less foot traffic for him to avoid, the better.

His boots crunched on the gritty, cracked sidewalk bordering the short chain-link fence that lined the perimeter of the Capuletas' property. Tall privacy hedges on the other side shielded his view of the back courtyard, the site of the sisters' first official performance as Mariachi Las Nubes more than ten years ago—a moment captured in a photograph on their website that showed a teenage Catalina standing alongside the other four sisters around her age, all dressed in their charros.

At fifteen or sixteen Catalina had already begun to exude her signature confidence and sass. They bloomed in her proud stance, impish smile, and the sparkle in her eyes. A force to be reckoned with, even at that young age.

He reached the front of the building at the same time a beat-up Ford truck slowed at the light, then turned onto Commerce Street in front of Casa Capuleta. Patricio ducked his head, tugging the brim of his hat lower. The last thing he wanted was for someone at the corner mercado to spot him. One social media post geotagging his location could potentially lead to hordes of paparazzi trolling the premises and hounding Catalina's familia. After everything that had gone down recently with one of the teens, protecting their privacy as long as he could remained of the utmost importance.

Following Arturo's instructions, Patricio strode down the paved path leading to the courtyard and the back entrance. Catalina and the rest of Mariachi Las Nubes should be in the middle of their Sunday rehearsal in one of the center's music rooms. That gave him time to reassure her parents of his intent to keep their daughter safe, and then he could slip out the back again. Unnoticed.

Moments later, he stood in front of apartment 2A, his boot toes brushing the woven MI CASA ES SU CASA mat. Hat in hand, he waited for an answer to his knock.

An unfamiliar antsiness tingled along the back of his neck, then marched like a swarm of army ants across his shoulders, moving en masse into his chest. The deadbolt clicked, and his gut clenched. Suddenly he felt like a teen here to meet his crush's parents, hoping to gain their approval before whisking their daughter away.

An average, everyday life moment that he had never experienced thanks to his unaverage upbringing. Having lost his mom during childbirth, he'd grown up on the road with his father or been left at home with nannies, tutors, and later vocal coaches, then Alberto. By the time he hit dating age, his career had been set in motion by his father and Padua. The only person he'd really wanted to spend time with had—

The Capuletas' front door swung open, halting what-ifs Patricio didn't bother with anymore.

"Bienvenido a nuestra casa." Berta Capuleta welcomed him to their home with a friendly smile, the soft lines arrowing out from the corners of her brown eyes deepening.

Arturo Capuleta stood behind his wife, sans the warm smile. Dressed in a short-sleeved, brown plaid western button-down, dark Wranglers, and boots, he appeared as rugged as his craggy features. Questions loomed in his dark eyes, but the thin line of his lips remained unmoving.

Pressing his black cowboy hat to his chest, Patricio tipped his head with respect. "Muchísimas gracias for meeting with me on such short notice."

"Ay, ni lo menciones," Berta assured him. "Really, don't mention it at all. We're honored to have you visit."

Arturo humphed under his breath, and his wife frowned at him over her shoulder. Known in the local mariachi comunidad as generous and easygoing, Arturo Capuleta exuded a definite protective-father vibe.

"Por favor, come in." Berta stepped back, elbowing her husband out of the way for Patricio to enter.

He eased by the couple with a mumbled "Gracias," his misgivings giving way to curiosity.

The front door opened to a large dining area, where a long, scarred wooden table held court. Six high-backed chairs lined each side with another chair at each end. Enough room for the eleven Capuletas and three more to break bread together on a regular basis. Framed pictures of their familia decorated the walls. An early one of the five older girls in full charro, one with the eight that comprised Las Nubes today. A trio of photographs featured them in pajamas gathered around a Christmas tree, in beach attire with the open water and a SOUTH PADRE ISLAND sign behind them, and out back in the courtyard with strings of lights sparkling overhead. Joy was a common theme.

The entire dining room oozed hearth and home in a way that made him long to linger. For someone who'd grown up eating meals alone, or with whomever had been paid to watch over him, rarely with the father who'd been consumed with his career, the thought of Capuleta familia dinners with everyone crowded around the well-used table seemed more storybook than real life.

A fictional world that a secret part of him yearned to step inside.

"Ven, we'll be more comfortable in the sala," Berta said.

Hooking an arm with her husband, she motioned for Patricio to follow her through the wide opening that connected the dining area to the kitchen, then into a supersize living room at the other end of the double apartment.

Moments later he sat beside her on a faded olive sofa with worn cushions and multicolored throw pillows. A watchful Arturo perched on the edge of a battered recliner. Patricio's nosy gaze trailed around the room—from the crocheted doily underneath the Virgen de la Guadalupe statue and half-melted candles in a place of honor in the far corner, to the keyboard with electrical tape wrapped around part of its cord, to the floral area rug with a faint red stain. He'd bet there was a story behind the stain, and he found himself wondering about it.

This was what a home should be like. Full of shared memories. Filled with a sense of belonging.

Catalina would be leaving all this behind to pursue her dreams.

He was aiding her in that endeavor. But he couldn't deny that a part of him would give up his Grammys, or at least one of them, for a chance to experience what she was walking away from in pursuit of the limelight.

"To what do we owe the honor of your visit, Patricio?" Berta asked.

"And why the secrecy?" Arturo threw in. "Especially from Catalina. ¿Hay algún problema?"

"No! There's no problem," Patricio rushed to assure them.

None with their daughter. Not exactly anyway. The problem was his. And he alone could fix it, despite Padua pushing a full-album col-laboration on him, a move that necessitated Patricio's game of duplicity.

Resting his hat on his bent knee, Patricio cleared his throat, swallowing his misgivings. "To be honest, I'm not sure Catalina would appreciate my reason for being here. Given her intense aversion to machismo or anything that smacks of it."

"Bueno, that's a sentiment shared by all our girls. We have raised them to know their value, and that this is not only a man's world." Berta's soft voice rang with pride.

Still seated stiffly on the edge of his recliner, Arturo gave a curt nod.

"I completely agree," Patricio said. "Unfortunately, we all know there are many who don't think the same way. Our industry can be rough for women performers, as well as for rookies new on the scene. Since it's my name on the marquee of every stadium or arena we play, I hold myself responsible for every member of my show. That now includes Catalina. And while I don't normally make home visits like this for others, I felt compelled to relieve any concerns you may have."

Berta reached over to clasp her husband's forearm. "You see, viejo, I told you this was a good move for our Cat. She is in good hands."

The older man's stiff shoulders relaxed. His skepticism slowly faded, while at the same time his wife's words shoveled a heap of pressure on top of Patricio.

She is in good hands.

"I can't promise you that life on the road will be easy for your daughter. Like most first-timers, she's in for a rude awakening. Long hours, cramped buses, living out of a suitcase. Pero les prometo esto . . ." Patricio nodded with certainty, confident in himself and in his ability to follow through on his promise to them. "Padua Records—*I* want what's best for Catalina. Knowing that everything she does is with the intent to make you and her sisters proud."

Tears pooled in Berta's brown eyes. "Gracias, Patricio. My faith in God and my daughter is strong, pero a mamá always worries."

Arturo's smile didn't quite reach friendly proportions, but he stood and extended his hand.

Patricio rose, and though he towered over the older man by a good five or six inches, Arturo cast a long shadow when it came to protecting his familia. As he should. From his place outside the boundaries of that shadow, Patricio stared at the Capuleta patriarch with admiration.

"I am entrusting you with one of our jewels." A father's love dripped from Arturo's words and his grip tightened. "Our Catalina is special. She shines brighter than a diamond under the spotlight. Sí, her emotions are quick-fire, often hotter than my vieja's homemade salsa, pero they come from a good heart."

"Believe me, I know. I've seen her in action," Patricio answered.

Catalina *was* all heart. In this business, if she wasn't careful, that could be a detriment to her.

But she was also savvy and talented and sexy as hell. The first two were key traits that, if given proper guidance, could help her go far. The last . . . bueno, the last he would try like hell to ignore.

His relationship with Catalina would remain all business. Nothing more.

"Your daughter has talent and drive and a will to be the best that may rival my own. And that's saying something."

Arturo's raspy chuckle had Patricio allowing himself a faint grin.

"Buena suerte. You're going to need it with our Catalina," the old man warned.

"Ay, viejo, stop before you scare him off." Berta swatted at her husband as she pushed off the worn sofa to stand between him and Patricio.

Arturo leaned closer. His nearly black eyes squinted with intensity, his humor from moments ago now gone. "Ten cuidado con ella, ¿me oyes?"

Oh yes, Patricio heard the older man loud and clear.

Be careful with her.

So many expectations and meanings and potential disappointments were wrapped up in that one sentence.

On Patricio's drive back to his rental home, Arturo's warning replayed in his head like an old vinyl album with the record player needle caught on a scratch: *Ten cuidado con ella. Be careful with her. Ten cuidado con ella. Be careful with her.*

He'd gone to Casa Capuleta intent on reassuring her parents, foolishly thinking that, by doing so, he'd feel less guilty about his ruse of working with her to buy him more time to finally break through this creative block. Unfortunately, while he had received her parents' blessing, the strings it came with meant that any sense of relief continued to elude him.

Instead, the disquiet inside him he hadn't been able to silence in ages only droned louder.

Chapter Five

"How's everyone feeling?"

At her older sister's question, Catalina paused with her brick-red lipstick hovering over her lower lip. She cut her gaze to Mariana's reflection in the mirror mounted above the long vanity shelf that took up an entire wall in their tiny, cramped dressing room backstage at the AT&T Center.

Pandemonium ensued around them, pretty much summing up how the other girls were feeling less than an hour before they would hit the stage as the opening act of Galán's tour kick-off concert.

A few padded chairs down at the vanity, already dressed in her black charro like the rest of them, Blanca held a small brown paper bag over her nose and mouth. The paper made a crunching sound as it retracted and expanded with each breath she sucked in, then blew out. The worrier in the bunch was in hyper-freak-out mode.

Between the enormity of tonight's show and Cat's imminent departure following it, Blanca had been an emotional tumbleweed lately. Guilt over leaving her sister behind jabbed like the tip of Blanca's violin bow in the center of Cat's chest.

Over in a corner, heads bent together, the twins engaged in a whispered conversation. One of Violeta's hands kept up a steady it's-gonna-be-okay pat-pat-pat on Sabrina's back.

The teens gathered in a tight circle around their instruments. Nina wasn't a performer—yet—but their newest foster sister was finally showing interest in being part of their group, tagging along for moral support. Poor Teresita, at thirteen the youngest but also wickedly talented on the guitar, nibbled her thumbnail to the quick. Fabiola gripped her violin's neck, in danger of crushing the poor instrument if she squeezed any tighter. And Claudia, at sixteen the oldest and thus the leader of the younger girls, struggled to keep her game face on, creating an almost comical smile-grimace combination.

Cat shot Mariana an "are you kidding me" scowl. How the hell did it look like they were feeling moments before performing in front of their largest audience?

Scared.

Nervous.

Out of their league.

Thrumming with anticipation and ready to kick ass.

Okay, so those last two were mostly Cat. Even Violeta, normally a close second to Cat when it came to feistiness, was a bit ashen. Though she was bravely putting on a good act for her twin.

But give Mariana a few minutes and she could pep talk the girls' preperformance nerves into a hum of excitement. Cat's oldest hermana gave a pregame talk better than Popovich, the legendary head coach of the San Antonio Spurs, who played in this very building. And that was saying something.

They were less than an hour away from stepping onto the stage at the AT&T Center. The freaking AT&T Center. Where mariachi greats and international pop stars and the Spurs held court.

And for tonight . . . so, too, did Mariachi Las Nubes.

"Who are the Battle of the Mariachi Band champions?" Mariana cried, arms raised.

Silence met her question.

In the mirror, Cat arched one of her artfully threaded brows.

Mariana wrinkled her nose at her, then clapped her hands in a rapid one-two. "Oye, I asked, who are the Battle of the Mariachi Bands champions?"

Cat pushed her chair away from the vanity and rose, turning to face the room. "We are."

One by one the others repeated the refrain as they slowly gathered to form a hand-holding circle.

"Exactly. We earned this. All of us," Mariana said, chin high, confidence bolstering her words. Like she did before every Las Nubes performance, she launched into her pep talk, knowing exactly what to say to calm her sisters' nerves while energizing their spirits.

Minutes later, as they brought their circle in for a big group hug, someone knocked on their dressing room door.

A female stagehand, wearing an earpiece with a bendable microphone that hugged her left cheek, poked her head inside. "Excuse me, ladies, I have a delivery for Blanca."

"For me?" Blanca's eyes lit with pleasure as the stagehand entered carrying a large bouquet of roses in a glass vase.

The sisters mobbed Blanca amid a string of excited cries.

"Who are they from?"

"Is there a card?"

"¡Ay, qué romántico!"

"Maybe they're from a secret admirer!"

"Ooh, there's a note!" Teresita pointed at a small pink envelope among the red roses and baby's breath.

Hugging the vase against her torso with one hand, Blanca snatched the envelope with the other before anyone else could. She pressed it to her chest, a pink corner peeking out from under the curve between her thumb and pointer finger, a stark contrast to the black wool of her short charro jacket. Guilt widened her eyes. She shuffled backward until she bumped against a metal folding chair in front of the vanity.

"¿Qué te pasa, chica?" Cat asked.

"N-n-nothing's wrong?" Blanca answered, her voice climbing octaves with each word. "These are probably, um, probably from the teachers at school. They've been, um, really excited for me. For us."

She spun around to set the vase down on the white laminate shelf, keeping her back to the group.

"That's so nice of them," Mariana said.

"Mm-hmm," Blanca answered, her jerky nod and furrowed brow odd reactions for someone who'd been brimming with surprised joy moments ago.

No one else seemed to pick up on Blanca's caginess, and with the mystery of the secret sender solved, most of the girls went back to their preperformance rituals: vocal warm-ups, makeup checks, charro adjustments, or instrument fine-tuning. Except for Cat, who studiously watched Blanca's reflection in the mirror.

Head ducked, Blanca carefully opened the envelope, then withdrew the small card. A dark blush stole up her cheeks as she read the message. A shy grin tugged at the corners of her red-painted mouth, and she pressed the card to her chest again with a soft sigh.

This was no "break a leg" bouquet from coworkers. Not unless Blanca had a thing for someone at the school. Possible, but doubtful. The only male teachers or staff she'd mentioned were married or not her type. So, who was the secret someone who had her sister smitten? And was it the same someone Blanca had been texting with during rehearsal recently?

When Blanca cast a furtive glance around the room, then tucked the card into the side pocket of her makeup case, instead of back on the plastic cardholder stick nestled among the flowers, Cat's curiosity turned to discomfort.

More important than who . . . *why* was Blanca keeping the identity a secret?

Unease slithered through Cat, a garden snake disturbing her preperformance euphoria.

She and Blanca might have come from the same DNA, but all the softhearted genes had skipped Cat and stockpiled in her younger sister. Blanca tended to give her heart easily and often wound up hurt. If this mystery guy turned out to be equally as pendejo as others before him and Blanca needed a shoulder to cry on while Cat was on tour . . .

Sure, the other girls and Mamá would be there for comfort. But Blanca and Cat had been through every traumatizing life experience together, big and small. She hated the idea of not being there if her little sister needed her.

Suddenly the garden snake morphed into a boa constrictor encircling Cat's chest, squeezing tighter and tighter until she struggled to draw in a breath.

After the concert tonight, she'd be hopping on one of the tour buses and leaving San Antonio in the rearview mirror. Leaving her familia. Las Nubes. Casa Capuleta. Blanca.

Just like their birth father had always left them.

The skeleton in her closet ran a bony finger down Cat's spine. Her shoulders shimmied with a shiver, and a sheen of nervous sweat prickled her upper lip. Cat swiped it away with the back of her hand and gave an angry shake of her head.

No. Not like that sinvergüenza. She was *nothing* like that shameless man, who didn't deserve the title of father.

She was leaving with her familia in her heart, seeking fame and fortune for them all. Not only for herself.

"Knock, knock!" Patricio Galán appeared in the open doorway.

Two of the younger girls squealed with delight, quickly clapping hands over their mouths. Eyes saucer-wide, they gaped with adoration at the disarming mariachi. Even casually dressed in a pair of black sweats cinched at his ankles and a gray tee with the words Hecho en México in bold black font, its short sleeves snug around his biceps, the man was devastatingly handsome. Add his sexy smile as he grabbed the doorframe and leaned into their small space and . . .

No wonder he was greeted with swoons and batting eyelashes.

Not from her, though.

After several rehearsals with him and his band this week and the sound check earlier today, Cat was becoming used to her body's unwanted reaction to the charisma known to make Patricio's countless admirers weak in the knees.

Actually, she found herself more intrigued by the man he was behind the scenes when the cameras were off. The one who seemed more comfortable concentrating on his music and choreography, the lighting, and the million other decisions he had deftly handled during sound check. Patient and confident, quick witted yet at times contemplative, always a consummate professional. There was something about watching the legend at work that she couldn't resist. Ay, talk about a freaking turn-on.

One she'd be wise to resist.

"I thought I'd come see how the Battle champions were holding up," Patricio said. He flashed his charming grin, and damn if lust didn't rush over her like a warm summer rain.

The calm Mariana's pep talk had brought a few moments ago fizzled in the sisters' surprise over Patricio's visit. A jittery, nervous exhilaration hummed in the air.

"Have you seen how many people are in the seats? Is there, like, a ton?" Teresita asked. She caught her lower lip between her teeth. Her sweet face pinched with alarm.

Patricio moved out of the doorway, hands outstretched as he stepped toward them. "Ten people, a hundred people, the number doesn't matter. Teresa, you do your magic on your guitar, like you did during the Battle, and they're going to eat it up like your mamá's best cooking."

A blush tinted Teresita's cheeks dusky rose, and Cat could have kissed Patricio for his sweet pep talk. So unlike the blunt "constructive feedback" he was fond of giving her during rehearsals.

"The same goes for the rest of you." Patricio trailed his gaze over each of the sisters as he spoke. "Las Nubes deserves to be out there tonight. Play like you're on the wooden stage under the strands of white lights in the Casa Capuleta courtyard entertaining your comunidad. That's who's out there. Nuestra gente. Our people. And they're here to see you. You're going to be great."

His gaze finally landed on Cat. Intent. Certain. And damn if it didn't make her heart flutter while at the same time hardened her resolve to prove him right, and countless others wrong.

Lifting her chin, she flared an eyebrow with a hell-yeah intent.

Patricio's lips curved in his sexy smirk. He shot her a playful wink and her stomach flip-flopped.

Preshow nervous energy, she assured herself. But the lie didn't calm her suddenly racing heart.

"Gracias for stopping by, Patricio," Mariana said. "It means a lot to all of us, right, girls?"

The others answered with a chorus of "Ay, Dios mío, yes" and "So much!"

Cat tipped her head in agreement.

He broke their staring contest first to shrug off the thanks and step back toward the door. "I'll let you ladies finish getting ready. Catalina, I need a word with you. Outside."

A softly spoken command, but one that pricked her ornery nature all the same. Did the man not know how to use the word "please"?

Without waiting for her response, Patricio turned and headed out, clearly expecting her to follow.

When she didn't move to do so, Sabrina elbowed Cat in the ribs.

"What are you waiting for? Go," Blanca chided, giving her a little shove from behind.

"Hurry, and we'll do our prayer circle when you get back." Mariana shooed her away. "Everyone, finish up. It's almost time."

With her sisters now bustling about the tiny room, Cat strode out. She had no idea what Patricio felt compelled to discuss minutes before Las Nubes went on, but she certainly didn't need the unwanted distraction the man presented.

Out in the hallway, she found Patricio leaning a shoulder against the wall, arms crossed. A relaxed pose that belied his intent gaze as she approached. Overhead, a fluorescent tube light flickered, mimicking the uncharacteristic jitters trembling through her.

She slowed her steps as two stagehands dressed all in black hurried by, talking into their headpieces. Farther down the hallway, still dressed in casual clothes, Luciano Gomez, one of the trumpet players in Patricio's band, ambled closer. Busy checking something on his phone, Luciano nearly bumped into a young man exiting the dressing room assigned to the comedian who would entertain the crowd in between the opening and main acts. When he caught Cat's eye, the trumpet player quickly glanced back at his phone and strode by with only a mumbled hola for her and Patricio.

"You called, Your Majesty?" Cat deadpanned, twirling a hand in front of her waist as she bowed.

Patricio blew out a breath on a laugh. "Funny. Maybe you should join Jorge for his act."

"I'm always up for a challenge."

"Good, because life on the road can be one." He pushed away from the wall to stand. Arms still crossed over his broad chest, feet planted wide, he struck an imposing stance she'd secretly named his I-mean-business pose. Usually seen whenever Alberto or George challenged him about an idea or demand. But the line of worry etched between Patricio's brows . . . that was something new she hadn't seen. "We didn't get a chance to talk after the sound check earlier. Did you get settled on your bus?"

"Yes, my suitcase and guitar are tucked away safely. I'm ready to hit the road to Houston after the concert."

"I've heard the bunks aren't always the most comfortable. If it's too bad, let Alberto know."

She grinned. "Oh, you've *heard* about them, huh? Because you ride in your tricked-out, fancy castle on wheels, so you've never actually slept in one of the lumpy bunks like the rest of us commoners. Am I right?"

He rolled his eyes—his typical reaction when she teased him about his El Príncipe moniker. Of course, his exasperation encouraged her even more.

"Any last-minute questions about our set?" he asked.

"Nope. I'm stellar. Just like our set will be. Especially since you finally took my advice about the intro to our last number."

Instead of Patricio firing back an answering jibe like he usually did when they sparred over their artistic differences, the worry line between his brows deepened. "Did your parents get their VIP passes? They'll need those to get backstage after the show if you all want to say goodbye."

"Uh-huh. They actually stopped by earlier when they arrived."

"Good. If you or anyone in your familia needs anything—"

"Hey." Drawing closer, she clasped his forearm, confused by his barrage of personal questions. Even more by the guarded concern she hadn't heard from him before. "What's going on here?"

He glanced down at her hand, curled around his arm. The toes of her black boots were inches away from his sneakers, crossing the boundary of his personal space. Too late, she realized that she'd broken one of her self-imposed rules: maintain a platonic distance at all times. Definitely no touching. The better to squelch her body's hyperawareness of him.

Behind him, a group of people turned the corner at the end of the hallway. Cognizant of how easily rumors caught fire based on a misinterpreted situation and a quote by an "anonymous source," Cat released Patricio's arm and took a giant step back. No need to give anyone the wrong idea about them before the tour had even started. Ever, really.

Patricio apparently didn't have the same qualms. Closing the giant-step distance she had just put between them, he cupped her shoulders and peered down at her.

Entranced by his serious expression, surprised by the welcome weight of his hands, Cat didn't move. Couldn't move.

"This is an important night for you," Patricio said, his deep voice huskier than normal. "For your entire familia. Big changes are ahead. Once you debut on that stage with me, eyes and cameras and gossip hounds will be on you like flies on honey."

"Good thing I'm so sweet," she teased.

Joking was a knee-jerk defense mechanism. Whenever fear or pressure or some other unwanted emotion threatened to strangle her, she laughed it off, faked confidence until hers returned or righted itself.

Patricio didn't laugh. Instead, his troubled frown darkened. "I'm serious, Catalina. You need to be ready for what's coming. And if something's too much or . . . if you have a problem, let me know."

Thrown by his sudden show of concern, anxious to get them back to their comfortable sparring routine, Cat gave his chest a playful pat. Bueno, she meant to. But somehow her palm stayed resting against the slope of his firm pec. The warmth of his body seeped through the thin material of his T-shirt, searing her palm.

Curling her fingers into a fist, she fought the urge to slide her hand to his nape and draw him closer. Instead, she dropped her arm to her side. "Look, it seems like your way of handling immediate stress is to jump into problem-solving mode. Mine is to laugh in its face while I bulldoze through. I've been waiting my whole life for tonight. And everything that comes with it. Believe me, I am more than ready."

He gazed down at her, his throat moving with his swallow. "Dios mío, you're fearless, aren't you?"

"A woman in this business has to be."

"Bravery isn't the absence of fear, Catalina. It's acknowledging that fear and strategically fighting for what you want."

"Good. Then I'm doing things right."

A mix of emotions she couldn't quite pinpoint—awe, desire, guilt?—flashed in his eyes. His fingers flexed on her shoulders, and for a gut-clenching moment, she thought he might pull her to him. Despite all her business-only self-chiding this past week, Cat wouldn't have been able to resist the temptation to lean into him, loop her arms around his waist. Feel her chest pressed against his. Catch a deeper whiff of his earthy, ginger-tinged cologne as she stretched onto her toes to taste his lips.

Behind her a walkie-talkie crackled, then screeched as another stagehand walked by. Cat ducked her head to hide the embarrassed blush heating her face. Once they were alone again, she glanced up at Patricio. Whatever indefinable emotion she had seen in his eyes moments ago had disappeared.

"You should get back to your sisters." He cleared a rasp from his voice and released his hold on her. "I'll see you onstage."

"It's a date." She patted the silk roses attached to the comb tucked into the top of her chignon, the same flowers embroidered along the side seams, waist, and lower back of her black skirt and down the sleeves of her charro jacket. "I'll be the one with red roses in her hair. Unless you've changed your charro accessories to match mine."

"Always ready with a wisecrack."

"Keeps you on your toes."

His bark of laughter bounced off the drab walls, the rich sound and his delighted grin eliciting whirls of pleasure that arced through her. "Get ready, Catalina Capuleta. After tonight, your life is going to change."

"I'm counting on it."

He arched a brow in that pensive smolder captured in an ad for a fancy men's cologne that, thanks to him, flew off the shelves as if it were bottles of water. She may or may not have snagged a few samplers at the mall when Patricio's first ad released a few years ago. Might have even spritzed it on a pillow a time or two. A fangirl move she would take to her grave.

Patricio motioned at someone behind her, and she glanced over her shoulder, surprised to find Luciano hanging out near the Las Nubes dressing room door. Odd that he would still be here, seeing as how most of Galán's team was set up in a different area.

Luciano tipped his head in greeting.

"Be careful what you wish for, Catalina," Patricio told her. "Like I've said before, life in the limelight isn't all it's cracked up to be."

A promise or a warning . . . she wasn't sure which he intended as he strode away, his bandmate at his side.

No matter. Patricio's words didn't intimidate her. Like that cheesy positivity mantra scrawled on a poster in her therapist's waiting room, she was shooting for the moon. If she missed, at least she'd land among the stars.

Undeterred, Cat hurried back to the dressing room. Inside she found her sisters gathered in their holding-hands circle waiting for her so they could say their preconcert prayer. Love for them swelled in her chest, tinged with a trickle of regret that this would be her last time playing with them for a while. But she would return. And she would rejoin Mariachi Las Nubes. Because she knew without a doubt that if she missed that moon she was shooting for, the stars she'd land among would be her familia.

And as long as she kept her head in the game with Galán, if she focused on business and didn't get sidetracked by fickle pleasure, her odds of a moon landing with him increased exponentially.

Chapter Six

Cheers and whistles and gritos filled the AT&T Center as Patricio patted the sweat off his face with a black hand towel. Midway through his concert and the audience still hummed with an excited, expectant energy.

For years he had fed off their adrenaline, like a beggar starving for nourishment. Over time, though, he had slowly come to understand that what the mass of fans offered was fleeting. It couldn't nourish a wounded soul. When the music quieted and the lights shut off and the seats emptied, he was left alone. Wanting. Craving a deeper connection he'd yet to experience.

It was a harsh reality that his father's rebukes, both private and in the press, continuously confirmed.

Always a consummate professional, though, Patricio squinted under the bright stage lights and grinned out at the crowd. He was El Príncipe, after all, giving the fans what they wanted. Following in the footsteps of El Rey. Yet *never* surpassing him.

"¡Muchísimas gracias!" he cried into the mic. "Like I said earlier, it's always a pleasure being back in San Antonio."

More celebratory gritos pierced the air with special cries from the locals.

Removing his mariachi sombrero, he held it against his chest and bowed slightly. "Agradezco mucho the warm hospitality during my extended stay here. And I also appreciate the incredible support for the Battle of the Mariachi Bands and Nuestros Niños. We raised an incredible amount of money for the Our Kids organization thanks to many of you here tonight."

He paused for the expected audience reaction, murmuring an "I love you, too" into the mic in answer to a smattering of "Te quiero, Patricio" cries. His wink into one of the moving video cameras set off a ripple of sighs and swoons, reactions he never took for granted, though he recognized that the adulation was mostly for the performer they adored. Not the *real* Patricio Galán.

There were parts of him his fans didn't—couldn't—know. Secret pieces he kept purposefully private. Unwilling to risk having his insecurities plastered all over the press or, worse, going viral on social media, he protected himself with the necessary game of masquerade.

"Speaking of the Battle, how about Mariachi Las Nubes and their powerhouse performance earlier this evening?" Hands raised high, he clapped along with the cheers. "Talented mujeres showing us how tradición and change can lead to beautiful artistry and music. Denme un grito for all the amazing mujeres in the house tonight!"

Cupping a hand behind an ear, he encouraged the Mexican cries of joy he had just called for. Had he been among the crowd, he would have joined in their appreciation, having been equally as awed by the Las Nubes performance.

After talking to Catalina, he should have gone back to his own dressing room. Normally he sequestered himself away from others before a show to avoid distractions. He'd go through his vocal warm-ups, run the full show in his head. Allow his adrenaline free rein, ramping himself up before he harnessed it, his need to give his best for the fans fighting against the ingrained habit of giving his father what the old man wanted—a talented son who never outshone him.

But a strange compulsion Patricio couldn't resist had driven him to forgo his usual preperformance ritual. Instead, disguised in a black hoodie and dark sunglasses, he'd stood in the shadows of the stage wings watching Las Nubes. Impressed by all the sisters. Enthralled by one in particular.

"Speaking of amazing women," he told the crowd, "I'd like to introduce one who's agreed to join me onstage for a few special numbers. A skilled singer-songwriter, one of Padua Records' newest talents, who, according to her, plans to keep me on my toes during our tour!" He winked at the crowd. "We'll see about that, ¿verdad?"

Catcalls and laughter rose from the audience. He chuckled, their anticipation heightening his own. Funny, Catalina wasn't even out here with him yet, and already the exhilaration of performing live that had eluded him lately slowly stretched and awakened from its long hibernation.

He lifted an arm and extended it toward stage right as rehearsed. "Por favor, give it up for Catalina Capuleta."

Red lips curved in her beguiling grin, delicate brows raised in that challenging stare she was wont to throw at him when he—rightfully, mind you—pushed her during rehearsal, Cat sauntered onstage. Her black charro skirt swished across the ankles of her heeled boots. The vines of red roses trailing down the skirt's side seams under the shiny gala swayed with the shake of her hips, and his fingers twitched with the urge to trace the embroidered vines and the curves beneath them.

Confidence straightened her shoulders and spine as she approached the microphone stand next to his. If Catalina was nervous about their set, there was no sign of it. In fact, she looked proud and poised and sexy as hell. Watching her draw near set his body on fire in a five-alarm way he knew could only spell disaster if he didn't find a way to douse the flames.

Instead of keeping a cautionary distance when she reached him, Patricio leaned toward her to kiss her cheek, a traditional greeting in their Latinx comunidad. A gesture he and Catalina had avoided by a silent, if purposeful, agreement over the past week.

Her eyes widened, but she recovered quickly, closing the distance between them and angling her face to accept his kiss.

Her skin was warm and soft against his lips. She smelled like face powder mixed with something musky and rich that quickened his pulse. Her hand rested on his chest, her fingers curling around the lapel of his charro jacket. Instinctively he swung his sombrero behind her, his arm circling her waist in a hug that felt natural but was over far too soon to sufficiently satisfy his desire to touch her, hold her. Have her.

Tiny specks of light flashed around the Center as fans snapped pics with their phones.

Catalina gently patted his chest and eased back. Grabbing her mic stand, she tipped it toward her mouth and shot him a coquettish grin that instantly sent his blood rushing south in a way that could turn unfortunate in front of thousands of onlookers.

"Ay, talk about a warm welcome. I may not be able to wash this cheek for at least a week," she murmured into her mic and caressed her face with her fingertips. "¿Qué piensan?"

The crowd let her know exactly what they thought with a chorus of resounding "yes" and "sí."

Patricio played along, puffing out his chest with pride. She batted her eyelashes and fanned herself with a hand as if overcome by his kiss. Whistles and catcalls echoed through the arena. Proof that, like him, the fans were charmed by Catalina's teasing.

"As the young girl who spent her entire allowance on Patricio's first album and mooned over the cover, my night has been made. It can't get any better than this."

"Oye, believe me, your night can *definitely* get better if I'm involved," he quipped, enjoying their verbal sparring.

"Promises, promises," Catalina drew out the words with a salacious grin and slow shake of her head. Jabbing her thumb at him, she played up to the crowd. "Ay, the ego on this one."

"¡Yo quiero un beso!" an older woman in the second row shouted.

"You're in great company, señora," Catalina shot back with a laugh. "There are many here who'd like a kiss from Patricio Galán, too."

"How 'bout one for me, Cat?"

Her husky laughter answered the call from a young stud in a tan cowboy hat and a tight-fitting white tee about five rows back. Patricio chuckled, but a spurt of uncalled-for jealousy burned through him.

"Oye, güey." Patricio shook a finger in the guy's direction. "I promised her papá I'd keep watch over her on the tour. Don't get me into trouble before we've even left town."

Catalina's brow puckered with a question, and Patricio realized he might have let slip his secret visit to Casa Capuleta and his conversation with her parents.

"I'm a big girl, I can take care of myself. Right, ladies?" Catalina crooked an elbow and raised a fist as if to show off her biceps, hidden under her charro jacket sleeve. High-pitched cheers from the women answered her. "Who knows? It might be *me* who winds up looking out for *you!*"

"Promises, promises." He singsonged her words back at her, eliciting lively laughter from his fans.

"Touché."

Catalina winked and he couldn't help but be smitten by her flirty banter. Inside his chest, the tight knot of ever-present tension unfurled as he grinned down at her. For the first time in ages, Patricio found himself relaxing onstage. Enjoying himself. Thanks to her.

Tugging her mic out of the stand, Catalina snagged the cord with one hand, then angled slightly to face both him and the audience. "Bueno, I'm thinking your fans are ready to hear you sing some more."

He waited for the cheers to quiet down. "I say we slow things down a bit, sing a few classic duets. Maybe try a new number I'm betting will become a classic."

"I'd take that bet and raise the ante."

Ay, she was cheeky. Confident. Captivating in all the right—probably also wrong—ways.

Behind them, the band kicked off the opening strains of Catalina's "No Me Olvides," her burning, pining, angsty, don't-forget-me ballad. The humor sparkling in her brown eyes softened to sincerity. "It's an honor to perform this with you tonight, Patricio."

"Likewise."

Honor woven with something that felt a lot like relief. Maybe even comfort.

Struck by the unfamiliar emotions rioting in his chest, he held out his hand. Catalina rested hers on top of his. Her fingertips curled around his pinkie, and it was as if she gave his heart a little squeeze. It felt right, standing here with her. Their verbal foreplay exciting him. Her smiles and presence warming him. Their voices about to blend in a way he felt certain would wow the crowd.

Closing her eyes, Catalina sang the opening lines. Her melodious voice filled the Center at the same time it filled an emptiness deep inside him.

Entranced, Patricio gazed at her, struck by the all too real possibility that, if he wasn't careful, he just might find himself in deep trouble.

Chapter Seven

The insufferable man was avoiding her.

No doubt about it.

Arms crossed, Cat squinted at the darkened bus windows of Patricio's palace on wheels. The toe of one ankle boot tapped her annoyance on the parking lot asphalt as she weighed her options.

Sulk back to her shared bus. Again.

Knock politely on the door and hear some excuse from Alberto. Again.

Bang on the damn door and demand Patricio see her.

Squinting up at the midday sun, she prayed for the patience her familia would say she rarely possessed.

Ha! The joke was on them. She'd been patient for four days.

Four. Freaking. Days.

After Friday night's concert in San Antonio, they had immediately hopped the buses and beelined to Houston for a Saturday night show. It'd been a fast turnaround with no room for error or anything that didn't involve prep for the concert.

She hadn't expected to work on songwriting with Patricio in the midst of all that. The man had been up to his eyeballs with sound check, troubleshooting problems, and any number of details that made her head spin. Not his, though. He had this way of calmly asking questions and thinking things through. His intensity and commitment to excellence made a girl wonder if he carried that same intensity to other activities. Like the kind that took place behind closed doors. Or up against them.

Of course, then he'd make a decision and start rattling off orders in that authoritative manner of his that had people jumping to carry them out. Cat rarely jumped for anyone. But somehow, with Patricio, she found herself doing his bidding. If begrudgingly.

So fine. With a performance that night, Saturday couldn't count on her wasted-days list. They'd all had a higher priority. But the three days since?

Mija, por favor, they totally counted.

And he had wasted each of them.

On Sunday, Patricio had given everyone the day off, ordering them to enjoy the break in Houston before they made the caravan trek overnight to Irving for Thursday night's show. Cat had gone to mass with two of the other girls on her bus but begged off a trip to the mall, thinking she and Patricio could get down to work. Nope. He'd gone to visit with friends, according to Alberto, who'd been left behind playing tour-bus butler, answering each of Cat's knocks.

Yesterday and this morning . . . the exasperating mariachi had left Alberto to pass along more excuses about why Patricio wasn't available.

Twice already, George Garcia had reached out to ask Cat how things were going with her and their superstar. More like super pain in the ass.

She didn't know why Patricio was playing this silly cat and mouse game when they had a ticking-clock deadline. Padua had made it clear that they wanted the two of them to write as many songs as possible for Patricio's new album by the end of the seven-week tour. That wasn't a lot of time to form a creative partnership.

Adding to the pressure, as a new talent out to prove herself, Cat felt certain Padua's "wanted" really meant "expected" when it came to her. El Príncipe might be able to jerk George and the other executives around, but she didn't have that luxury.

It was past time they got to work.

Decision made, she raised her fist and pounded on the bus door.

Moments later it slid open with a barely audible pneumatic hiss. Alberto stood on the middle step, a slightly pained look on his round face. "Hola, Catalina, it's good to see you again."

Again, because she'd been here a little over an hour ago. And shortly after breakfast.

"Hi, Alberto. Still looking dapper in your suit. I'm living for the day when you surprise me in shorts and a tee or . . . ay, dare I suggest"—she pressed a hand to her chest in mock surprise—"sweats!"

"Don't hold your breath. Or better yet, do!"

Patricio's taunt from somewhere in the bowels of the behemoth bus drew Alberto's attention away from her long enough for Cat to deftly sidestep the older man and scurry up the steps.

"Oh, I—un momen—whoops!" Alberto's hands fluttered in the air as he tried to halt her progress and nearly palmed one of her boobs.

Eyes widening with horror, he stumbled backward. The heel of his black orthopedic dress shoe caught on the top step, and he started toppling in slow-motion like a towering oak felled by an axe.

"¡Ay! ¡Cuidado!" Cat grabbed one of his flailing arms to stop him from collapsing onto the wood floor. Only, the older man was heavier than she anticipated, and she pitched forward with his weight. Her repeated "watch it" turned into a yelp of surprise as gravity and his momentum pulled her toward the floor with him.

Seconds before she would have landed sprawled on top of Alberto and his round belly, a muscular arm looped around her waist from behind, hauling her up. Her back slammed into the solid wall of Patricio's chest, and the air rushed out of her in a guttural *oomph*.

"I got you." His deep voice rumbled against her ear. The vibration traveled down her neck into her chest, sparking wicked curls of lust that pebbled her nipples.

The material of her cropped tee bunched up, leaving her abdomen exposed to the warmth of his bare forearm. With her legs dangling off the ground, her butt wound up cradled intimately against his pelvis where the button on his jeans poked her through her leggings. Damn if the sensation didn't have her thinking about what lay behind that button and zipper. Desire pulsed between her legs, and she squeezed them together.

Shocked by her body's intense reaction to being held by him, she wiggled for him to set her down.

Rather than release her, Patricio's hold tightened. She grabbed on to his forearm. Truthfully, she couldn't have said whether she wanted him to let go or keep her tucked against him.

Alberto blinked up at her from his seat on the wood flooring. Shocked disbelief slackened his jaw.

That made two of them.

So much for the power of a surprise attack on her part.

"You okay?" Patricio ducked closer, and his scruffy jaw scraped her temple. His spice-tinged cologne clung to her next inhalation.

The combustion building from his torso pressed along the length of her backside, plus the strength of his arms wrapped around her and his heady scent enveloping her, had Cat on instant sensory overload.

"¿Estás bien?" he repeated, and all she could manage was to nod mutely. Her loose, messy bun wobbled, the hair tie's hold on her long locks as precarious as her ability to rein in this raging, uncontrollable awareness of Patricio's seductive appeal.

Desperate to put a respectable distance between them and regain some semblance of control, she squeezed his forearm and squirmed for him to let go.

Big mistake.

The friction of her butt against the front of his jeans set off a clash of warning alarms and let's-get-it-on cheers in her head.

"Whoa!" Patricio grunted.

His free hand palmed her hip, pushing her away from his pelvis. Lust arrowed from his fingertips across her belly and lower. He loosened his hold on her waist, and she yelped, stumbling as her feet hit the floor.

Thankfully, Alberto had managed to scramble to his own feet already. The older man grasped her elbow before she tripped over him.

"Gracias," she muttered, tugging down her top and steadying herself.

Of course, her ponytail holder chose that moment to give up the fight. It slid from her hair, sending the locks tumbling over her shoulders and into her face. She swiped the curtain of hair out of her eyes to glare at Patricio. The insufferable man had wisely backed away after unceremoniously dropping her.

"Looks like you're alive and well. If in need of a shave," she shot at him.

"Who said I wasn't? I've been busy."

He motioned to a rectangular table in between two brown leather-upholstered, padded booth seats, one of which butted up against a matching couch that ran along the right side of the bus's front lounge area. Muted sunlight streamed through the slatted blinds covering the dark, tinted windows. It glinted off the table's shiny surface and the glass tumbler nestled in one of the cup holders carved into the table, a precaution against spilled drinks when the bus was in motion.

Cat had seen photographs of Patricio's home on the road in a *People en Español* article several years ago. She and her sisters had oohed and aahed over the lavishly customized tour bus and joked about the perks they'd want when Las Nubes had one of their own. But this was her first time making it through the hallowed door to check out the bus firsthand. Until a few moments ago, Alberto had been a staunch sentry barring unwanted visitors. Namely her.

Ay, the girls were gonna flip, demanding all the juicy details when they video chatted later tonight. Still, she tried to play it cool. No sense getting caught ogling the man's private quarters. She was here for business, not pleasure.

"Busy, huh? Doing what?" she asked, casting a furtive glance around the bus.

A matching brown leather-upholstered couch-bench ran the entire length of the lounge area's left side. Bright red and yellow throw pillows added a homey vibe, and she imagined Patricio sprawled on the cushions, his dark head resting on a pillow. Or her lap.

Cat shook off the tantalizing image and trailed her gaze to one of two supersize televisions that hung in the center of the windows on both sides of the bus. Soccer players jockeyed over a black-and-white ball, chasing each other across a verdant field on one screen, the sound muted.

"Working on ideas for the album?" she prodded when Patricio didn't answer.

"Among other things, but yeah," he said.

Alberto brought a fist to his mouth as he cleared his throat. His bushy brows angled together in a warning scowl Cat recognized well. She'd seen it on her parents' faces whenever she or one of her sisters tried playing a little fast and loose with the truth.

Arms crossed, Patricio scowled back.

Some kind of silent exchange took place between the two men. Alberto's gaze slid to her, then back to Patricio, who gave a quick shake of his head. Whatever mental argument they were having, it clearly involved her.

"Is there something I should be aware of?" she asked.

"Not at all," Patricio asserted.

Alberto grumbled something under his breath but didn't elaborate.

Hands stuffed in his front jeans pockets, Patricio strode from the lounge into the kitchen area. Mottled black-and-light-brown ceramic countertops flanked a stainless steel sink on the left with a microwave / convection oven and a two-burner stove top on the right. If memory served her correctly, somewhere behind the mix of gleaming wooden and brushed metal cabinet doors hid a refrigerator/freezer for the specially prepared meals he was known to order in. If she opened another, she should find the temperature-controlled wine rack. Additions to his home away from home that had garnered praise from the journalist writing the *People en Español* article.

Most stars traveled back to their residences in between weekend shows, while their band and crew stayed in hotels at the next city. Patricio was known to camp out on his bus. Bueno, "camp" being a relative word. This place was a far cry from roughing it.

But forget convection ovens and wine racks. What Cat *reeeeeeally* wanted to see lay beyond a closed pocket door in the glistening wood walls that separated the kitchen space from the private suite that took up the entire back half.

She wasn't interested in testing the comfort of the queen-size bed that slid out for use. Por favor, she had no plans of becoming one of Patricio's groupies.

Nor did she care about the fancy treadmill exercise station that helped him maintain the gorgeous physique his tailor-made leather charro clung to onstage.

Uh-uh. Her music-loving heart raced at the chance to play around with the small recording studio he had installed, complete with a mixing station, multiple monitors, and surround sound. Supposedly Patricio had written many of the songs for his last two albums in his mobile studio while on the road.

That was exactly what they needed to be doing now. Together.

"I'd love to hear what you've come up with," she said.

"I'm still tossing around ideas. Thinking."

"Thinking is good." She sat down on one of the bench seats flanking the table. "Sharing those thoughts with your cowriter is even better."

"I'd invite you to make yourself at home, but . . ." Patricio frowned. "You already are."

"Gracias for the warm welcome." Cat batted her eyelashes with a saccharine-sweet smile for Patricio, then swiveled to offer Alberto an apology. "Perdóname for the minor kerfuffle. I hope your backside's not too sore."

"¡Qué—Oh, no, estoy bien!" Alberto reached behind to rub his butt, then winced and shifted to tuck in his button-down shirt with bashful motions.

Patricio chuckled at the older man's obvious embarrassment. "I can't remember the last time someone's gotten the better of you, viejo. You're losing your touch."

Alberto answered with a *humph* as he finger-combed his thinning salt-and-pepper hair into place.

"Or maybe I'm just that good at not taking no for an answer," Cat challenged.

"One of your many talents." That sarcastic smirk Patricio had perfected tilted a corner of his mouth.

"More proof of how lucky you are to team up with me. Speaking of which, George asked for a progress update when he called earlier to see how I was settling in," Cat shared.

"He did?"

"Mm-hmm. Apparently he didn't think he was getting a straight answer from you. Funny, I feel the same way." Elbows planted on the table, she steepled her hands under her chin and stared up at Patricio, daring him to try and make up another excuse.

The infuriating man leaned against the sink behind him, hands loosely gripping the countertop edge, black boots crossed at the ankles as if he didn't have a care in the world. A state of mind she didn't have the luxury of enjoying. This gig could make or break her career. He knew that and yet . . .

The sound of a wind chime tinkled from Alberto's pocket. He pulled out his phone, his expression brightening when he read the caller's name. A huge grin plumped his round cheeks.

"It's Magdalena. My wife," he added, jiggling his phone at Cat. "I'll take this outside so you two can talk. Patricio, remember what we discussed, okay?"

"Nag, nag, nag," the singer bemoaned. He followed Alberto to the top of the steps, shooing his assistant with a flick of his wrist. "Go on, get out of here. Send Magda my love and ask her to please give you a hard time for giving me a hard time."

"Never!" Alberto called when he stepped onto the parking lot asphalt.

"Oye, you know she will. I'm her favorite!"

Despite her annoyance with Patricio, Cat grinned at the men's banter, more evidence of their close relationship—more tío and nephew than assistant and superstar.

The older man's "hola, mi amor" greeting to his beloved was cut off when Patricio closed the bus door.

The sounds of the traffic passing by on the busy street alongside the hotel's back parking lot disappeared, leaving Cat and Patricio in a muted silence. He strolled back to the kitchen, pushing up the long sleeves of his black Henley again. The muscles in his forearms rippled, the dusting of dark hair against his bronze skin reminding her of his strength, the surprising sense of security she had felt when he'd grabbed her around the waist to keep her from falling earlier.

She forced herself to look away and stop her mind's unwelcome meandering. On the muted TV behind him as he walked by, a player on the Mexico team sank the soccer ball into their opponent's net. The men dogpiled on top of each other in celebration—the same tackle-hug her younger sisters had shared on the sala floor at home, the morning they'd found out Mariachi Las Nubes had moved on to the second round of the competition.

They had worked so damn hard to prove themselves worthy. To do their part in chipping away at the annoying glass ceiling that often kept female mariachis offstage or relegated to playing only backup. She owed it to them, to the students in her all-girls mariachi class at the community center, *to herself*, to not let Patricio and whatever megastar moodiness he had going on stop her from giving this opportunity with Padua Records her best shot.

"Would you like something to drink?" Patricio tugged open a long cabinet door to reveal the fridge.

"Water's fine. Thanks," Cat answered.

"With bubbles or without? Flavored? Plain?"

She laughed. Of course his fridge contained bottled-water options. Probably lined up in neat rows alongside the gourmet meals for his 80/20 diet plan. Meanwhile, over on the much smaller, much less tricked-out bus for the peons, she'd been happy to find the dorm-size fridge stocked with spring water and Gatorade the first night. The box of microwave popcorn and bag of M&M's stashed in another cabinet had provided her with suitable comfort food after the tearful goodbye with her familia.

"Without, please," she answered. "I save the bubbles for my celebratory drinks, preferably in a champagne flute."

"Duly noted. For when you win your Grammy."

"Which won't happen unless we get to work."

Patricio grunted at her needling. Striding toward her, he broke the seal on a bottle of water, then handed it to her as he slid into the other side of the booth. His feet tangled with hers under the table, and she started at the intimacy of his ankle sliding along her lower calf.

She shifted, angling her legs to avoid more contact. There was plenty of room for the two of them. No doubt the bus had been custom designed with his specific height and build in mind. Still, the booth felt smaller, more intimate, with him filling the seat across from her.

"I jotted down some notes this morning." He gestured toward the leather notebook that sat open between them, a silver pen nestled in the seam of the bound pages. Lines of text in a messy script filled one full page and half of another. Some lines had been crossed out. Several repeatedly. A few were circled, two marked with an asterisk.

"May I?" Cat touched the top corner of the notebook, waiting for his permission.

When her ideas were percolating, still in that nebulous stage, she tended to keep them to herself. Patricio might be the same.

For her, the genesis of a lyric or a melody might come from a tickle in her subconscious. Or a niggling sensation building, churning in her chest. Sometimes her muse whispered an enchanting idea in her ear. However it started, the seed of the idea required nurturing and care. Time to sink into her being and fully form before it was ready to be shared.

Every once in a while, a song poured out of her. Notes and chords, words and phrases tumbling over each other, and she raced to get it all written down before it disappeared. That's when she grabbed her phone and gave thanks for her voice-memo app.

Some days, she scribbled in a lined notebook much like Patricio's or typed haltingly into the notes app on her cell, the words hovering on the edge of her consciousness but unable to make the leap into the outside world.

The writing process was sacred. It could also be fickle and frustrating, much like Patricio's recent behavior.

"Go ahead," Patricio answered. "There's nothing much useful, though."

"Modesty? From you?" she teased, brows raised in mock surprise.

He huffed a breath between his teeth. A corner of his mouth trembled as if fighting a grin, but ultimately it tipped in the opposite direction with his admission. "I'm still trying to grasp that elusive . . . something. It's there. But it's not. Y'know?"

His tiny shoulder hitch said "no big deal." But the worry divot between his brows . . . the way his gaze skittered over the pages, then dashed away . . . those anxious tells were a far cry from Patricio's typical cocky assurance.

Curious, she slid the notebook closer.

This was her first real peek into the mind of the man whose talent had earned him accolades she dreamed of. Their two weeks of rehearsals before the San Antonio concert had been so hectic, they hadn't spent much—any, really—time discussing his vision for this album, his first since his crossover album had skyrocketed up the pop and Latin charts.

Millions around the globe had sung his praises. Fans had clamored for his concert tickets.

Surprisingly, though, there had also been a small faction of haters—mariachi traditionalists, his father included, who made it clear they believed Patricio had sold out. Gone over to the dark side of commercial music instead of staying true to his heritage. El Rey had even proclaimed his displeasure with his son's decision in several interviews.

Pretty shitty move if you asked her. And she knew a thing or two about shitty moves by fathers.

To his credit, Patricio had refused to comment publicly.

As someone who regularly bucked similar small-minded traditionalists and often faced the wrath of their rebukes but rarely kept quiet, she'd been impressed with his restraint.

"Let's see what you've got," she murmured.

"Wait!" Stretching forward, he flattened a large hand over his chicken scratch.

Cat tilted her head in question.

"If I show you mine, you'll have to show me yours," he grumbled.

Laughter bubbled out of her.

He scowled his displeasure.

"I didn't fall for that line from Carlito Pérez in fifth grade. And he was our class hottie. Doubtful I'm falling for it now. But good try." She winked and tried to slide the notebook out from under his grasp.

Patricio didn't budge. His fingertips pressed into the paper, tendons and blood vessels popping up along the back of his hand. The intensity in his gaze sharpened.

"That was a joke," she said, drawing out the last word. "Look, I know what it means to collaborate. We're a team, right?"

He slid his gaze to the far windows, where Alberto could be seen talking on the phone outside. Patricio's lips thinned as if he were forcibly keeping words inside. Strange reactions to what she had thought was a rhetorical question.

Something was off. She didn't know why or what. But she was certain of it. Odds were good that Alberto probably knew what Patricio was hiding, based on the two men's silent exchanges and the old man's cryptic remarks. And while she wanted to ask, she doubted Alberto would betray Patricio's trust by confiding in her. Hell, she didn't expect him to.

This was a problem she'd have to figure out on her own. And she would. Her success—her promise to her familia—depended on Patricio eventually trusting her enough to bare his musical soul. A trust she wanted to earn, if he would only let her.

"This is *your* album, Patricio. Yes, we're a team, but it's only right that you and your vision should take the lead." She gently patted the back of his hand, relieved when he took the hint and loosened his death grip. "Just don't get too used to it."

Patricio sagged back in his cushioned seat with a shake of his head. "Madre de Dios, you never let up."

"Pedal to the metal. Always." She grinned at his eye roll. "Now, let's see what you've got for me."

Running a finger slowly down each line of text, she scanned his notes. This was one of her favorite parts of the creative process. The idea dump. Reading over someone else's thoughts. Opening her mind and heart to whatever grabbed her or teased her inner muse out to play.

Within seconds, the synergy that can come of brainstorming with someone began to shimmer inside her. Whether he realized it or not, hidden in the subtext of Patricio's bold scrawl lay a theme. A message. One that craftily made itself known and spoke to her.

Roots—binding, life-giving, gnarled

Nuestra historia. Our history.

Made in Mexico. Hecho en México.

Mamá's favorite rancheras

Canciones de nuestra historia, followed by a list of old classics by Antonio Aguilar, Pedro Infante, Jorge Negrete, José Alfredo Jiménez, Vicente Fernández, Rocío Dúrcal, Lucha Villa, and several other musical icons who had blazed the trail in mariachi.

Revenge— crossed out, then circled, or maybe it was the other way around. She couldn't be sure if it was a keep or delete idea.

Tradición y modernidad

Prove him wr—

This one interested her mostly because the unfinished thought had been crossed out so many times, she could barely make it out.

Reality vs. persona

Also crossed out, though still legible.

Familia y traición

The last entry—family and betrayal—had been underlined. Multiple times. With an intensity that left deep grooves in the paper. An asterisk had been scrawled at the end of the entry for added emphasis. A sign that perhaps his father's denigration in the press over Patricio's successful pop album had hit harder than he let on publicly.

From the age of ten, when she had first arrived at Casa Capuleta, Cat had been a lucky recipient of unconditional love and support from Arturo Capuleta. Papo would never turn his back on her or any of her sisters.

Her asshole birth father? That was another story. The cabrón had willingly done so, repeatedly. Hell, his name wasn't even on her birth certificate. Gracias a Dios for small favors, because that one removed a tie to the man she hoped to never see again.

But how to cope with a slap in the face from the man the entire mariachi world maintained on a pedestal? Worse, they expected you to do the same.

That was a raw deal.

Patricio may not have made a statement in the press, but this list—the themes of familia, roots, betrayal, and history—spoke volumes.

"Bueno, you're right *and* you're wrong," she told him.

He arched a brow in his signature sardonic glare. "I am rarely wrong, especially when it comes to my music. But I'll bite. Explain yourself."

"You're right, there's not much on your list."

His nostrils flared and she caught the tightening of his jaw muscles.

Ooh, she'd hit a nerve. Maybe someone else on this bus wasn't as good with criticism, constructive or otherwise, as he advised others to be. Her, specifically.

Interesting.

"You're also unequivocally wrong," she pushed. "I say, there's plenty to work with here. It's emotional, raw. Universal. Actually, it's really good."

She nudged the notebook toward him. He eyed it for several weighty seconds, his expression grim. Then he nodded slowly, and the tautness in his broad shoulders eased. The worry line between his brows relaxed. His nod grew more pronounced, confident. That smug grin of his made its reappearance, and she realized with a jolt that she needed it to. Needed his annoying conceit because it made her raise her hackles.

Arrogant megastar? Him, she could easily handle.

Broody son wounded by his parent's disdain? That guy hit her heart in a way that could ultimately prove detrimental.

"*Really good*, huh?" Satisfaction danced around the edges of his question as he ran a finger along the notebook's leather edge.

"Sure. But I can make it better." She gave a little head toss that sent her loose hair swaying around her shoulders.

He laughed. A rich, hearty sound that wrapped around her with the warmth of her favorite comfy sweatshirt. Scooping up the pen, he clicked it open. "Let's get started."

Chapter Eight

Patricio gazed out at the sea of middle schoolers filling the wooden bleachers at the Nuestros Niños Club in Irving, Texas, Wednesday afternoon. Standing beside him at the gymnasium's center court, Catalina smiled warmly at the young girl who had shyly posed a question from her seat in the second row.

"Was I nervous getting up on that huge stage in front of thousands of fans at the AT&T Center for my first concert?" Catalina repeated, ensuring the rest of the kids heard the question. "Hmm, would you like to take a guess?"

The young girl and several others around her nodded, eyes wide with awe.

"Sí, I won't lie, I definitely was." Tucking her hair behind her ear, Catalina took a few steps to her right. The students tracked her path, drawn by her story. She spoke with passion but in a friendly, approachable way the kids seemed to relate to. Even Patricio found himself mesmerized by her.

Watching her effortlessly connect with the kids, he relaxed for the first time since he'd spotted the group of photographers pulling up behind his rental car in the parking lot. This was supposed to have been a private meet and greet for the club. No live press asking probing personal questions. But once they had arrived, barring the reporters and their crew from entering would have drawn unwanted negative attention.

"And I'll be nervous tomorrow night when we hit the stage at the Pavilion, here in Irving," Catalina continued. "Pero before every performance or, really, *any* time I'm faced with something important and I feel my stomach start to get all jittery and jumbly . . ." Fingers bent like a claw, she circled her hand in front of her midsection, then flattened her palm to quickly *thump-thump* over her heart. "Or when my pulse quickens and pounds in my ears. You know what helps?"

Collectively the students shook their heads.

"I take all that energy—'cuz that's what it feels like, like electricity zipping through me—and I turn it into fuel, feeding my determination to kick a—kick butt." She chuckled at her near blooper and turned to the club's director with an expression that mimicked the grimace emoji she had texted him, along with an eye-roll face, in response to one of his jokes.

Laughter tittered through the crowd.

"Then I go out on that stage and give my absolute best." Her amber eyes alight with enthusiasm, Catalina crossed in front of Patricio as she spoke, her boots eating up the distance to the left side of the bleachers.

Enthralled by her animated speech, the kids shifted to follow her progress.

The cameras lined up along the top center row and huddled at the bottom corners near the gym doors trained on her every movement.

Even Patricio couldn't take his eyes off her. Hell, he hadn't been able to stop thinking about Catalina ever since she and Mariachi Las Nubes had blown away the competition in the first round of the Battle, and each round after that. Then, when she joined him onstage for the San Antonio concert and again in Houston, he'd been zapped by the electricity she spoke of now. It made him—*she* made him—feel alive in a way he hadn't for a while now.

His growing infatuation with her playful smirks and overflowing confidence . . . his inability to stop imagining her in his arms, his lips and tongue and hands exploring every delectable inch of her body, discovering her erogenous zones, and turning her husky laughter to moans of pleasure. Madre de Dios, even now, in a gym packed with hormonal teens and a gaggle of paparazzi cameras trained on him, Patricio found himself turned on by her wit and charm.

That's why he had ghosted her the past few days, scrambling to suppress this infernal attraction that could only spell trouble for his ill-thought-out plan. Of course, he should have known that Catalina would be undeterred, almost literally tackling Alberto to the ground as she finagled her way onto Patricio's bus yesterday.

"Because when it comes down to it, doing our best—or trying our hardest—is all we can ask of ourselves," Catalina continued, her ease in connecting with the kids reminding Patricio of her role teaching music lessons at the Casa Capuleta Community Center. "My parents have always told my eight sisters and me that if—" She broke off on a laugh at the smattering of "no me digas," the "you don't say" twittering through the crowd in one variation or another in both Spanish and English. "Yeah, you heard that right. There are *nine* of us Capuleta siblings. All girls."

"I've met them, and let me tell you, her parents are saints," Patricio added. Catalina sent him a wide smile, love for her familia shining on her beautiful face. His chest tightened with a sensation he chose not to define.

"Yes, they are," she agreed, then turned back to face the kids. "My papá and mamá believe that, at the end of the day, if you can look yourself in the mirror and honestly say 'I tried my best,' pues eso es lo más importante. Or, because we don't all speak Spanish here, that's what's most important."

Her parents' wise words sounded so simple when she shared them. A basic premise to live by. Only, not for someone who'd been conditioned to do the opposite. To never overshadow the one person whose approval he had always sought.

"But something else that helps calm my preshow nerves is my sister Mariana's pep talks. Those are the best! And you know who else happens to give a pretty good pregame pep talk? This guy." Catalina jerked a thumb in Patricio's direction.

He pressed a hand to his chest and mouthed the word "me?" She nodded, but he couldn't recall what she might be referring to.

Her expression encouraging, she peered up at him as she made her way back to his side. Today she'd left her hair loose, the wavy locks tumbling around her shoulders and down her back, a dark satiny curtain against her red, long-sleeved blouse. The bright color matched her short nails and the stain on her full lips—a stain he'd dreamed about wiping off with his kiss. Slow and languid. Hot and intense.

Mind-blowing and . . . and completely inappropriate for their business-only relationship.

And yet . . . it was like Catalina possessed some sort of magnetic force. One that compelled him to want to be around her. With her.

Yesterday, after she had bulldozed her way onto his bus, they'd sat at the table brainstorming together and he'd been blown away by her talent, marveling at how naturally her mind wove words and phrases with musical notes she hummed, beats she tapped out with her fingertips or with the butt of her hand on the table. The pure joy in her process had even convinced his recalcitrant muse to join the fun.

"Do the words 'bravery' and 'fear' ring a bell?" she prodded, pulling Patricio from his rambling thoughts of yesterday and back to their current situation with their interested audience.

"Bravery and fe—ahhhh, San Antonio, right?" he asked, remembering their talk in the hallway before Mariachi Las Nubes had opened his concert.

Her eyes brightened as if their shared memory brought her the same pleasure it did him. She motioned for him to share the story with the kids, and he obliged.

"We're often told that we shouldn't be afraid. In the mariachi world, in our Latinx culture and the world in general, there's a lot of machismo pride. I don't know how many times I've heard 'sé un hombre'—be a man." He pitched his voice lower and held up a tight fist. "Suck it up. Be brave. But bravery isn't the absence of fear. It's recognizing that fear and not letting it stop us."

Unconsciously he reached for Catalina's hand, unaware that he had until she threaded her fingers with his in a tight clasp. He slanted a glance at her and caught the proud tilt of her chin, the confident curve of her mouth. Buoyed by their united front, he continued. "Whether you're a mariachi singer, a teacher, a military member, a nurse, a video game phenom, or whatever it is you choose to pursue, if you follow Catalina's advice and try your best—if you face your fears, use them to help you make smart or at least informed decisions—bueno, you'll be on the right track."

"Excellent advice for all of us, and the perfect note on which to end our special visit." The club's director, a tall, wiry Afro-Latina woman with a beaming smile, short braids, and a reputation for fighting bureaucracy for her kids, stepped out from among a group of staff and volunteers gathered near the side doors on the right. "Muchísimas gracias, Patricio and Catalina, for taking the time to visit with us."

Applause broke out in the gym. The students rose, moving like a shape-shifting blob toward center court, cell phones primed to snap selfies. Thankfully the volunteers and staff stepped in, directing the kids to form a line before pandemonium ensued.

An hour later, Patricio and Catalina still stood at center court, having agreed to answer a few questions from the press once the kids had left.

"I appreciate your patience with allowing the students to have priority," Patricio told the small group—reporters and camera teams from two local stations, along with three freelancers working for various online entertainment sites.

In actuality, he wanted to ask how the hell they'd managed to find out about this unannounced event. But that was an issue for Alberto or George to dig into.

Instead, Patricio turned on the superstar charisma and fielded the usual questions:

How does it feel to be back on tour? "It's been my second home for as long as I can remember. Feels good to visit with the fans." Really, he meant: "Loneliness dogs my steps wherever I go, sometimes even my place in Puerto Vallarta; performing for my fans offers a sense of connection with others, even if it's only surface level."

Any chance of a combined concert with your father? "Not at this time. Our calendars are full and set far in advance." Really, he meant: "No way in hell."

When's your next album coming out? "I'm working on that now. Anticipation makes the heart grow fonder, right?"

Will it be another crossover like fans have asked for, or are you following your father's admonition that you honor tradition? This question made him pause. Rebuttals and denials jostled for position on the tip of his tongue. He bit them back, unwilling to put his personal struggles with his father on display.

Catalina, who'd been surprisingly silent during the barrage of questions aimed at him, hooked her right arm through his left, drawing the journalists' attention to her. "I've actually been fortunate enough to get a peek at what Patricio's cooking up for us, music-wise. Aaaand while I won't reveal any secrets, I think it's safe to say, if you're a *real* Patricio Galán fan, you're gonna be over-the-moon pleased."

Patricio ducked his head to hide the *what are you talking about* glare he shot her from the reporters' prying eyes.

It was a good thing one of them felt confident about his next album. Other than thematic phrases and plays on words, rhythms she had pounded against the table or shushed through her teeth beatbox-style yesterday, everything still felt unclear to him. Ideas more like whirls of wispy smoke that slipped through his fingers when he tried to grasp them.

It wasn't just her he'd been avoiding the past few days.

The keyboard set up beside the mixing station on the bus? He'd given it a wide berth.

His favorite guitar? Still propped in the corner near his closet, untouched.

Hell, he hadn't even bothered closing the foldaway bed in the mornings, turning his private space from bedroom to music room. Instead, the bed lay open all day, the sheets a tangled mess. Proof of his nights of restless sleep.

Used to be, his dreams were haunted by his father's scathing comments to the press. Then Catalina had burst onto his bus with her come-hell-or-high-water-we're-doing-this attitude, nearly tackling Alberto to the floor, and Patricio had reacted without thinking, scooping her into his arms to stop her fall. A move that brought him in pulse-pounding contact with her alluring curves. The slope of her hip burning his palm, her round ass cradled by his crotch. Lust had blazed a fiery trail through him leaving him singed and smoldering.

His restless sleep last night had a completely different, far more enticing, though equally bothersome, cause. Her.

"So, as well as singing a set during your concert, are the two of you working on the album together?" one of the local reporters asked.

"I think it's safe to say that Padua has signed Catalina because of her many talents," Patricio answered.

The truth. If also a runaround answer, given his secret compulsion to write this album on his own, thus proving himself to his father.

"Ay, you really know how to make a girl blush." Catalina nudged him playfully with her elbow; then her cheeky grin softened as she addressed the reporters. "Honestly, everything that has happened since

Mariachi Las Nubes won the Battle is a dream come true. I'm thrilled to be part of the tour."

The lone female reporter, who looked to be in her early twenties, held out her cell, making it clear that she was voice recording the interview. "Social media is buzzing with clips of your performances together. You share sensational chemistry. Now you're writing music and making secret appearances. Your fans would love to find out if the two of you might be . . . y'know . . . hiding a more personal secret."

A sly smile on her lips, the girl jiggled her cell back and forth between Patricio and Catalina as if it might entice them to reveal her misguided innuendo.

He was experienced enough to not make a big deal out of her blatant info digging. A seasoned pap, or one hungry enough, could sniff out a story from even the slightest whiff of nervous sweat.

Catalina, still new at the paparazzi game, released his arm like it was a live electrical wire, her hazel eyes silver dollar wide. "No! There's nothing—I mean, I don't—uh, we don't . . ." Her tan cheeks darkened with a soft blush, and she held up both hands as if to ward off the young journalist's nosiness.

"Look, I get that part of your job is to ferret out a good scoop," Patricio chided. "But all that's going on here is a mutual respect for each other's talent."

"El Rey is known for his tour romances. You can't blame us for wondering if this might be a case of the apple not falling far from the tree," the young reporter persisted.

"That's enough," Patricio warned, not bothering to temper the anger sharpening his tone. He was used to intrusive speculation about his personal life, but the insinuation was disrespectful to Catalina, who was just getting started in this business and didn't warrant the negative press.

Before he could cut the interview short, Catalina stepped forward, one hand fisted on a hip, her expression icy. "Questions and comments like yours are why women in our industry continue to have doors closed in our faces and hurdles put in our way."

The girl swallowed, but she still held out her phone, clearly not backing down.

"I'm damn good at my craft," Catalina said. "I am great at my job. Hard work and dedication—that's what my parents taught me. *That's* what earned me my deal with Padua and my spot on this tour. Gentlemen"—she dipped her head at the others in the group—"it's been a pleasure chatting. I hope your stories focus on the kids and Nuestros Niños. Maybe also on the need for more female mariachi whose names are in lights at the top of concert venue marquees."

Glancing over her shoulder, she eyed Patricio expectantly. "If you're ready to go, I have a video chat dinner date with my familia. Casa Capuleta House Rules say latecomers get dish duty. And believe me, my sisters will hold me to it the first night I'm back home."

With a diva toss of her hair, Catalina strode away.

Aware of the cameras, Patricio silently cheered her righteous indignation as he bid the journalists goodbye. Then he followed behind her, admiring the saucy shake of her hips and the *are you coming or what* expression she sent him as she pushed open the gymnasium door.

Chapter Nine

Cat awoke in her hotel room Thursday morning to the stutter-stop of something vibrating on the nightstand. Rolling over, she squinted at the sliver of sunlight streaming through the crack where the thick blackout curtains didn't quite meet. She rubbed the sleep from her eyes to peer at the hotel's digital clock. 8:35 a.m. glowed in bright block font.

Her phone vibrated again, then stopped. Vibrated, then stopped.

It couldn't be social media notifications. Those had been turned off since the morning after the first concert, when a picture of her and Patricio had been posted on his fan club's Instagram account. By midday, her number of followers had ballooned from a few thousand to more than twenty-five thousand and climbing.

It was great exposure for a newcomer. But even she, who thrived in the spotlight, had been taken aback.

The quick vibration-stop-vibration-stop pattern started up again, and she stretched out an arm to grab her cell. A little red circle with the number forty-seven stamped her text message app.

Forty-seven? ¿Qué carajo?

She bolted upright, repeating her initial "what the hell" as she watched the number increase to forty-eight. Palming her hair out of her face, she opened the app. A long string of new messages from friends and acquaintances greeted her. She scrolled through them, scanning the opening words that were visible on the app's home screen. All of them seemed to be some combination of "Felicidades, girl . . ." or "Way to go . . ." or, from one of her high school friends perpetually on the man-hunt, "You snagged a real . . ."

What was going on? Her joining the tour and signing with Padua was weeks-old news. These new notes of congratulations over the past few hours made no sense.

Warily she eyed the top of the list, where the most recent messages sat waiting to be opened: three from George Garcia, four from Alberto, twenty-one in her "Battle Champs" sister thread, and, directly below, one from Patricio.

While she dithered over which to read first, her thumb accidentally tapped Patricio's name. The screen shifted as his message opened.

Ignore the headline. They're digging where there's no treasure.
Instead, show them what you've got tonight onstage.

Headline? Digging for treasure? What did he—¡Madre de Dios! She slapped a hand to her forehead as realization struck.

The fucking interview yesterday. The young blonde eager to get a scoop or, at the very least, write an article with the potential of going viral. Even if it skirted the truth.

Cat's stomach clenched with dread as she tapped over to George's thread. No doubt the producer had shared the link.

Sure enough, the second of his three "this will blow over" messages included a link to a page in the Entertainment section of *Pa' la Gente*, an online magazine. Based on the article's title, "The 4-1-1 on Patricio Galán's Newest 'Partner' (wink)," *For the People* didn't concern itself with truth as much as with chisme.

A quick skim of the article mostly proved Cat's point. Sure, the young woman mentioned Nuestros Niños, and there were a few sentences about Mariachi Las Nubes and Casa Capuleta's Community Center. But most of the limited word count focused on her background—her birth mom's deportation and tragic death, her unaccounted-for birth father, the years she and Blanca had spent in the system before landing on Arturo and Berta's MI CASA ES SU CASA welcome mat. The genesis of Las Nubes. Her reputation as an ambitious, often labeled "brash," mariachi clawing her way to the top by any means. Even a mention and link to a copy of the feminist rant video Cat had posted, then taken down during the Battle. And, more damning, a photo of her and Patricio holding hands during yesterday's meet and greet at Nuestros Niños, along with a mention of "how close" they seemed.

This chick had done her homework, and then some. If only her angle had been more "female mariachi fights her way to new heights" instead of "scrappy no-name has her sights set on snagging El Príncipe." Of course, the second pic—this one of Cat linking arms with Patricio while they were being interviewed, her smiling up at him like he was a hot fudge sundae she wanted to devour—didn't freaking help.

The unfairness of the article's slant had anger and frustration roiling in her chest. They pushed up her throat in a low growl.

Her phone vibrated in her hand, surprising her, and she dropped it onto her lap.

Another text from Patricio popped up in a banner at the top of the screen: We need to talk. I'm heading . . .

She tapped the notification to finish reading his message: . . . to your room. Be ready to let me in.

Let him in?

Scandalized, she glanced down at her oversize red sleep tee, the words "Latina AF" in black script across the front. Registered the fact that she didn't have on any pants. And—a quick swipe confirmed—dried slobber crusted the edge of her mouth.

Holy crap! She started to respond with Give me ten. But those little blue dots hovered on her screen, signaling that he was typing.

Sure enough, another text appeared: On my way.

¡Madre de Dios! Leaping off her bed, Cat raced to change and wash up. The white sheet tangled around her left foot and she tumbled to the floor. She winced at the rug burn on her bare knees but hopped up, huffed a curse at the sheet, and scrambled to the bathroom.

Moments later, teeth brushed and face washed, she had one leg in a pair of exercise shorts she had snagged from the pile of clothes in the corner when a soft knock sounded on her door.

What the hell? Had he run from his bus or what?

Cat hop-stepped into the shorts, her eyes scanning her night-stand, the squat dresser / entertainment center, and the shelf above the tiny fridge and one-cup coffee maker, searching for, but not find-ing, a ponytail holder or claw clip for her hair. Not wanting Patricio to be spotted lurking outside, she muttered "F it" and hurried to let him in.

As soon as she opened the door wide enough, Patricio slipped inside, pushing it closed behind him. Despite her outrage at the arti-cle's petty slant and her flabbergasted shock that he would think it wise to meet in her room—of all places!—a bark of laughter burst from her when the bathroom light illuminated his getup.

She slapped a hand over her mouth, but it did little to stifle her giggles.

Dressed in black—of course—he sported a pair of worn sweatpants and a roomy hoodie, the strings pulled tight and tied in a lopsided bow under his chin. Even the oval of his face peeking out of the hoodie was mostly hidden, thanks to the ski-goggle-size dark glasses covering his eyes. He looked like a hit man in a bad B movie on his way to whack a mobster.

Patricio frowned. Or rather, his forehead above the huge glasses wrinkled and his mouth below them tipped downward. That was all she could see of his face.

"What's so funny?" he grumbled.

"I'm wondering how often you try to go incognito and if it's ever really worked for you." She eyed him up and down, from his black sneakers to the sweatpants hanging loose on his hips to the baggy sweatshirt, its hood hugging his head.

"Says the woman who looks like she stuck her finger in the light socket. Those '80s hair bands ain't got nothing on you."

She wrinkled her nose at his dig and barely checked the urge to smooth her bedhead.

Without waiting for an invitation, he moved deeper into her room. "Did a tornado blow through here or what?"

"Neatness is more Mariana and Blanca's strong points. I prefer the lived-in look."

"You nailed it." Reaching the rolling, ergonomic desk chair, he picked up the lacy bra hanging over the backrest.

Cat had never been accused of being modest. She felt comfortable in her skin and with her curves. The only person she dressed to impress was herself. If she felt good in an outfit, who cared what someone else thought?

However, the sight of her favorite bra cradled in Patricio's large palm did strange things to her. Lusty, toe-curly things she did not want to feel or fantasize about.

She marched over to him and snatched the lacy item out of his hand. "If I wanted maid service, I wouldn't hang the Do Not Disturb sign on the door."

"You'll want to put away your unmentionables before letting them in," he said, his mouth twitching with his smirk.

She ignored the jab and clasped her hands, along with the bra, behind her back.

Patricio moved her comfy fleece robe from its usual spot—draped across the seat and armrests—to the cluttered desktop. The lavender material with bold fuchsia swirls pooled over her journal, laptop, and the empty bag of microwave popcorn from her late-night movie-streaming snack. After familia FaceTime with her parents and sisters, she'd had a hard time settling down for the evening. Thinking about everything she was missing at home.

Wondering if her birth father had ever felt a similar sense of loss. Then hating the small part of her that cared, no matter how hard she tried to squash it.

Hence the empty popcorn bag on the desk. The M&M's wrapper in the trash. The mini bottle of red blend in the recycle bin. And the plastic cup with a deep purple circle of dried wine rimming the bottom on the nightstand. Remnants from her raid on the hotel's wannabe bodega in the lobby.

Had she known Patricio planned to drop by, she would have tidied . . . ha! Who was she kidding? She would have suggested they meet somewhere else. As it was, Dios save them if he'd been spotted leaving his bus at the back of the parking lot to sneak up here.

Patricio started to sit in the desk chair but froze midsquat and gestured at the blackout curtains. "Do you mind? It's a little . . ."

Batcave-ish?

Gloomy?

Clandestine?

That last one played havoc with her already-haywire nerves. With the curtains still drawn, the room lay in muted darkness. Rays of light peeked around the edges, casting long, thin beams across the carpet and her unmade bed. Yesterday's jeans lay on the floor in front of the nightstand, her blouse a puddle of red on the splotchy brown carpet. Both hastily discarded. Only, not because she and her lover had been impatient to touch, taste, feel.

More like, she'd thrown off her clothes while fighting lonely, guilt-ridden tears she hadn't expected. In that moment, all she'd wanted was her pj's, comfort snacks, a warm bed, and a feel-good movie on the screen.

"Uh, give me a sec," she mumbled when Patricio motioned at the curtains again.

Scampering around the small room, Cat gathered up discarded clothes, a bath towel, her boots, and the chanclas she'd slipped on for her provisions run to the lobby and then kicked off upon her return. In the classic company's-coming-clean-quick move, she tossed everything into the closet and slid the door shut.

Too late she realized she should have held on to her bra and popped into the bathroom to put it on.

It's all good, she pep-talked herself.

Smoothing her hands over her hair, she held her head high and made her way to the window. She turned her head away and caught Patricio doing the same when she reached behind the decorative curtain to tug one of the blackout drapes open. Bright early-morning sunlight invaded the room.

Patricio had removed his sunglasses in the dimness, and now he squinted at her, brow furrowed with a scowl.

"If you snuck over here to check up on me, I'm fine," she told him, settling on the foot of her bed, facing him.

"First of all, I didn't sneak anywhere."

"Oh, okay. So your Rocky-running-through-the-streets-of-Philly outfit is just a new look for you?"

"Hilarious." He pulled the string tie loose and skimmed the hoodie off his head.

Unfairly, his disheveled wavy black hair gave him a sexy, roguish appeal. No '80s-rock-band jokes for him.

"You didn't reply to Alberto," he chided. "Or George."

"I was up late watching a movie, so I set my phone to Do Not Disturb until eight thirty and slept in. What's the big—"

"Or me."

Something in his tone—more like unease than the annoyance she expected—stalled her flip remark.

This was new. In the nearly two months since they'd first met during the Battle of the Mariachi Bands, Patricio had run the gamut from arrogant to demanding, taunting to teasing. Even smoldery.

Back in San Antonio, when he stopped by her dressing room before Mariachi Las Nubes had opened his show, Patricio had seemed a little concerned. But the emotion now blanketing his handsome face smacked too much of pity, and she refused to be pitied, by anyone. Especially if it was because of her past.

Straightening her shoulders, she pushed down the edginess still lingering from the emotional pit she'd fallen into last night, focusing instead on her irritation with the unfair portrayal of her in the article.

"I've dealt with crappy press before," she told Patricio. "Machismo and the patriarchy and traditionalists who think my sisters and I and others like us don't belong. At least not in the spotlight."

"This is different. It calls your character into question." Leaning forward, he rested his elbows on his knees, his dark eyes peering into hers. Searching, gauging, as if he could see into the hidden corners of her soul. The secret places where she shoved the memories and emotions she didn't care to deal with. The ones he did not need to be aware of.

She blinked and looked away, deliberately conceding in their staring contest to protect herself. "Look, it is what it is. Am I pissed that a woman wrote that bitchy article? Sure. Will being pissed off change anything? No." Dragging in a shaky breath, she wedged her fingers through her hair, combing it back off her face. "It might feel good for a little while. But the best revenge is to prove them wrong. Show them what I'm capable of. Show *him* how it should be done."

Patricio drew back with a frown. "Him who?"

"What?"

"You said 'him': 'Show *him* how it should be done.' Who were you—"

"No one." Appalled by her Freudian slip, Cat hopped off the bed. "I meant, you know, a collective 'him.' Like, the patriarchy. That's all."

Liar.

The only person outside of familia she ever discussed her birth father with was her therapist. The cabrón had done nothing to help her get where she was today, so the bastard didn't warrant mention in any conversation she had with Patricio. That didn't mean the anger stoking her determination to succeed didn't flare, singeing emotions still raw from last night.

Frustrated tears pricked her eyes, and she stepped toward the tiny alcove with the microwave, fridge, and coffee maker before he could notice.

Patricio clasped her wrist, stopping her.

"What's going on? If someone back in San Antonio or"—his tone darkened, a rough edge sharpening his words—"on my tour is giving you a hard time, say the word and I'll take care of it."

"There's no need."

"But you're not denying that *there is* an 'it.'"

"Don't put words in my mouth. Let's drop the topic."

"Catalina."

She groaned, frustrated by his pestering. "Do I look like a damsel in distress who needs saving?"

His gaze made a leisurely stroll down her faded LATINA AF tee and exercise shorts, following the length of her legs to her bare feet, then back up again. She shivered at the interest sparking in his black-coffee eyes when he met her gaze. The pad of his thumb stroked the sensitive skin on her inner wrist in a slow, sensual caress. Awareness skittered up her arm, a match to the flame of lust. The juncture between her thighs tightened with need.

She was a damsel in distress, all right, but foolishly, saving was not what her body craved.

"You might scare some people off with your snarky attitude and mouthy tees. But I see this." He cupped her jaw, sliding his hand until his thumb touched the outside corner of her right eye, where a tear had pooled.

Her eyes fluttered closed, the entire side of her face on fire from his gentle touch. Heat spread down her neck and into her chest. Her nipples pebbled, straining against her cotton shirt.

"I've felt the slash of your sharp tongue," Patricio said, chuckling when she wrinkled her nose in complaint. Then his expression sobered, his gaze softening as he stared down at her. "But I've also witnessed the way you use it to inspire others—your sisters, your students, the kids yesterday. I know how much your music means to you. It shows in every performance and is why the fans adore you."

"What's with all this sweet talk? You're gonna make me blush," she joked, playfully swatting at his stomach in an attempt to shift the charged mood. Her fingers snagged on the front pouch pocket of Patricio's hoodie. She left them there, reluctant to let go of him.

"Whatever secrets you have, they're yours to keep," he promised. "Pero you know people will dig. They'll make shit up to sell magazines or get more clicks. Be prepared, and try not to let it, or them, get to you."

Moved by his unexpected concern, she nodded, her throat clogged by a sudden rush of tears.

"Behind those bright lights you seek, Cat, there's a lonely darkness. I hate to think of your spark being dimmed because of it. Or by anyone. You deserve better." He loosened his grip on her wrist, his hand sliding in a warm trail up her arm to cup her shoulder.

His gaze dropped to her mouth, then back up to meet hers again. Unable to resist his pull, Cat leaned toward him. Her fingers tugged on his hoodie pocket. Desire flared in his eyes in the seconds before they closed, his head drawing nearer. She sucked in a breath and his earthy scent bombarded her. Lust took over and she stretched up on her toes. Eager for his kiss.

A knock sounded on the door. They both froze. Eyes wide with shock, their lips a faint touch apart. The second tap at the door had panic gripping her at the thought that someone might have followed him.

"Catalina?" a hushed voice called. "It's Alberto. Checking to make sure everything is, uh, as it should be?"

The breath she'd been holding rushed out on a relieved sigh. Patricio straightened, a pained look tautening his angular features.

"¡Dios mío, ese viejo! I swear, he's got a parental sixth sense or something. His timing . . ." Patricio's hand slid from her jaw, his fingertips skimming her neck, her collarbone . . . tickling her skin, and leaving a delicious trail of pinprickly awareness.

"It's for the best," she murmured.

Actually, Alberto's timing was impeccable. The absolute last thing she needed was to put truth to that damn article's insinuation by kissing Patricio. No matter how badly she wanted to taste his lips. Feel his hands on her body while she explored his, stoking the fire his touch kindled inside her.

Instead, legs wobbly, Cat stepped away. The backs of her calves bumped her mattress, a stark reminder that they were stretching the boundaries of temptation. That she was dangerously close to making a costly mistake.

"You should go," she said. "We both have a busy day before tonight's concert."

Patricio reached for his oversize sunglasses on the desk next to her comfy robe. "Keep your chin up. Let your performance do the convincing."

"Oh, it will. Believe me."

"That's what I like to hear." He winked, making her silly heart flutter. Then he slipped on his glasses, pulled the hood over his head and tied the bow, and left.

As soon as the door closed behind him, Cat collapsed onto her bed with a muttered groan.

Madre de Dios, that had been close. Too close.

And yet, recalling his words of caution, his sincerity and gentle touch, the way her body burned for his . . . Parts of her complained that it hadn't been close enough. *He* hadn't been close enough. Not nearly.

Chapter Ten

Late Monday afternoon, Patricio sipped his añejo tequila and watched the employees at work on the other side of the plate glass window separating the private tasting room from the distillery at Verona Tequila. Hints of caramel and custard with a lingering essence of dark chocolate teased his taste buds as the liquid burned an invigorating path down his throat, into his chest.

But neither his favorite drink nor a day spent shadowing the tequilero, learning the intricacies of the craft distillery's unique process, which blended traditional with modern techniques, had dispelled the unsettled thoughts swarming in his head. The ones starring Catalina Capuleta and her stunning mix of strength and vulnerability.

In spite of the online fervor sparked by the less-than-flattering article, Thursday evening Catalina had wowed the crowd in Irving. As he'd known she would. And he had no doubt she'd continue to do so, especially if she followed his advice and stayed away from social media. Too bad he hadn't followed Alberto's advice and stayed away from her hotel room.

Talk about making another pendejo move! Something he normally avoided due to his father's constant reminders that everything Patricio did reflected on the legacy Vicente coveted.

But when it came to Catalina . . . Bueno, rational thought had a tendency to flee from Patricio's brain like the bandidos of Pancho Villa's era.

The woman excited him with her coy glances and mesmerizing talent and intrigued him with the flashes of vulnerability beneath her strength. Somehow, she managed to get under his skin in a way no one ever had. As he'd read the article's suggestive headline, the twisting of her "scrappy childhood," and the not-so-subtle subtext implying her scheme to use him as a rung on her stepladder to fame, guilt had trickled through him.

If anyone was using the other, it was him. She didn't deserve the reporter's low blow.

As soon as the article had hit the internet, Alberto, the father of two girls, had flown into protective papá mode. George had called almost immediately to confirm his instinct that the interview's slant was bogus, also eager to discuss potential damage-control maneuvers. When Catalina didn't respond to their texts or calls, the two older men had grown increasingly troubled. When she ignored Patricio's message, his apprehension mushroomed.

He wanted to blame his furtive race across the hotel's parking lot and up the four flights of stairs on the promise he had given her parents. But it wasn't the only reason. It definitely wasn't the main one.

The tears shining in her hazel eyes were the first crack he'd seen in her tough-girl facade. Her bravery as she fought to keep the hurt at bay. The jealousy that knifed his side at the thought of some mysterious "him" she had alluded to, then refused to discuss. They all coalesced in a huge tidal wave of remorse, awe, and desire that had crashed over him. Its tumultuous undertow tossed and turned, leaving him out of breath and uncertain which way was up. Nearly pushing him—them—past a line in the sand they wouldn't have been able to uncross.

Their near kiss had changed the dynamic between them. No one else had mentioned anything, but Patricio had sensed it during their concert later that evening. And he'd bet his shares in the distillery that Catalina had as well.

She was a naturally demonstrative performer. Her passion—onstage, with her music, in life—was one of her many traits that drew him to her. Depending on the duet they sang together, she might slide him a beguiling over-the-shoulder glance, clutch her heart on one of those angsty lyrics she teased him about, or shake her fist at the cheating lover she lamented. She was also a toucher, cupping his elbow as she sang to him, laying her hand with her red-painted nails on his forearm, linking their fingers when he held his hand out for hers, pressing against his side when he looped an arm around her waist to draw her near when they shared a microphone.

Thursday night in Irving and Saturday in Hidalgo, Catalina sang her freaking heart out. She grinned and flirted and joked with the fans. She blew kisses to the shouts of "¡Te adoro, Cat!" All while keeping a respectable Catholic-school, hands-off distance from him.

He should have been relieved. The tweaks to their interplay meant less chance for photographs that could be misconstrued in the tabloids and on the internet.

Should have, sí. But he hadn't been. He missed her innocent touches. Couldn't stop thinking about what might have happened if Alberto hadn't knocked on Catalina's hotel room door. Imagining the sweet taste of her mouth. Picturing himself peeling that LATINA AF tee off her body to free her breasts, cupping their luscious weight in his palms, unencumbered by the sexy bra she had snatched from his fingers with a blush staining her cheeks.

Wild fantasies he owed it to her to excise from his brain.

He was already being duplicitous about the album. Patricio refused to compound his deceit by following in his father's footsteps and bedding one of his backup singers. No way would he do that and risk hurting Catalina.

Seeking time apart to get his head screwed on straight, Patricio had hopped his private jet immediately after Saturday's concert in Hidalgo and flown to Guadalajara.

George had been far from pleased. Wearing his executive producer hat, Patricio's closest friend had whined about his agreement to work with Catalina on the road in between concerts. Right now, though, he needed distance to regain his perspective, and the media required a distraction. Something else to talk about.

The latter had easily materialized, thanks to an intimate dinner with a former Miss Mexico—a friend who didn't mind pretending they were more if it helped keep her and her charitable foundation in the press. As he had anticipated, local paparazzi had photographed the two of them seated at a small table on the private outdoor balcony of a trendy restaurant. Heads pressed together, ostensibly whispering sweet nothings to each other. In reality, discussing her next fundraiser and her search for an up-and-coming performer.

Patricio nearly bit his tongue to bleeding but still hadn't stopped himself from recommending Catalina for the gig.

In the end, his dinner date had failed to squelch thoughts of his tempting writing partner. However, George's complaints about Patricio jetting off for fun in Guadalajara and nearby Tequila had quieted this morning in the face of an "intimate dinner" photograph and its matching headline: "Mexican Royalty Once Again Get Cozy."

Catalina had posted her own pictures on social media, more proof that the two of them were not spending time together. One series of photos showed her and a mixed group of tour members clowning around while dining at a local Whataburger. In another, the group relaxed in the hot tub and pool at their hotel in El Paso.

Though he and Catalina hadn't coordinated their efforts to debunk the idea that they were romantically involved, it was clear they'd been on the same wavelength.

"A ver, ¿qué piensas?" Gustavo Cruz asked. The master distiller at Verona Tequila, like his father before him, strolled into the room, a copita with a finger of their latest añejo cradled in his calloused palm, an interested gleam in his eyes as he waited for Patricio to share his thoughts.

Patricio sniffed the liquid in his own glass, breathing deeply and catching the hints of agave, caramel, custard, and chocolate. He knew the dedication, patience, and years it took for Gustavo to create his award-winning tequila. The company's commitment to craftsmanship and superb spirits had drawn Patricio's attention when he'd been looking to invest in a local, familia-run business. Their dedication showed in the quality of their product and the speed with which the limited-edition bottles flew off the shelves.

"I'd say you have another winner on your hands," he told Gustavo, before taking another sip.

Pride filled the older man's face, darkly tanned from his time in the sun tending the rows of blue agave plants on his familia's farm. "When I first heard of your interest in investing in us, I assumed it would be in name only. We've all seen celebrities dabble with other companies. Many simply serve as figureheads or the new face of the spirit to increase sales, sabes?"

Yeah, Patricio did know. He was familiar with those tactics. People more interested in the financial investment than in the craft, history, and people involved.

"¿Pero tú? You come and get your hands dirty in the fields," Gustavo said. "You study our fermentation, distillation, barrel aging, and bottling like a student, hungry to learn. And you are becoming a master taster."

The old man winked, and Patricio chuckled at the good-natured teasing. "I meant what I said, this is an investment in tradición y cultura. You, your father, and your grandfather before him have created a legacy for your familia. As well as our people."

Gustavo ducked his head in appreciation. "Like you and your father. Our familia businesses may be different, but our desire to continue what our fathers started, to grow and exceed expectations. That is what we drink to, no?"

The older man raised his glass in salute.

Patricio hesitated for a millisecond, the untruth growing harder to stomach. Then habit kicked in, ingrained by years of living in his father's looming shadow rather than beside him in the spotlight. Smiling, he raised his glass. "Familia y tradición."

He wondered how different his career, his life, might be with a father who held the same views as Gustavo's, each generation improving on the legacy. Or who believed his child was destined for bigger and brighter, like Arturo Capuleta believed with Catalina.

That wasn't the case with him. Vicente Galán craved *all* the spotlight. He made a point of reminding anyone who listened that Patricio's talent came from him, his DNA. Always placing an emphasis on "mi" when he introduced Patricio as "mi hijo." His son would always be following in the footsteps of greatness—a burden and a blessing Patricio was expected to bear.

Catalina looked forward to video chats with her parents and sisters.

Patricio . . . He dodged any and all communication with his father. He made a concerted effort to limit public appearances with his viejo and relied on George to make that clear with other Padua Records execs. Even in private, he spent as little time as possible in his father's company. Pretending to be something less than what you wanted to be left a person mentally exhausted and unfulfilled. Only a glutton for punishment sought out more opportunities to feel that way.

On the other side of the window, a short, middle-aged man with glasses waved to Gustavo from the distillery. The tequilero excused himself and left, only to appear moments later when he joined the employee. Heads together, the two men peered at something on a tablet the employee held.

Off to the right, displayed on an exposed brick wall, hung photographs of Gustavo's father and grandfather. Others showed images of the distillery over the years. Accolades and award plaques told of their growing success, the generations building upon and improving what had come before.

That's what Patricio longed to be a part of with his father. Unfortunately, he had begun to accept that it might never come to fruition.

Interestingly enough, he and Catalina seemed to both have more than their love for music in common—a secret nemesis neither cared to discuss. He'd wager his only remaining bottle of last year's Verona Tequila añejo that a man in her past was at least partially to blame for the tears that had glistened in her beautiful eyes the morning of their almost-kiss. That her headstrong determination was fed by a need to prove the nameless "him" wrong.

Patricio's nemesis expected him to bring pride and recognition to the familia name while staying in his prescribed place. It was a soul-sucking mental tug-of-war that had rendered his creative muse mute and often left him battling loneliness, even when surrounded by thousands of fans.

The very real possibility that the press and its constant hounding or the secret heartbreak in her past might eventually wear her down saddened him. He didn't want a life like his for her. But how was he supposed to protect Catalina as he had promised? How could he get close enough for her to become comfortable confiding in him, trusting him, without risking another charged situation like the one in her hotel room?

Patricio had two more days before he was scheduled to meet the tour in El Paso. It wasn't much time to figure out a solution to his dilemma. But he would.

A lot of people were counting on him. Most especially her.

Chapter Eleven

"So, how's the songwriting going?"

Cat wrinkled her nose at her older sister's question.

Mariana reached for something outside the tablet's camera view, her hand reappearing holding a serving dish filled with refried beans, freshly grated cotija cheese melting on top.

Cat poked at her microwave dinner, a sad version of soggy enchiladas, bland Mexican rice, and a grayish-brown concoction the box claimed was refried beans. They tasted nothing like her mamá's homemade version.

Glancing back at her tablet, she gazed longingly at Mariana's, Blanca's, Mamá's, and Violeta's plates, the only ones visible on the screen. It was Wednesday night familia dinner at Casa Capuleta. Las Nubes had finished their weekly rehearsal, and they'd all gathered around the long dinner table in her childhood home. Everyone was present, even Cat, virtually.

As they'd done this past Sunday over barbacoa breakfast tacos after mass and the previous Wednesday for dinner after her and Patricio's visit to Nuestros Niños—the site of her infamous interview—Cat joined via someone's cell phone or tablet. The miracles of modern technology. You could take the girl out of San Antonio's West Side, but you couldn't take the West Side, or her familia traditions, out of the girl.

And tonight this West Side chica needed her home fix.

"What's with your huele mal face?" Mamá asked, dishing up a steaming beef enchilada, cheese and red sauce dripping off the ends.

Her expression might say something smelled bad, but Cat knew what didn't: the home-cooked meal everyone was digging into at Casa Capuleta. She couldn't actually see them because of the screen's angle, but if she closed her eyes, she could picture the darker flecks of chili powder, taste the tangy tomato-based sauce on her tongue. Her stomach rebelling, she picked at her dinner, her nose wrinkling even more.

"¿Qué pasa, mija?" Mamá pressed.

Blanca, Mariana, and Violeta stared at the camera with differing levels of interest. Blanca's, as usual, leaned more toward troubled; she'd wind up with an ulcer at some point, the worrywart. Mariana's intuitive gaze scanned Cat's image searching for signs or symptoms of illness, like she did with her ER patients. No doubt Violeta would tell Cat she needed a better concealer for the dark circles under her eyes. To which Cat would respond, "Bite me, I'm not wearing any." Thus earning an *oye language* glare from Mamá.

Just like old times.

"It's nothing and something. I'm not sure which," Cat said on a beleaguered sigh. "The songwriting collaboration with him's been a bust, and this meal . . ." She forked a piece of the bland enchilada and held it up to her tablet camera.

"Ew!"

"Bleh!"

"Gross!" Blanca, Mariana, and Violeta complained in unison.

"Hey, I wanna see!" Teresita's voice chimed in from the other end of the table.

A hand hovered over the camera before covering it completely. The screen went black, then the tinny sound of utensils clattering onto ceramic plates mixed with a rustling and a thump that indicated the tablet being passed down.

"Hi, Cat!" Teresita's sweet, braces-filled smile greeted her. "It's so good to see you! ¡Me haces falta!"

"I miss you, too, chiquita. How was your guitar practice this week?"

"Stellar!"

"That's what I like to hear. Just 'cuz I'm not there, don't let yourself slack with practice, okay?" Cat waited for her youngest sister, one of the most talented guitarists on the Texas mariachi circuit even at thirteen, to nod. Once Teresita had given her a thumbs-up, the tablet made the circuit of those seated at her end of the table, from Teresita to Fabiola, Claudia, then Nina—the teens ultimately trying to fit all their heads within the rectangle so they could take a screenshot with Cat before passing the tablet along. Sabrina slid into view, waving and sharing an "I miss you," her soft smile a contrast to her twin's sly grin.

Finally, their father's craggy face appeared, framed by the sala behind him with their well-worn sofa on one side and the TV and keyboard on the other. Late-evening sunlight streamed through the window blinds behind him, creating a halo around his salt-and-pepper hair. He wore one of his typical plaid flannel shirts with silver snaps, and she knew that if she were there to rest her head on his shoulder for comfort, the soft material would smell of his piney aftershave. The same brand he'd worn for as long as she could remember.

"Hola, mija, how's our rising superstar?" Papo winked, the laugh lines around his eyes deepening.

Love for her biggest cheerleader swelled in Cat's chest and she blew him a kiss.

"Tell me, why are you having trouble with the songwriting?" Papo asked.

"Ay, Patricio is a hard man to pin down," she complained.

"According to the chismosa who wrote that story last week, you're doing a good job getting your Cat claws in him," Violeta called out.

Papo frowned at her from his end of the table, and Cat heard an "ow, I was just kidding," which probably meant one of her other sisters had given Violeta either the back-of-the-head slap or under-the-table kick the brat deserved.

"Don't even mention the yellow journalism that rag published!" Cat warned. "I hope no one's been poking around the Center trying to dig up info and bothering you or any of the students."

Papo shook his head. "Don't worry about that, mija. Between Tonio and me, we've got it covered. You keep working hard like you always do. Don't listen to those chismosas. We know who and what you are. So does Padua and Patricio. He promised me—" Papo broke off. His gaze cut somewhere above the camera, and a beat later he gave an almost imperceptible nod. "Bueno, we know he'll take care of you."

"What do you mean 'he promised'? When did you—?"

"It does not matter." Papo shook his head, then tapped his fork on the green vine decorating the outer rim of his plate. "What's important is meeting the terms of your contract with Padua. I'm sure they know how busy Patricio is—perhaps they can help by scheduling time for you two to meet."

Cat pushed her now-cold meal away and leaned back in the hotel room desk chair. "Maybe. It certainly doesn't seem like it's a priority to him. I mean, he skipped town as soon as our concert in Hidalgo finished Saturday night, and I haven't heard from him since."

"He's in Guadalajara," one of the teens piped in off-screen. "Wining and dining and, from the looks of the pictures, a lot more. With Miss Mexico. Bueno, she was Miss Mexico a couple years ago."

Wining and dining and more. Yeah, Cat had seen pics and read the corresponding captions that popped up in her social media feeds. Good for him. The jerk.

Not that Cat was jealous of the slender, statuesque former cover model who "worked tirelessly for her charity," or so *People en Español* had noted in the caption accompanying their photograph of El Príncipe and his Beauty Queen. At least the "royal couple's" hot date had pulled interest away from Cat, a win-win for them all.

The only thing the woman had that Cat wanted was Patricio's time. Miss Mexico could have all the "and more" he offered. Cat wasn't interested in any of it.

Mentirosa.

The taunt whispered in her ear, her subconscious calling her out for the liar she was.

After their near kiss a week ago, she had made a point of changing her behavior onstage, worried she might melt into a puddle of lust if he touched her. Dios forbid he put his arm around her and gently tug her to his side like he normally did when they sang "Somos Novios." Or softly trace her jaw with his knuckle when he crooned the lyric in "No Me Olvides" about how he missed seeing her beautiful face in the morning. The first time he had caressed her jaw during their Houston concert, she nearly missed her next line.

She had wondered if deliberately keeping her distance from him and ignoring her instincts while performing might have been an overreaction. But Patricio running away to play footsie with some model? That was too much. Por favor, there was work to be done!

Sabrina leaned closer to Papo, her brown ponytail swinging in front of his chest as she chimed in, "I read something about Patricio spending time in Tequila, about an hour outside the city, touring the craft distillery he invested in recently. He actually walked the agave fields, worked in the distillery itself, and got hands-on while there. The photos are pretty cool."

"Bueno, pues, I need him to be hands-on with the music for his next album," Cat snarled. "I don't care if he's drinking expensive tequila while we work, I just need him here. Present. His creativity engaged, not his social calendar."

"Mija, talk to his assistant or to George from Padua," her mamá advised. Papo tapped the tablet screen with his index finger, flipping the camera to show the other end of the table, where her mom sat.

"Your papo is right—scheduling time might be the only way. Galán is a busy man."

"I am, too, Mamá."

"Yeah, busy eating at Whataburger and getting pruney in the hot tub," Violeta shot back, her lips spread in her teasing grin. "Blanca's been mooning over the pic of you with the young trumpet player and two other girls."

"Cállate!" Blanca's angry scowl accompanied her cry for Violeta to shut up. "Quit stirring the pozole pot when you don't even know what you're talking about!"

"Oh really? Then whose IG feed were you scrolling after rehearsal earlier with that goofy grin on your face?" Violeta challenged.

Her expression mutinous, Blanca leaned over to clap a hand over Violeta's mouth. "I told you not to—"

"Wait a sec, are you talking about Luciano Gomez?" Cat asked.

Blanca shot Cat a guilty side-eye. She bit her bottom lip, her usual tell when there was something she was trying not to say in a bid to avoid a sister squabble. Violeta pried Blanca's hand off her mouth with a muttered complaint, then nodded in response to Cat's question when Blanca ignored it.

Cat jerked back, her big-sis radar on alert. The plastic desk chair rolled away from the desk, and she grabbed the edge to stop herself.

Luciano Gomez? The same guy who'd been hanging around the Mariachi Las Nubes dressing room before she and her sisters opened Galán's San Antonio concert? The night the secret-admirer flowers had been delivered for Blanca, and she'd slyly tucked away the card without showing any of them?

Now that Cat thought about it, Luciano *had* asked about her sisters several times. Even going so far as to suggest that some of them should fly out for a weekend of shows. Had he been hinting about one sister in particular?

"Blanca, is there something going on I should know about?" Cat asked, her tone sharp.

Her sister pressed her lips together, refusing to answer.

Cat looked at Mariana, who shrugged, her face scrunched in a *beats me* grimace.

"Are you sure it was Luciano? Closely cropped dark hair. He's short but kinda buff?" Cat directed her questions to Violeta, but she seemed to sense that something more than sisterly teasing was going on here and finally heeded Blanca's earlier "shut up" cry.

"Friendly smile," Cat pressed, her anxiety mounting. "But more importantly, a mariachi. Which means off limits!"

Blanca flinched at Cat's raised voice. Her fingers nervously fiddled with her fork as she ducked her head to avoid making eye contact.

"Blanca, we have a pact," Cat insisted. "A promise. No one like . . . no one who's—" She broke off, betrayal and disbelief storm-trooping through her chest in heavy, steel-toed boots. "It's for your own good!"

"Mija, there's no need to yell," Mamá gently scolded. "Especially at the table."

Cat gave a tight-lipped nod of apology to Mamá, but the memory of her birth mother's gut-wrenching sobs, night after night, taunted her. Huddled with her sister in their shared twin bed, Cat had sworn they would never wind up like that. Never give their heart to or place their trust in a man whose mistress was music. His only true love—dreams of music stardom. Blowing into town on a whim, making piecrust promises to settle down, then slinking off without an adios when the next "big gig" called.

"Look at me, Blanca," Cat pleaded. "Is there something you're keeping from me?" She stared at the top of her younger sister's head, willing Blanca to look up and tell her that Violeta had this all wrong. That the secret admirer Cat had wondered—and worried—about was not Luciano.

Eyes downcast, Blanca poked at the refried beans on her plate and stayed mum.

"You two can discuss this later. Pero con calma, Catalina," Mamá warned.

The power of her parental *I mean business* expression carried through the tablet screen, and again Cat nodded respectfully. Although "calm" didn't even begin to describe her current emotional state.

Odds were low she'd be any closer to it when she finally cornered Blanca.

"Bueno, we all have a busy weekend ahead." Mamá wiped her mouth with a napkin before continuing. "Catalina, you have your concerts and making progress on the album with Patricio. Here at Casa Capuleta, on Friday we have the girls' mariachi class concert. On Saturday, Las Nubes will play at the Vargases' fiftieth-anniversary celebration in the courtyard, then for the parish picnic at the Basilica on Sunday. We'll miss having you here with us, mija."

The irony of their mom listing the events Cat would miss, on the heels of her learning about Blanca's potential dalliance with a mariachi who wouldn't be around for special moments either, was not lost on Cat.

She had half a mind to hang up and go bang on Luciano's door. Demand he leave her tenderhearted sister alone. First, though, she needed to talk some sense into Blanca, which would be easier without the others around.

The notification for an incoming call flashed on Cat's tablet screen.

"Oooh, Alberto's calling me. I should take this," she said.

"Sí, mija, go. Que Dios te bendiga," her mom said.

A mix of her mom's "God bless you" wish and cries of "break a leg" and "besos" accompanied by smooching sounds warmed her heart as she tapped the icon to answer Alberto.

Five minutes later, she'd been apprised that Patricio had arrived in El Paso and, even more exciting, she was being summoned to El Príncipe's bus for a meeting with the wardrobe team at 9:00 a.m.

Apparently, Padua wanted to make a change. She liked wearing her Las Nubes charro; it made her feel close to her sisters—a loving reminder of where she had come from and what was most important to her.

But if Padua felt she needed something a little flashier, she'd find a way to tie it back to her familia and, while she was at it, maybe shake things up a bit. Make a push to wear pants. Thumb her nose at those traditionalists who decreed women mariachi should perform only in skirts.

If she was climbing that ladder of success, she didn't have to sleep her way to the top like that pinche article had implied. But wearing pants could make kicking ass a little easier, and that was exactly what she planned to do. Starting with convincing Patricio to schedule their work time and get down to the business of cowriting a Grammy-winning album.

Slapping her hands together, Cat rubbed them briskly. A cackle of gleeful laughter burst from her. Ay, 9:00 a.m. "go" time couldn't get here fast enough.

Chapter Twelve

The door to Galán's palatial bus opened with a quiet hiss. Alberto, dressed in his typical dapper suit—this one navy—and shiny black dress shoes, waved to her from the top of the stairs with a welcoming smile.

Cat finger-waved back, surprisingly pleased to see the friendly gate-keeper/assistant/conscience of the perturbing star, who'd been gallivanting around Guadalajara while ghosting her since Sunday. Today that frustrating behavior would come to a stop.

Determination giving her a little extra *oomph*, she tap-danced up the steps.

"¡Hola! So nice to see you, Catalina," Alberto greeted her, shuffling back to make room. Probably hoping to avoid the disaster from her last bus-storming visit. "I caught some of your social media posts. Looks like you've had an enjoyable week with the others." The older man leaned in for a hello kiss on the cheek as she reached him.

"Sí, it's been fun." She waggled a reproving finger at him. "Pero no me están pagando por divertirme."

"What? Who says you're not getting paid to have fun? Such a travesty!"

Cat spun around at Patricio's booming voice.

Arms crossed in front of his broad chest, biceps straining the short sleeves of his tee, feet planted wide like Mr. Clean's yummy evil twin in black and with a full head of gorgeously thick, wavy hair, he stood in front of the closed pocket door separating the front lounge area from his private quarters. Home to the recording studio on wheels she had yet to get her eyes on.

Not for long, though. She was done with him avoiding her all the time.

Bueno, other than when he'd sneaked into her hotel room and nearly melted her panties off with that almost kiss. His minty breath caressing her lips. The warmth of his hands—

¡Basta! She was *not* reliving that anymore. Nor was her imagination taking their rendezvous anywhere further. Like, to her bed. Or her shower. Or the desk—

She gave herself a mental head thunk and another "Enough" warning. Just like she had reminded Blanca last night, even thinking about getting involved with a mariachi was a fool's errand!

That was not Catalina's mission this morning.

"Actually, there's a real travesty you and I need to discuss," she threw at Patricio, jutting her chin to look down her nose at him. Despite her height disadvantage of almost a foot.

"Do what you love, and you'll never work a day in your life—isn't that what they say?" He flashed his roguish grin and winked. All teasing and playful, like he hadn't left her high and dry, stuck sidestepping George's text asking for a progress check yesterday.

"Oh, I love my job. No question about that." Mimicking his crossed arms, Cat advanced on him, stopping a few feet away, where the cream carpet met the kitchen's wood flooring. "My issue's with coworkers who are a pain in the ass when it comes to collaborating. Ditching work to jet off for fun and frolic and tequila-making side hustles."

Behind her, Alberto snickered.

"Who would do such a thing?" Patricio tsked and slowly shook his head, but the twitch of his lips belied his mock concern. "Tell me who it is, and I'll set them straight."

"Oh, no need. I'm a pro at handling big egos and patronizing behavior." Cupping a hand around her mouth, she leaned forward as if sharing a secret. "You know what they say, the bigger the ego, the smaller the—"

"Ahhh, such a sense of humor. I'd love to hear more of your unscientifically proven theories, pero we have a lot of work to do. There's no time for tomfoolery today."

"Tomfool—oye, you're the—"

Clasping her shoulders, he turned her around to face the front of the bus. "Catalina, say hello to Gordo Sanchez y Carmen Rivera. The talented duo is here to discuss the design for your new charro."

¡Madre de Dios! Spotting the two guests for the first time, Cat back-stepped in surprise. She bumped into Patricio, her shoulder blades pressing against his firm chest with a breath-sucking jolt.

The Carmen Rivera and Gordo Sanchez. Here. On Patricio's bus. Waiting to meet with her!

And she'd been so incensed by Patricio's flippant attitude, she'd completely overlooked the famed fashion designers when she barged in.

Gordo—a total misnomer because there didn't seem to be an ounce of fat on his wiry body—was around Cat's age. Sprawled on the short couch, dressed in his signature ripped jeans, well-worn Doc Martens, and a long-sleeved, old-school Selena concert tee, the fashion phenom gave Cat a two-fingered salute. Carmen, an icon in her industry, sat at the booth table, her brunette hair slicked back in a low chignon that drew attention to the sharp cheekbones, ski-slope nose, and pointy chin of her lightly lined face. A navy cardigan with pearlized buttons tucked under the Peter Pan collar of her pale-blue blouse exuded a prim-and-proper style that, under normal circumstances, should have conflicted with Gordo's scruffy tour-crew vibe. Instead, together the two created the surprising yin-yang fashion power duo known as RS Designs.

Several papers with sketches of charros and charro pieces were scattered across the tabletop in front of Carmen. Notes in a neat script adorned the white space around the drawings. Swatches of material attached by a clip flapped from a corner of each page.

"Un placer," Carmen said, her voice a husky smoker's alto. She gestured to the open booth seat across from her, inviting Cat to sit.

Dios mío, talk about a pinch-me moment! Cat barely stopped herself from blurting out, "No, the pleasure's all mine!"

Carmen Rivera had been dressing the who's who in- and outside the entertainment industry for as long as Cat had been ripping pages out of fan magazines to tape on her bedroom wall. Telenovela stars. Grammy winners. Royalty on the big screen and in real life.

Up-and-comer Gordo had joined Carmen's design house several years ago, bringing a young, hip vibe. Together, the two had merged to create highly sought-after haute couture that Cat and her sisters salivated over but could never afford.

Y ahora . . . excitement danced a cumbia in Cat's chest . . . now they were creating an RS Designs charro for her.

She twisted at the waist to throw Galán a wide-eyed *holy shit* glance. He gave her shoulders a supportive squeeze that shouldn't have made her heart flutter but did. Only, there was no time to worry about her reaction. Instead, she hurried to shake hands with Gordo, then joined Carmen at the table.

Patricio chuckled as he settled next to Alberto on the longer couch along the other side of the bus. Probably laughing at her newbie giddiness. Whatever.

Her earlier icy-hot frustration with him melted in the glow of her delight.

"It is such an honor to meet you both." Cat angled to press her back against the bus's sidewall so she could include Gordo, seated on the small couch behind her.

"¡Ay, chica, por favor!" He playfully slapped her hand on the padded backrest between them. "A chance to meet the singer-songwriter who's stealing the show from El Príncipe? Girl, I started packing my carry-on as soon as Padua called."

"Stealing the show? Pfft," Patricio huffed. "Who's the one with more signs proposing marriage in the audience?"

"I don't know," Alberto chimed in. "We've had quite a few inquiries about when Catalina would start holding meet and greets after the concerts."

"I'd love to!"

"I don't know. You have to be careful. Some fans can be a little handsy. Especially with female performers," Patricio cautioned.

Cat batted away his lame reasoning with a flick of her wrist. "I'm more than capable of putting anyone in their place if needed. When have you known me to hold back when someone's being a jerk?"

"Ooh, spunky! I love it!" Gordo clapped his hands, a mischievous grin carving grooves on either side of his mouth.

"You call it spunk. I call it attitude," Patricio complained.

"Sounds like someone else I've been dressing for years now," Carmen chimed in. "Don't you agree, Alberto?"

The older man nodded, leaning away to avoid the elbow Patricio jabbed at his side.

Cat lapped up the good-natured teasing at his expense. It didn't happen too often.

He harrumphed, but couldn't hide his amused smile.

The rustle of papers on the table drew Cat's attention. Carmen spread out the four sketches with their swatches of material—three black with different-colored embroidery and one red, the embroidery in a metallic thread. All four drawings were of charros with skirts.

"So, these are the ones Padua liked the best out of the ideas Gordo and I sent over," Carmen said, fingering the edges of each page like a loving parent adoring her offspring.

"When I saw the designs earlier, I told these two that you deserve better."

Cat gasped at Patricio's rudeness. "Don't listen to him." She held up a hand and made a jerky, back-and-forth motion, as if his words were a stain she could rub out.

"Only the best for my new duet partner," he added, lazily stretching out his legs.

"¡Qué malo!" Cat chided, mortified by his pretentious behavior with the fashion legends.

"Mean? Me? When?" Patricio teased, rushing on before she could answer. Probably because he knew she'd willingly provide a list of examples. "From the very beginning, I've told George and the others at Padua, only the best of everything for Catalina Capuleta."

Ha! He should have sent that memo to himself. So far, he'd only given her the best dodge job.

"You deserve the royal treatment when you're joining mariachi royalty, no?" He flashed his sexy bedroom smirk, poking fun at her for all the times she had teased him about his moniker.

Cat rolled her eyes so hard, she nearly made herself seasick. "Ignore him. All of these are beautiful, and he knows it," she told Carmen.

And they were. Except for the one change she wanted. One that would make a statement she'd go down fighting for.

"I'd be honored to wear any of them. Really. But . . . I'm wondering if . . . or, there are two requests I need to make . . ." She traced a finger along the outline of the skirt in the sketch closest to her, loath to come across as ungrateful or, worse, arrogant like El Príncipe himself. "If I'm not wearing my Las Nubes charro, I'd like to include roses in the embroidery of the new one. A touch of familia, if you will. And, equally as important, I'd prefer to have you design a charro with pants."

Carmen arched a brow, her gaze sliding past Cat to lock with Gordo's. A thousand words Cat couldn't decipher were silently exchanged between the duo. On the other side of the bus, Alberto pressed a hand to his paunch, indicating that his belly might be experiencing the same jittery mass-of-nerves reaction as Cat's. Patricio's dark brows furrowed, but she couldn't tell if it was in confusion or if a "hell no"—a common reaction among traditionalists—was forthcoming.

After several quiet seconds, Gordo hopped up off the couch. One tattoo-sleeved arm punching a fist in the air, he slid into the booth on Carmen's side. "I knew I had it right!"

"No need to gloat," Carmen muttered, groaning when Gordo threw an arm over her shoulder to pull her in for a hug.

"We sent Padua two sketches with pants," the young designer explained. "Word is, they were vetoed by the older executives. We weren't given names."

"Tradición. It's hard to change," Carmen said matter-of-factly.

"But if enough of us don't push, it never will," Cat answered. "If my sisters and I and so many others before us and now don't keep trying to jab an ice pick in that damn glass ceiling, it'll never shatter."

"Pero esos viejos—those old men in the old guard—changing their minds isn't easy," Alberto noted.

Cat shrugged, and the wide-necked tee she wore over her exercise bra slid off her right shoulder. "I don't expect it to be. But that doesn't mean I stop trying. They don't scare me."

A tiny white lie. The last thing she wanted to do was piss off any record executives who might already be annoyed that she had yet to produce a single song with Patricio.

"Out of these, is there one that calls to you the most?" Carmen spread her hands over the four sketches.

Gordo fished a cell phone out of his back pocket, then thumbed at the screen. "I might be able to access my drawings of the charro pants that were axed."

"Is it that important to you?" Patricio's voice held that calm, deliberative tone she had noticed the first time she watched him go through sound check before a concert. Unfazed by problems, big or small. Pensively, deftly troubleshooting, then delegating with confidence and command.

Her style was more "act first, think later"—a habit that mostly worked. Until it didn't. Then she'd face a new mess to clean up.

Patricio straightened on the dark brown leather cushion. Forearms resting on his knees, he leaned forward, his expression assessing. Intent. All signs of his earlier tomfoolery and teasing erased.

"Yes, it's that important to me," she answered. "It's a visual statement. A silent, powerful message that says, 'I'm here. Mujeres like me are here. We're equally as dedicated to our tradición y cultura. Equally as proud to wear full charro like the originators of our music.'"

His lips a stern line, Patricio dipped his chin in a brisk nod. "Then we make that statement."

"We might want to—"

"Should you consid—"

Alberto and Carmen spoke at the same time, both breaking off when Patricio stood. Even casually dressed in black sneakers and sweatpants, his black tee hugging his broad chest and shoulders, he still bore that commanding patrón aura that silenced their arguments. Demanded everyone take heed. Promised to get the job done.

It bordered on condescending. But it was also powerful. And, oddly, a freaking turn-on.

"You create the charro Catalina wants," Patricio told Carmen and Gordo, his tone brooking no argument. "And when she hits that stage in Vegas, she makes her statement. We make that statement with her. With Catalina front and center."

His gaze shifted from Cat, to the sketches on the table, then back to lock on her again. She gulped, ensnared by the sensation that, despite their bickering and the distance he continuously put between them, it was important to Patricio that she feel seen, heard . . . understood. Respected.

Gratitude and affection welled in her chest. His lips curved with an encouraging smile, and damn if it didn't make him even sexier.

Picking up the sketch with the swatch of deep red material with black-and-gold embroidery, she handed the paper to Carmen. She'd been ready to take this step for ages. Only, she had never expected that, when it happened, Patricio Galán would be standing by her side.

Chapter Thirteen

It was past midnight when Patricio heaved a tired sigh and wiped the sweat off his brow with the black hand towel draped around his neck. After a final wave for the fans still gathered across the parking lot on the other side of the steel barricades, he made his way up the steps onto his bus.

A shower, a copita of tequila neat, and sleep. That's what he needed, in that specific order.

Unfortunately, when he reached the top step, he found George and Catalina on board. His longtime friend and producer had already poured himself a copita from one of the new bottles of Verona Tequila Patricio had brought back with him on Wednesday.

"Didn't realize I was hosting an after-party," he grumbled.

"If you were, I wouldn't be attending," Catalina answered, her peeved tone proof that she was still annoyed he'd wound up canceling their songwriting session after their arrival in Albuquerque yesterday.

He *had* been battling a headache, but even to his own ears, the reason sounded as lame as "the dog ate my homework."

Never mind that the headache was born out of his mind-spinning enigma—how to help Catalina while helping himself. While also ignoring an attraction that, if acted upon, could damage her reputation just as she was rising, and paint him the same mujeriego shade as his father. Worse, any hint that he was following in his father's womanizing footsteps would negate Patricio's promise to the parents she video chatted with practically every day.

With an exaggerated sigh, Catalina stretched out on the longer sofa, linking her hands behind her head. The pose arched her back, stretching the thin material of her shirt over the outline of her full breasts. Lust fireballed through him, heading straight for his cock. He shifted and forced himself to look away.

"I have my own party that promises to be way more fun," she announced in a testy tone. "With the only hot air blowing courtesy of the desert wind. I'm only riding back to the hotel with you per George's request."

George arched a brow, eyeing Patricio over the rim of his glass as he took a sip. Great. His friend hadn't missed her waspish attitude.

Patricio bit back a sigh.

He deserved it, mostly. His original plan to awaken his muse from hibernation by working alongside Catalina and her boundless creative energy was floundering. For a number of reasons.

At the top of that list: his heightened awareness of her.

Even now, exhausted from the physical and mental toll performing live took on him lately, a strange internal radar pinged incessantly, alerting him that Catalina Capuleta was in the vicinity. Looking far too comfortable in his private space. As if she belonged here. Giving him a hard time for not getting work done and at the same time making him grow hard with raging lust.

She hadn't wasted any time changing out of her charro and handing it off to wardrobe for dry cleaning before their concert in Phoenix on Thursday. Dressed in a pair of pink-and-black cross-trainers, black leggings that hugged her curves, and another one of those blousy shirts—this one bright pink—that let the slope of her shoulder play peekaboo with his libido, she looked ready to hit the gym for Zumba or yoga. Or maybe get cozy on a hotel couch or bed for a night in . . .

That idea had his thoughts U-turning back to the private party she had gloated about. Where was it exactly? And with whom?

He slammed the mental brakes on the questions. The answers didn't matter. Or they shouldn't.

"Freddie, we're ready to roll," Patricio called out to his driver. The sooner they got back to the hotel, the sooner she'd be off his bus. Leaving only her musky, floral scent behind to tease him.

"Where's Alberto?" George asked.

"He flew back to Guadalajara this afternoon for his youngest grand-daughter's piano recital." The bus started, and with George taking up one couch and Catalina the other, Patricio opted for a booth seat at the table.

"Good show tonight," George said.

Patricio's mumbled "gracias" mixed with Catalina's. Neither elaborated.

George rattled the ice in his glass. "Is the hostility I'm sensing here the reason for the uptick in what most fans are labeling sexual tension during your set?"

"Excuse me?" Catalina bolted upright.

"Ching—" Patricio threw his towel at George as he bit off the curse.

"That article and the few it spawned are full of crap." Catalina drove a hand through her hair, combing the long, wavy locks away from her face, scrubbed free of makeup and still beautiful. Even with her annoyed scowl. "There's nothing going on between us. Hell, not even songwriting, because I can't get him to keep a freaking scheduled brainstorm session."

Patricio felt her pissed-off glare like a burn of shame across the back of his neck. He should stop this sham and level with George. Admit his creativity block.

Pride kept him from spitting out the words.

"It's been hectic the past two weeks," he explained. Another lame excuse. "Flying to Guadalajara wasn't planned, but the trip did clip the thread the paparazzi were using to tie the two of us together."

"I'll give you that." George nodded, his expression pensive. Or—mierda—more like worried. Patricio muttered an even stronger curse than "shit" at his friend and producer's next words. "But there's absolutely zero progress on the new album?"

Patricio shrugged, hating the disappointed sigh that expanded and then deflated George's chest.

"I've got a couple song ideas. Some lyrics and a strong chorus for one," Catalina volunteered. "I went off the notes from that first day, but I'm not sure if they're exactly what you're looking for. Or if it's something Padua might want for another artist."

Patricio could have kissed her for that suggestion. But for a million and one reasons he'd been repeating to himself lately, he didn't. Without even knowing it, she had positioned herself perfectly in his thus-far-thwarted game of chess. Relief settled on his shoulder, bumping aside the misgivings and frustration that had taken up long-term residence.

"Mira, güey." George scooted forward on the couch, motioning with his tequila glass at Patricio. "I know you've been struggling since that mess with your—"

"I'm handling it." His father was not a topic he wished to discuss in front of Catalina.

"He mentioned to another exec that you haven't been answering his calls," George pressed.

"I'm busy."

"Fine, but you should know, there's talk of him being in Vegas in a couple weeks." George rattled the ice in his glass again, the sound rattling Patricio's cage because he knew—he fucking knew—what was coming. "Vicente will be there the same time as your tour."

"Not happening. It'll be a cold day—drop it." Patricio cut his gaze to Catalina.

Still lying on his couch, now with one knee crooked, the curve of her hamstring and calf muscles making his hands itch to trace them with his palm, she stared with interest at him and George. Questions loomed in her hazel eyes, along with something else . . . something a helluva lot like empathy?

He had no idea why her understanding touched something inside him. And no doubt it was smarter for him not to dig for the answer. Still, despite his unwillingness to share his private shame out loud, the pang of wanting a connection with someone—no, with *her*—speared his heart.

"Look, with Alberto in Guadalajara, why don't you head to your beach place for the next few days," George suggested. "Get away from the tour, the business, the paparazzi, and let the ocean do its magic—or whatever it is you claim it does—on you."

Elbows on the table, Patricio scrubbed his hands over his face, too tired to think but desperate to jump at the reprieve. The only thing he remembered having on his schedule was a Wednesday evening charity event in Phoenix. That gave him three days to spend communing at the beach. If he got lucky, the ocean breeze might finally tease his muse into coming out to play.

"It's not a bad idea," he mumbled behind his hands. Unplugging would get him away from whatever shitshow his father was trying to finagle in Vegas. It would also give him time to work on his own music without the guilt of giving Catalina the runaround.

"When have I ever had a bad idea?" George demanded, tongue in cheek.

Patricio plopped back on the padded leather seat and shot his friend a *yeah right* glare.

The bus slowed and made a sharp right turn into the hotel parking lot, continuing toward the area behind the building where they'd been assigned a row of spaces.

"Great! Then it's all squared away," George said. "You and Catalina will head down to Puerto Vallarta in the morning, and we'll see you both in Phoenix on Wednesday."

"Wait, what?" Catalina hopped to her feet, disbelief stamping her face.

"That is not what I had in mind," Patricio muttered.

"Too bad." The sober expression on George's face made it clear that, while he understood the beach house was Patricio's sanctuary, a place where few outsiders had been welcomed, he had not interrupted his weekend by flying from LA to Albuquerque on a Saturday as a friend. He was here on Padua business. With one specific goal—get the record label's second-generation superstar back on track.

"Give me a little more time," Patricio pleaded, despising the weakness in his voice.

His mouth twisted with a grimace, George shook his head. "I've tried. I can't hold off the others much longer. Here, you're pulled in too many directions. The threat of cameras and paps lurking is a constant distraction."

Tires screeching on asphalt, the bus suddenly jerked to an abrupt halt. Catalina stumbled on her feet, her mouth open in surprise. Reacting on instinct, Patricio slid from the booth, darting in front of her to keep her from slamming into the table's edge.

She landed against his chest with a muffled "oof," her hair billowing around them, her face buried in the open V-neck of his button-down shirt. He cradled her soft curves in his arms as his lungs filled with her alluring scent.

"Sorry, jefe!" Freddie called from the driver's seat. "Damn pendejo with a camera popped out from between two cars. As much as these dudes annoy the shit outa me, running over him's not an option."

Elbows bent, George lifted his palms in a clear *I rest my case* sign. "Take advantage of the solitude and inspiring view to put your creative minds together. See what happens."

Patricio pressed his lips to silence the groan trying to push its way out. With Catalina currently nestled in his arms, his crotch reacting to her nearness, putting their minds together was the least of his worries.

She blinked up at him, a riot of emotions swirling in her amber eyes—shock, unease, awareness.

Qué desmadre. See what happens? "Disaster" was exactly what might come of him and Catalina being alone at his beachside retreat.

Avoiding temptation 24-7 didn't sound relaxing. Or creative well refilling. Hell, if he were his muse, he'd stay in hiding to avoid the tension.

"Go enjoy your after-party, then sleep in tomorrow—bueno, today. I'll have the jet on call to fly you down around noon," George said, pulling his phone out of his pocket to set his diabolical plan in motion.

"That works for me." Lips spread in a satisfied smirk, Catalina winked and patted Patricio's chest playfully. "Good thing I packed my bikini."

≈

"I don't know how you ever leave this place. The view is absolutely gorgeous. How can we not write amazing music with this for inspiration?" Awe dripped from Catalina's words, and a pleased warmth stole over Patricio.

She'd been quiet and standoffish the entire flight to Puerto Vallarta, treating him to more of the same in his Range Rover on the drive to his oceanfront property. Either still pissed at him for his boorish behavior or hungover from partying last night. Or both.

But the moment the foliage flanking each side of the private road leading to his beach house cleared and his home came into view, her mood brightened with her murmured "Wow!"

Now he followed her gaze past the wide infinity pool off the back deck to the calm Bahía de Banderas just beyond and the watercolor sunset spanning the sky above the bay. Early-flowering trees stretched their gnarly branches, adding shades of green, pink, and red to the picturesque panorama. Bordering the pool and spa area, colorful clusters of lantana invited butterflies to stop and linger.

His private property extended for acres in either direction, but one of his favorite spots lay at the end of the stone path that carved its way through the tropical foliage, ending at a thatched-roof hut that jutted out over the rocks and sandy beach below. A spectacular place to relax and soak up the peace of Mother Nature's eye-catching atardecer sinking into the bay waters.

Few things in life were more perfect than the sunset over the ocean, a smooth tequila in one hand and a partner you could trust clasping the other. He had yet to find the latter, but the tequila tasted better with this view.

The breeze shifted, catching a lock of hair that had slipped loose from Catalina's low ponytail. It blew across her face to snag on her glossy lips. Without thinking, he lifted a hand to tuck the silky lock behind her ear. She beat him to it—saving him from a misstep—crooking a finger to deal with the errant strands, all the while keeping her gaze on the sun's artful display on the horizon.

Patricio had seen the view a million times before. But sharing it with her now felt . . . different. A little more breathtaking. More awe-inspiring. Though he couldn't bring himself to examine why or what that might mean.

His goals over the next few days entailed muse reviving, songwriting, soft pitching Catalina's own idea to write for other Padua artists, and keeping her resolutely in the friend zone.

"Ay, what my sisters would give to be here right now," she murmured.

He figured she might be missing her close-knit familia and started to ask how she was holding up with the separation. Instead, he drew back in surprise when her soft sigh turned into a chuckle that morphed into a cackle of evil laughter.

"They are going to be green with envy. And I am gonna *love* rubbing it in!" Arms lifted to bounce in a raise-the-roof motion, Catalina happy danced around him, coming dangerously close to the edge of the pool.

"Oye, watch it!" Patricio grabbed the billowy material of her short sundress, dragging her back a few steps.

"Oops! Gracias." She grinned, mischief lighting her hazel eyes. Then, as if a light bulb had switched off inside her, her smile dimmed. "Oh, don't worry. I promise not to give them a video tour of your house or anything. This is your private space. And I am well aware that you've only shared a few pictures of it. Plus, the one interview you gave from that amazing lookout spot, which, I'm guessing, is the thatched roof–looking thing peeking out from behind those coconut palm and other trees over there."

Rising on her toes, she craned her neck and pointed toward his thinking place, its rooftop barely visible through the foliage and in the fading sunlight.

"You're saying you'd earn some serious big-sister cred if they got an insider's view?"

"Oh, definitely."

"When are you video chatting with them again?"

Stepping closer to the pool, she hunkered down and tugged up the elastic at the end of her puffy, long sleeve to dip her hand in the water. "We had familia breakfast tacos this morning, and we're supposed to—"

"Wait, you actually ate together?"

"Uh-huh." Pushing her hand through and out of the water, she sent droplets flying in the air to sprinkle across the deep end. A flurry of concentric circles floated over the still surface. "Every Sunday after eight a.m. mass, Papo stops to pick up barbacoa tacos for everyone. Ay, I'm hoping I can find some in Phoenix when we're there later this week.

Then, one night a week before or after Las Nubes rehearsal, we meet for familia dinner. The time usually depends on whether or not Mariana's worked a shift at the hospital that day because that affects rehearsal. Why do you ask?"

Why did he ask?

Because to the young boy who had eaten most meals alone or with nannies growing up . . . the teen who came to view familia meals with his father as business meetings where talk of the industry and lessons learned and knowing his place in the hierarchy were the main points of discussion . . . and the man facing the realization that for all the riches he possessed and the adulation he received from many, he lived a solitary life . . . to all three of them, the idea of regular meals with loved ones sounded like something out of a sitcom. One he'd give anything to step inside.

He pictured the supersize dining table at the Capuletas' place in San Antonio. The familia photographs on the walls, snapshots and formal portraits capturing special moments over the years. After having witnessed the sisters in action behind the scenes during rehearsals, he easily envisioned them sharing raucous meals ripe with laughter, teasing, and affection.

How Catalina could give that up for the limelight and lonely life on the road left his mind boggled. And, though he wouldn't admit it, hungry to experience it.

"You said that this is the first time you've been away for an extended period. Do you miss them?" he asked.

Hell, he missed just watching their interactions. He couldn't begin to imagine—

"Sí, me hacen falta. But phone calls and video chats help. This is only a couple months. Fingers crossed my next gig is bigger—"

"¡Oye!" Hands fisted on his hips, he shot her an affronted scowl. "Who's a bigger tour name than me?"

She laughed and splashed water at him. He jumped back to avoid the spray, and dark wet spots splattered, then spread across the wooden deck.

Still crouched by the edge of the pool, she tilted her head and gazed up at him. Her long ponytail swung behind her to dangle over the water's surface. The cheekiness she typically threw at him melted away. A gentle smile curved her full lips while certainty blazed in her warm honey-colored eyes. Her expression radiated with an intensity of love that had Patricio catching his breath. Wondering how it might feel if *he* were the recipient of something as beautiful and fierce.

"No matter what happens, Casa Capuleta and San Antonio will always be a place I call home. My parents and sisters and I, we'll always have each other's backs."

A simple statement of unguarded truth that opened a floodgate of emotions inside him. Jealousy, awe, yearning.

"I've said this before, but are you sure this life is what you want?" he asked, his own internal struggle seeping out onto the pool deck.

"What do you mean?"

"A career like mine, like the one you are determined to achieve, it requires a lot of sacrifice. A lot of time apart from loved ones and familia responsibilities."

A frown dipped between her brows. Her mouth pursed and she pushed herself to stand. "Why is it that so many men can have a successful, demanding career, and no one worries about their 'familia responsibilities'? Yet with a woman, she's often expected to choose between the two."

He blinked, caught off guard by her sudden vehemence.

"Why are the men who choose career over familia praised, while society, especially in our culture, often questions and condemns a woman who does the same?"

"That's not what I'm saying."

"¿Pues, qué? Exactly *what* are you saying?"

By now the sun had mostly set, leaving the darkening sky a swirl of deep purples and midnight blues in a moody backdrop behind her. The solar lights lining the perimeter of the deck flickered on, giving the area a hazy glow. Behind him, the lights from the sala and kitchen area reflected like splotches of gold in her fiery eyes.

"I'm saying, when it comes to you, Catalina Capuleta—" Stepping closer, he grasped her upper arms, grounding himself and her in this moment. "Forget everyone else and what they say. I know your familia is important. Your dedication to them is one of the things I admire most about you. Your relationship with your familia is . . . Bueno, it's something I envy."

Surprise flitted across her face. Probably his, too. The admission had slipped out, his subconscious willing him to give her the truth.

Catalina bit her lip. Her brow puckered, and for the first time since they'd met, indecision seemed to hold her in its grasp. She sucked in, then released, an audible breath. Her expression cleared and she gazed up at him intently, as if she'd come to some kind of decision.

"I don't know exactly what happened with you before I came onto the scene and signed with Padua. I have my theories. But either way, I can't help wondering if too much out there"—elbow crooked, she motioned in a small circle at her side, as if indicating the world in general—"is messing with in here." Her palm splayed on the center of his chest for a heart-stopping second before she raised her hand to press her cool fingertips to his left temple. "And here."

He couldn't answer. Couldn't bring himself to force another lie meant to cover up his weakness past the grapefruit-size knot in his throat.

"That's why you're having trouble writing," she continued, her voice matter-of-fact but soft and understanding. Her nonjudgment quieted the turmoil raging within him. "Maybe Alberto knows. I doubt much can slip by him. But George doesn't. At least, I doubt he knows how bad it really is. Am I right?"

The best Patricio could do was lift a shoulder in a half-assed shrug. Pride and shame kept even a simple "yes" locked inside.

How could he admit how long he had held back, never pushing the envelope creatively, cognizant of his father's expectation that Patricio "know his place." Stepping into a different arena with his last album, one where competing with his father was not a concern, had been a way to stretch himself. Spread his wings without worry of overshadowing El Rey. And *still* his viejo had found fault.

"I think George was right," she told him. "Unplugging from distractions will do you good. Hopefully it'll do us both good. Mark my words, amazing things will come of our time here. I mean, how can we not be inspired in a place as breathtaking as this?" She spun around to face Mother Nature's playground, now shrouded by the night's cloak.

The moon hung low in the darkened sky. Its glow draped the mountains protecting the bay and trailed a wavery silver path across the calm water. Above them, stars glittered on a velvety backdrop. If they ventured down to the hut with a flashlight to guide their way, the stars would sparkle even brighter. Just like Cat, with her vibrant spirit and the strength of her conviction, had brightened his gloomy world.

Suddenly, an all-consuming need to hold her close swept over him. It would be so easy to step behind her and wrap his arms around her in a tight hug. To confide in her and allow her enthusiastic energy to buoy him. But holding her wouldn't be enough. One whiff of her tantalizing scent mingled with the salty ocean air could tip him over the edge. He'd give in to this unrelenting urge to taste her lips, caress the soft skin along her elegant neck, and ignite the flames of desire that had blazed in her eyes when he'd run to check on her in her hotel room.

Instead, he kept his feet firmly planted a friendly distance away. Hands safely stuffed in his pant pockets. He could not act on his attraction. It would disrespect her parents. It would disrespect her. He already risked her wrath should his duplicity come to light; he refused to make things worse by acting on his desire and risking her reputation.

"I don't know about you"—Cat tossed him a playful glance over her shoulder—"but tomorrow, I plan to splash around in this pool and soak up some sun on one of those comfy loungers that make me dream about hunky cabana boys who'll bring me frozen drinks."

"A cabana boy, I am not. Hunky? I've been called worse."

Her throaty chuckle teased a smile of his own. She moved to his side, angling her head and batting her eyelashes with exaggerated flirtation. "So, I can count on you to whip up a refreshing umbrella drink? Maybe with that tequila you're so fond of."

"Ay, mujer, por favor. Verona Tequila is a one-of-its-kind spirit you sip and appreciate. Throwing it in a blender with sugar and fruit juice would be a disgrace." He tugged her ponytail playfully, relieved she was no longer giving him the cold shoulder.

She wrinkled her nose in complaint, but her eyes smiled up at him. "Fine. You can sip yours. I want a brain freeze with my drink. I'm sure you have something else I can use for a daiquiri. The main point I'm trying to make is this." Looping her arms around one of his, she hugged it tight. Her cushiony breasts pressed against his biceps, and the air backed up in his lungs. "A partnership should be mutually beneficial."

Sí, and he could think of plenty mutually beneficial acts he'd like to do with her. Right now. On one of the lounge chairs by the pool.

"Writing music together will help me get where I want to go," she rambled on, and he shifted his stance, trying to relieve the pressure building behind his zipper. "Let me help you get past this block or rut or rough pat—"

"Okay, okay," he grumbled. "It's not like you're searching for the perfect word for a lyric in a song about my struggles. If I wasn't blocked, I could write an entire damn album about them."

"See! You're already getting the mood!" Releasing his arm, she stepped back and happy clapped with an excited grin.

Immediately he missed her warmth. Her touch. He was definitely in the mood . . . for something.

But Catalina was on a different wavelength—one that involved working, rather than playing, together—and he'd seen her in action during the Battle and their concert rehearsals. Once an idea struck, she went full steam ahead. Naysayers be damned.

Which was exactly what he wanted—to silence the naysayers and push past this block. If he couldn't do that now, with her, Padua would force another writer on him. And he didn't want someone else.

He wanted Catalina.

"In the morning, I'll show you what I've been fiddling with. You can let me know what you think, and we'll go from there. Like my mamá used to tell us when we complained about Saturday morning chores, many hands make light work. With my hands . . ." She held hers up, palms toward him. "And yours . . ." She waited, wiggling her fingers until he mimicked her jazz hands. "We'll write the best damn songs Padua Records has ever produced. Of course, my unparalleled talent makes that a given."

He let his head fall back as he groaned up at the sky.

Her mischievous cackle filled the night air, and for the first time in months, he found himself looking forward to sitting down to make music. Because of her.

Chapter Fourteen

"That is so corny!" Rolling her eyes, Cat flopped from her side onto her back, sinking into the supersize square pillow beneath her.

Overhead, exposed wood beams and slender poles arrowed toward the circular skylight in the center of the hut's thatched roof. The tail of a wispy white cloud and the pale-blue sky peeked through the opening.

"Oye, who are you calling corny?" A small yellow pillow with red tassels on the corners landed on her stomach, then toppled to the colorful woven rug, punctuating Patricio's complaint. "You're the one talking about some 'I'm on fire, I angst, I die' emotion that mariachi and ranchera fans crave."

"I'm on fire, I angst . . . ?" She tapped her mechanical pencil on her chin as she repeated his accusation under her breath, drawing a blank as to what he meant.

"Our first rehearsal at the rental home in San Antonio," he explained. "You were patting yourself on the back about why the audience loved 'No Me Olvides.'"

"First of all"—sitting up, she crossed her legs and pointed her pencil at him, lounging on a cushy, red clay–colored beanbag several feet away—"that song resonates because it's about two people forced to part to live happier lives. I've always said, love yourself like you want your lover to, and you'll be okay."

"Not sure a song about pleasuring yourself is a good direction for this album. But it'll be fun for you to try and convince me."

She frowned. "Pleasuring yourself?"

Dios mío, how did he— Patricio winked and she realized he was teasing. The wise guy was simply giving her single-woman-in-a-healthy-relationship-with-herself mantra a Kama Sutra twist they had no business discussing or, worse, visualizing, with each other.

His beach home already oozed "romantic getaway" instead of "tropical work retreat." Especially this oblong hut with its den-of-iniquity decor, complete with a fully stocked bamboo wet bar and array of colorful pillows in all shapes and sizes that beckoned you to lie down and make yourself comfortable. Open on the two short sides, the hut provided a spectacular view of the house and grounds behind it and the bay and beach directly below.

However, for her, this trip was business. Nothing more.

That meant not getting carried away like she had last night, hugging his arm while making her appeal for him to accept their partnership. Theirs had to remain a platonic relationship. But the way her breasts had ached for his touch while cushioned against his firm biceps. Uh, totally not platonic. Even now her pulse giddy-upped at the memory. His "pleasuring yourself" joke—as if the guy knew what she'd been up to in her bedroom last night—did not help.

Time to drag them back to the friend zone.

So far this morning, they'd managed to break bread amicably, if with a little needling in the process. Him criticizing the amount of butter she used to fry her eggs. Her turning up her nose at the puke-green, supposedly-good-for-you smoothie he failed to convince her to taste. No 80/20 diet for her—unless that eighty involved savory Mexican food like her mamá made and the twenty was filled with desserts.

More important than their food bickering, Patricio actually liked her revenge-driven song, and they'd made progress on her idea. Moving their work session from the music room inside to the beach-lookout hut had proven to be the perfect oasis to tap into their creative energy.

"Secondly!" She motioned at him with the pencil again. "The correct quote is 'I burn, I pine, I perish.' You need to brush up on your Shakespeare, güey."

He blew a *pffft* through his lips and hitched a lazy shoulder. "Shakespeare, ni que Shakespeare. Most of my fans go for the Latin-lover appeal." He struck a lazy pose on the beanbag, one that was far too sexy for her own good.

"Nuh-uh." Determined to keep things light, Cat picked up the yellow pillow he'd thrown and tossed it back. "You did *not* just go there."

His cocky smirk flashed. The rolled-up sleeves of his white linen shirt slid to the top of his muscular forearms as he stretched his arms high, then linked his fingers to tuck his hands behind his head on the beanbag. "When you got it, flaunt it."

"Ay. Dios. Mío. The ego on this one." She dropped her pencil in the crease of her songwriting notebook, set it next to her guitar on the brightly colored woven rug, and hopped to her feet.

Patricio's laughter followed her to the edge of the hut floor and out onto the brushed-concrete deck. A large netted area attached to the deck jutted out about fifteen feet, looming over the rocks and sea foam–topped waves below.

She stopped with her toes barely touching the netting's steel-bar frame. Face raised to the sun, she closed her eyes and sucked in a deep breath, almost tasting the salty water on her tongue.

"Vente conmigo." Patricio's invitation to join him had her peeking her eyes open with suspicion.

Standing in the middle of the net, he bent his knees and gave a tiny bounce. The nylon strips rippled under his feet, and she held her breath, petrified one of them might break loose, sending him tumbling onto the sharp rocks below.

"Uh, no thanks." She shook her head and shuffled back a half step. "I don't have a death wish."

"C'mon, I didn't think you were the skittish type."

"I have never been accused of having my head in the clouds. More like, my feet on the ground. Which is where I prefer to keep them firmly planted. Not—whoa!" She yelped as he stepped toward her, arms flapping at his sides to keep his balance on the unstable net.

"Just try it," he urged. He held out his hand, the angles of his chiseled face softened by his reassuring expression. "Seriously, it's a comfortable place for a nap."

"We should be working. Not napping."

"All work and no play . . ."

"Gets an album written," she finished.

His grin widened, his straight teeth a row of bright white against his bronze skin. "You're relentless."

"Determined."

"Scared."

"Prudent. Which isn't a word typically used to describe me. But this . . ." She glanced down at the supersize hammock and winced.

"Vente." Patricio bent his fingers back and forth, beckoning her.

Her gaze cut from his face to his open palm to the water crashing onto the rocks below. Tentatively, she lifted a hand. Then quickly pulled it back. Her fingers wiggled, stretching toward his.

"Trust me." His husky whisper washed over her, allaying her fear.

Placing her palm in his, she gingerly stepped onto the netting. It sank under her foot, and she yelped again.

"I got you," he promised, tightening his grip on her hand and reaching for the other. The sincerity in his Americano-coffee eyes led her to believe him.

The breeze whipped her short sundress around her upper thighs, plastering the soft yellow cotton to her torso. Several strands from her loose ponytail draped across her cheek, and she turned her head into the wind so it could blow the hair out of her face. The warmth of his hands cradling hers and the appeal of his encouraging smile calmed and quickened her pulse at the same time.

He led her several feet out, then slowly bent his knees, nodding for her to do the same. Her fingers squeezed a death grip on his as they lowered until they sat cross-legged, facing each other.

"See, that was easy," he said.

"For you, maybe. For me?" She tipped to the side and peeked at the sandy rocks. Another wave crashed against them. Water sprayed into the air, catching on the wind and sending a refreshing mist that skimmed over them.

Patricio released her and lay back—eyes closed, elbows bent, hands cushioning his head. "Try to relax. Let the sound of the water lull you to rest. Savor the warmth of the sun's rays on your face. Enjoy the breeze teasing your hair, caressing your skin."

Damn, he had a way with words. No wonder his songs resonated with listeners. His lyrical advice sure as hell resonated with her.

Hesitantly, Catalina stretched out beside him. One of her knees brushed the side seam of his black-and-red tiki-print board shorts, and he scooted his hips to make room for her. The netting undulated and she sucked in a breath.

"¿Estás bien?" He turned his head to squint at her.

The netting's two-inch-wide nylon strips dipped under her weight, pressing into her skin. It was almost like lying in a hammock in the courtyard at Casa Capuleta, and she found herself releasing the tension in her muscles. "Sí, I'm good."

They lay like that for a while, side by side with only the sounds of crashing waves and the occasional squawk of a bird interrupting their companionable silence. Cat listened to his slow, even breaths, hyper-aware of his proximity.

His fingertips brushed the back of her hand, and she swiveled her head to face him.

"I'm going to grab something from the house. You stay," he added when she started to sit up. "I'll be right back."

Once again, she stiffened as he made his way across the net to safety. The netting rippled and swayed, and she willed herself to move with it rather than freak out. Soon enough the motion slowed. Her anxiety dissipated and her eyes, initially scrunched closed in fear, remained closed against the sun's glare.

She must have dozed off, because the next thing she knew, Patricio was calling to her from the shadows inside the hut.

"I brought us a post-lunch snack, si tienes hambre." He raised a serving tray, and she realized that, yes, she was hungry. Their grilled chicken and kale salad hadn't filled her enough to last until dinner.

"Gimme a sec," she called back.

Standing on the wobbly net without the reassurance of his hold was a no go. Instead, she crawled to the edge, releasing a sigh of relief when she reached the steel beam connecting the net to the concrete deck.

"Grace is not your middle name, huh?" Patricio asked as she clambered to her feet.

"Cabrón must be yours, though," she shot back.

"How about Cabana Boy instead?" He held up a wavy-shaped glass filled with a peachy-orange frozen drink, a piece of fresh mango hanging on the rim.

"Get out of here! You made me a daiquiri?" She hurried forward, touched by his thoughtfulness. "I take back most of the snide remarks I've made about you."

"Hold up." Instead of handing her the drink, he lifted it high out of her reach. "Only most? And who have you been bad-mouthing me to?"

"Just a little," she hedged. He squinted a glare at her, and she quickly added, "But to be fair, until recently, you deserved it."

His moody *humph* didn't mean he forgave all her chisme, but he passed her drink over and she didn't waste any time sampling it. She hummed her satisfaction at the sweet rum and mango flavors titillating her taste buds, then followed him to a squat dark-stained wooden table surrounded by pillows.

He set down the tray loaded with a plate of fresh mango, pineapple, cantaloupe, and papaya; a small dish with a variety of raw nuts; a beveled glass of his craft tequila; and, surprisingly, her cell phone.

She picked up her cell and eyed him with an unspoken question.

"It was vibrating on the kitchen counter when I went up. Looks like you missed a call from Blanca," he replied.

"What? No!" Cat sank onto a sunflower pillow with a frustrated groan. "That girl's been dodging my calls for days because she knows I'm right. Figures I miss her when she finally works up the courage to talk."

"Give her a quick call."

"She probably won't answer." Disappointed, Cat sucked on her straw and watched Patricio toss several walnut halves into his mouth, then lean back to prop an elbow on the mountain of pillows beside him.

With the top two buttons of his white linen shirt undone, exposing the curves of his tanned pec muscles, and his dark, wavy hair beachy windblown, he was the epitome of one of his sexy cologne ads come to life. Sinful and provocative. Making it far too easy for her to picture them lying on a bed of pillows, bathed in the moonglow filtering through the skylight. Exploring and tasting and—damn him for giving her creative imagination this idea—*pleasuring* each other.

"Something going on between you two?" he asked.

"Hmm?" She blinked at him, lost in her lusty musings. Which, she reminded herself, she should put a stop to.

"Blanca's your birth sister. Also, the more quiet one in your group, verdad?"

"Mm-hmm." She took another sip of her daiquiri and considered whether to bring up Patricio's band member. The man behind Blanca's passive-aggressive phone silence and the knot of fear and frustration in Cat's stomach. "¿Te puedo preguntar algo?"

"With you, that could be a loaded question. But, sure, what do you want to ask?"

"What can you tell me about Luciano?"

"Gomez?" Patricio speared a chunk of pineapple with a toothpick, pausing with the fruit halfway to his mouth when she nodded. "He's been with me for a few years. Good kid. Talented trumpeter. Stays out of trouble on the road and works hard." Patricio slipped the fruit in his mouth. Her gaze zeroed in on his lips as they closed around the toothpick before he slid it out and set it aside. The tip of his tongue swept over his bottom lip, licking away a drop of pineapple juice. She squeezed her thighs together and swallowed the lusty moan building in her throat.

He chewed and swallowed before continuing. "His papá played and toured for years with a few other bands before he passed away. He had a heart attack, about six months before Luciano came on board. ¿Por qué?"

Why?

A risky question to answer, since she refused to reveal the real reason behind her "no mariachis" rule. There was no need for Patricio to know the impetus for the vow she had extracted from Blanca when they were kids. A vow her sister now seemed intent on breaking.

Carefully considering her response, Cat speared a slice of papaya and nibbled on the sweet fruit. "Apparently, according to the story I got from Violeta, one of the twins, he and Blanca connected during rehearsals for the tour kick-off concert in San Antonio. I found out last week that they've remained in contact."

"Interesting."

That was one word for it. She preferred "disastrous."

"If I knew Luciano better, I'd give him a heads-up." Playing it cool so as to not pique Patricio's interest, Cat took her time deciding which cube of mango to select. "I can't help feeling like I should let him know that Blanca and I have the same unbreakable rule: no dating mariachis."

"¿De veras?"

"Yes, really." She raised her brows, mimicking Patricio's surprised expression.

"Do *all* of the Capuleta girls?" He swirled the añejo in his short glass but abruptly stopped, nearly spilling the expensive spirit. "Wait, no, they don't. Mariana and Angelo, they're together, verdad?"

Cat nodded, mentally tiptoeing through options for how this conversation could go, like a chess player strategizing her game. "Just Blanca and me. We're biological sisters. Our pact doesn't include the other girls. But there's no breaking it. We swore to not be like—we just won't."

"So, this 'unbreakable rule' stems from something that happened before you arrived at Casa Capuleta."

It was more statement than question. Cat chose to treat it as such and not reply. Patricio tapped a finger on his glass rim, his face pensive. That deliberative problem-solving nature of his, which, as a hothead, she normally admired, now made her antsy.

"Is it safe to guess that with Luciano having found his way into the picture," Patricio eventually said, "you're worried Blanca might consider changing her stance?"

"No. That won't happen. I won't let it."

Patricio eyed her in silence for several weighty beats. "You know, you can't actually control whether it happens or not."

She speared a pineapple chunk with so much force the toothpick broke in half. A fractured piece stuck out of the fruit, the tip jagged and splintered. Her therapist would advise that she examine the fear clawing at her chest. Talk it through. Journal about it. Cat channeled all those emotions into her music. That's how she coped. Pain and joy, fear and hope . . . they were all fodder for her songs. Like the revenge anthem she and Patricio had brainstormed for most of the day. She understood that emotion well, as did he, apparently.

"Hey." Patricio's voice was as gentle as his touch, warm hands deftly removing the piece of toothpick from her clenched fingers, then wrapping around hers. "It's going to be okay. You and Blanca have a tight bond. I've witnessed the close relationship all you Capuletas share. That's definitely unbreakable. Give her a call. Talk this out. But word of advice, if you don't mind: watch that temper of yours. Something tells me Blanca will shut down. Like you said before, passive aggressive is her specialty, right?"

There it was . . . that unflappable, decisive manner of his that defused tension when a problem arose. Now it worked its magic on her. No, *he* worked his magic on her, dulling the alarm bells clanging inside her.

"Gracias," she murmured.

He gave her hand a quick squeeze, then released her and leaned back on the pillows with a sexy, sweet smile that tugged at her heart. "Partners, verdad?"

Cat nodded, grabbing on to that reminder of why she was here like the lifeline to reality she currently needed.

A soft buzz interrupted the quiet.

"Jefe, ¿estás allí?" a voice crackled over a speaker mounted on one of the wood beams above the bamboo bar.

"Sí, I'm here," Patricio answered.

"A black Cadillac SUV crossed the property boundary line on the main road a few minutes ago. Alberto called with a message. Said he couldn't reach you on your phone. Looks like Vicente is headed this way."

Patricio's entire demeanor one-eightied at his father's name. His relaxed posture stiffened. His warm expression shifted, and a stoic mask slipped over his features. His hands fisted and he rose with a disgusted snarl.

Apparently their tropical retreat was about to be invaded. Unplugging to leave your distractions behind didn't work if your main distraction came knocking on your door.

Chapter Fifteen

"¿Qué haces aquí?" Patricio demanded. Not bothering to wait for his father to make it up the brick stairs to the front stoop, he stepped onto the burnished red tile to block the doorway.

One shiny black boot on the bottom step, Vicente paused, nonplussed. "I am here to visit, mijo. Does a father need a reason to visit his only son?"

"Some do. *You* do."

"Por favor, no seas así."

"Don't be like what?" Patricio shrugged, feigning an indifference he didn't feel but refusing to give his old man the satisfaction of knowing he could get under Patricio's skin. That his approval mattered.

"¡Ay, basta!" With an angry swipe of his hand emphasizing his "enough already" order, Vicente scowled and continued up the steps. His bootheels crunched on the gritty brick, then landed with heavy thuds on the stoop's tile. Head high, chest puffed with ego, he pushed past Patricio as if he had been invited inside. "Stop being so petulant. It does not become a Galán."

Patricio pivoted on his beach loafer to follow—always fucking expected to follow—the old man. He slammed the heavy door behind him. The round mirror hanging above the matching distressed wood credenza rattled on the nearby wall.

Ahead of him, Vicente strode through the foyer and into the wide sala with its wall of windows overlooking the infinity pool and the gleaming waters of Bahía de Banderas. The sun had sneaked behind a cluster of thick clouds, leaving a dull pall that blanketed the deck area and the property creeping around it.

Patricio shot a worried glance at the spiral staircase as he reached the living room area. Catalina had followed him from the hut back to the house after his security guard had called to warn of his father's imminent arrival. Their mood sedate, conversation minimal, he'd set the tray of snacks on the granite kitchen counter and suggested she hang out in her room on the second floor. For her sake, it was best she stay away from his father's antagonism.

Mango daiquiri in one hand, her songwriting journal in the other, she had stopped halfway up the stairs, concern pinching her features. His "I'm fine" was answered with her brisk nod, her lips pressed in a serious line. A silent message that felt a helluva lot like a partner's *you've got this*.

Although he hadn't shared with her anything about the problems with his father—the futility of meeting his viejo's expectations, the impotence of holding a piece of himself back to stroke the old man's inflated ego—somehow, despite her growing up with an incredibly supportive father, Catalina seemed to understand. As if somehow a shared pain connected them. Though Patricio had no idea how that could be possible.

"¿Dónde está?" Vicente demanded. He pivoted on his bootheel, searching the open living area.

Patricio shook his head. "Where's who?"

"¿La nueva cantante, la escritora?"

Fuck! There was only one new singer-songwriter his father meant, and there was no way Patricio would subject Catalina to him. Not in Vicente's current snit. Or without witnesses the megastar wouldn't risk alienating.

"I don't know what you're talking about," Patricio hedged. He crossed to the kitchen, stopping at the breakfast bar. Thankfully Catalina had taken her drink upstairs, leaving only a single glass on the snack tray. "I'm busy, so tell me whatever it is that had you driving out of your way to barge in here. Then go."

"Mijo, how can you behave like this with your viejo? After everything I have done to pave the way for you."

"Are you kidding me with this?" Hands fisted at his sides, Patricio spun to face his father. Outside the sky had darkened as quickly as Patricio's mood. Gray clouds swooped in, turning the bay a stormy deep blue.

"I came to meet the woman the press loves and who has the fans crying for more of her. Cuidado, mijo. If you're not careful, she will steal your thunder. And whose name is it on the marquee? Galán!" Vicente thumped a fist to his chest with boastful pride.

That's what the old man craved. His name in lights. On the lips of fans. At the top of music charts and in the tabloids. The problem was . . .

"It's my name up there, viejo. Not yours." The words Patricio would normally keep to himself scraped his throat as they forced their way out.

"*Our* familia name. Handed down from generación a generación. Our familia tree has strong roots, here in Jalisco. Específicamente en Guadalajara, the birthplace of mariachi. We must always honor the one before us. The stronger branch from which we grow. El padre siempre viene primero."

The father always comes first.

That simple statement defined Patricio's entire life. Every significant moment, good and bad, boiled down to his father's warped belief that his place was rightfully ahead of his son's.

Striding over to join Patricio at the breakfast bar, Vicente set his misty-gray Stetson, its matching band adorned with his initials in 14K gold, on the granite counter. Without the hat, Patricio noticed his viejo's thick, wavy hair was more a distinguished gray these days. The lines creasing his forehead, around his eyes and mouth, were more pronounced.

The benevolent smile Vicente bestowed on him said his father had already put their disagreement behind him. Willing to forgive Patricio for a son's transgressions. Even if the son believed he had done nothing wrong.

How could a successful album with two Grammys, several Top Ten hits, and crowds that sang the lyrics along with him at packed concerts be considered a transgression? A stain on a career many dreamed of?

How could a father expect his son to give less than his best? To be content in the shadows?

A wave of inevitability crashed over Patricio like the salty water slowly wearing away the rocks along the beach below. Weary of this constant battle with his father and with himself, he heaved a heavy sigh and asked, "What do you want, viejo?"

Puzzlement angled his father's bushy brows together. It was comical—almost—how unfazed the old man was by the damage an ego like his could do to another.

"I will be in Las Vegas at the same times as your Friday and Saturday concerts. My management team is meeting with Park MGM representatives to finalize discussions about my short-term fall residency at Dolby Live, where you happen to be performing."

This was a new development. Vicente had never been interested in staying in one place. He preferred being on the move. Going from city to city with new women to woo along the way. But life on the road took a toll. It drained a body, especially an aging one. And for some, it drained the soul.

When Patricio didn't respond with his congratulations or a suitable amount of praise for this new development, Vicente frowned but continued. "Padua, MGM, and I think it would be good to have a dual concert on Saturday. Vicente y Patricio."

"No."

"The fans will love it. Ticket sales will increase—"

"My concert is already sold out. Fans are expecting the show I'm doing now."

"So, we give them more. Make the show better."

"It's already better. The set with Catalina has been the perfect addition. There's no need to change anything else."

"¡Ay, qué terco eres!" his father bellowed.

Better hardheaded than hard-hearted.

No, that wasn't exactly fair. Frustrated, Patricio scrubbed a hand over his eyes and forehead, as if doing so would scrub away spiteful thoughts like that one. His father loved him. Just . . . in his own unhealthy way.

"You don't see the benefit now, pero más tarde . . . sí, later, you will," his father bulldozed on. "Padua can handle all the logistics, and we'll see—"

"No!" Patricio slammed the side of his fist on the granite counter. Pain shot up his arm. He ignored it. Just like his father ignored his wishes. "We will see nothing. I have a show. You have meetings. That's what will take place in Vegas. I've already agreed to sing a duet with you at the Latin Grammys later this year. That's enough, viejo."

"Mira, cabrón, this is a smart move."

"For you. Not for me. I won't—"

"Ay, what a wonderful surprise!"

At Catalina's delighted cry, Vicente and Patricio swiveled toward the spiral staircase. She stood at the top in a flowy, pale-pink dress with short, capped sleeves. The dress's design cut a straight line across her chest, giving a delicious peek of her cleavage. The pink material hugged her torso before falling to skim her apple red–painted toes. Her long locks had been loosened from their earlier ponytail and left to tumble with abandon. But her smile . . .

Damn, how that sassy smirk of hers sucker punched him every time. That mischievous sparkle in her hazel eyes never failed to tease a smile from him. And the jut of her chin that said she was ready to take on her next challenge made him swell with pride in her.

Only, Patricio didn't want that next challenge to be his father.

"Gracias for coming all this way to meet me, Vicente. Es un placer." She floated down the stairs like an avenging angel.

His father rushed forward to meet her at the bottom, his trademark charm dripping from his greeting. "The pleasure is all mine."

Catalina rounded the spiral steps, her gaze locked on Patricio's. Determination glinted at him, and she dipped her chin. An infinitesimal movement. Still, its meaning pierced his chest—*I got this. I got you.*

Alberto had often come to Patricio's rescue in the past, especially when he was a teen. George did his best to pull his weight and influence at Padua to help Patricio maintain his distance. A few tutors and nannies over the years had bravely tried to speak up for him. Tried, failed, and been fired.

Sure, he might have misread Catalina's unspoken message. She could simply be taking advantage of an opportunity to meet El Rey, a man whose influence could aid her career. Maybe she wasn't purposefully interrupting the father-son disagreement to protect Patricio before it blew up. But something told him her intent was the latter.

Vicente reached out to help her—unnecessarily—down the final step. He bent to kiss the back of her hand, and Catalina threw Patricio a wink.

A chuckle rumbled in his chest. He coughed to cover it, surprised by his levity. It wasn't an emotion he often felt around his father.

"I was going to suggest we head outside to the patio, but it looks like the day has suddenly turned dreary," Catalina said, and damn if her overly sulky tone didn't have Patricio's lips twitching with a grin.

Holding on to her hand, Vicente led her to the three-seater sofa. Handcrafted in Italy, the wooden-framed sofa, with its channeled seat and backrests in nubuck leather, was one of Patricio's favorite finds during his search for unique pieces for his oasis. Now, he would forever picture Catalina leaning against the bubble cushions, her dark hair draping like silk over the pale leather. Her sun-kissed skin a golden tan glowing against the soft pink of her dress. Her magnetism dazzling the slickest ladies' man Patricio knew.

In no time, Vicente was singing his own praises, regaling his new audience with stories from his past. Offering sage advice to a "beautiful, talented artist" and warning her to "be wary of falling for the appeal of commercial pop music."

It wasn't easy, but seated on the ottoman angled beside the sofa, Patricio bit his tongue. No use refuting his father's unsolicited guidance. The pop-versus-mariachi argument with his viejo would, at best, end in a stalemate. At worst, another father-son shouting match Catalina didn't need to experience.

"Actually, Patricio's pop album is one of my favorites," she admitted, surprising Patricio. This was welcome news to him.

Vicente patted her hand where it rested on a bubble cushion between them and treated her to a patronizing smile that Patricio knew would be like nails on a chalkboard to her.

"Listen to the voice of experience, mija," his father chided. "Like I keep telling mijo, El Rey knows best. Trust me."

"Bueno, mi mamá always told me that trust must be earned. I will, however, take your words under advisement. In good time."

"She is cheeky, this one, no?" Vicente directed his words at Patricio but tilted his graying head at Catalina. "But she will come to see that I am always right. Like you have, mijo."

Patricio's ire simmered hotter. The amount of time he could spend in his father's lofty company before he exploded with outrage was quickly dwindling like a fiery wick on a stick of dynamite.

Catalina's pursed lips were the first sign of her annoyance at Vicente's heavy-handed counsel, which leaned more toward must-follow directives. "*She* is right here. And *I* prefer following my creativity's lead, writing music that moves me and my fans. I will not be pigeon-holed or 'set in my place' by anyone. Especially not by the patriarchy. Or outdated principles."

"Cuidado, mija," Vicente warned. Based on the way his father's right eye twitched, she had hit a nerve. "You are new, inexperienced, pero this business takes hard work, and you will soon learn your place."

"Enough!" Patricio shoved off the ottoman to grab his father's arm, dragging the old man from the sofa and to the foyer.

"¿Pero qué es esto?" Vicente blustered.

"*This* is me showing you the door," Patricio growled.

Catalina scurried behind them, having grabbed Vicente's Stetson off the breakfast bar.

"You asked about the show in Vegas, and I said no. You wanted to meet Catalina, and you have. Ahora . . ." Patricio drew to a halt at the front door. "Now, we need to get back to work."

Vicente huffed his disapproval. He made a show of straightening his shirt, tucking it in, and making sure none of the snap buttons had come undone.

Catalina held out his hat. "No offense intended, Vicente. But my parents have also taught me that respect goes both ways. I look forward to writing a song for you, someday. And I do appreciate you coming to meet me."

Without waiting for him to respond, Catalina rose up on her toes and pressed a chaste kiss on his cheek.

"Dios lo bendiga," she murmured.

Vicente repeated the common "God bless you" farewell, probably more out of habit, based on his confused frown.

Patricio didn't even bother with a goodbye. He dipped his chin at his father, who responded likewise. Then, after a stern glance from Patricio to Catalina, Vicente left without another word.

The door closed behind him with a metallic click of the latch. Patricio twisted the dead bolt for good measure. Catalina stood beside him, her eyes wide, questions looming in them like the dark clouds that had rolled in earlier. With his father gone, the tension that had been building inside Patricio, stretching his patience like a balloon threatening to pop, slowly eased away.

Normally, he felt browbeaten and worn after time in Vicente's company. Today . . . today his anger was tinted with hope, thanks to Catalina. Before he thought twice about it, Patricio clasped her hand and tugged her to him.

She came willingly, slipping her arms around his waist and laying her head on the front of his shoulder. He wrapped her in his arms, palms splayed on her back to press her closer.

"You were amazing," he whispered.

"Amazing's kinda my MO."

He chuckled, and she burrowed deeper in his embrace. Her nose dipped under the material of his linen shirt to brush his bare skin. Desire sparked through him, swift and hot. His left hand slid higher to caress the smooth skin above the edge of her bodice. Slow, languid brushes that teased him with the need to touch more of her.

"It was gutsy, standing up to him like that," he said. "Few have ever had my back the way you did. Gracias."

"Anytime, partner."

He hugged her tightly, knowing he shouldn't relish how perfectly she fit against him. The way her soft curves melded to his. The heady aphrodisiac of her scent filling his lungs.

Just a few minutes. That's all he wanted. What could one hug hurt?

Then she lifted her head and gazed up at him. Her arms tightened around his waist. Desire turned her hazel irises to burnished gold, and he lost the battle with temptation.

Slowly, he dipped his head, giving her time to back away. Say no. Stop him. Instead, she craned her neck, tipping her chin to angle her mouth toward his. Her eyes fluttered closed. And he finally . . . *finally* . . . tasted the sweetness of her lips.

Chapter Sixteen

She'd meant to simply offer him some comfort. That's all.

But the moment Cat laid her head on Patricio's chest, touched his warm skin with her nose and cheek, she knew she was fooling herself. A platonic hug wasn't going to be enough.

Then he went and called her amazing. Thanked her for having his back, even though his father had been an ass and no way in hell could she have stayed silent.

Then his fingers had caressed the skin along her upper back, and desire furled low in her belly. Ribbons of heat and need spiraled through her until she thought she might combust.

Easing back, she looked up at him. Maybe one kiss. One taste of his mouth would assuage the lust quickening her pulse.

An echoing desire flared in his dark eyes, heightening her need for him, and she tightened her hold around his waist. As if he understood, his head lowered, slowly coming closer.

¡Sí! The word echoed in her mind in the seconds before she closed her eyes and gave herself up to the moment.

His lips touched hers. Warm. Gentle. A soft brush of skin to skin. She gasped, and the sound lit a fuse that ignited between them.

His mouth crushed hers. Their kiss was frantic. Tongues licking and tasting. Lips devouring. Teeth nibbling. His hands were in her hair, cradling her nape, angling her head so he could take more, give more.

Her fingers explored the muscles along his broad back through his linen shirt. Eager to feel his bare skin, she felt for the shirt buttons. In no time they were undone, the material falling open. She skimmed her hands over his pecs, along his washboard abs, then up to push his shirt off his shoulders. He released her long enough to let the material slide down his arms to the tile floor, then pulled her close again, his mouth seeking hers.

She moaned with pleasure, and his tongue swept into her mouth, tangling with hers. Savoring, caressing, teasing. He broke their kiss to gently scrape his teeth on the curve of her chin. Soothed it with a swipe of his tongue. Then he blazed a delectable trail of nibbling kisses down her neck, along her clavicle, to the cleavage straining at the top of her bodice as her chest heaved with her quickening breath. She arched her back, her body begging for more of his exploration. Her breasts aching for his lips.

"Eres tan bella," he murmured, his breath warm on her skin.

"You make me *feel* beautiful," she told him, gasping with pleasure as his mouth closed over her right breast, suckling her nipple through the thin cotton of her dress. Unencumbered by a bra, the nipple swelled, pebbling at his heated ministrations. His hand cupped her other breast, kneading and massaging, his thumb flicking over her nipple in delicious swoops that sent pleasure arrowing to her sex.

She dug her hands in his thick hair, gasping as lust swept over her. He continued lavishing her breasts with attention, and she pressed her pelvis against him, eager to satisfy the desire pulsing between her legs. His rigid hardness throbbed along her lower belly. Reaching down, she covered him with a hand. He groaned and bucked into her palm.

His hands moved to cup her jaw, and he took her mouth again in a greedy kiss.

"I want you so bad," he growled, nipping her lower lip with his teeth, then caressing it with his tongue.

"Yes," she murmured, pressing her hand against his hard cock.

Suddenly he bent and slipped an arm behind her knees, scooping her off her feet. She clasped her hands around his neck, taking advantage of her position to trace the shell of his ear with her nose. Following the same path with her tongue before sucking his soft lobe into the warmth of her mouth.

Patricio strode to the leather couch, where he laid her down, then sat on the edge of the bubble cushion near her hip. Gently, he combed her hair off her forehead, tucking it behind her ear.

"So soft," he whispered. "So beautiful."

He trailed a finger along her jaw, continuing the sensual path to outline her lips. Opening her mouth, she drew his fingertip into her warmth. She bit the fleshy pad, then laved it with her tongue.

He stared down at her, his lips kiss swollen. His eyes dark pools of desire. His pants tented with his arousal. She placed her hand over him, and his erection throbbed against her palm, making her grow wet with her own arousal. Her body craved his; there was no longer any use denying it.

But in this moment of calm after the initial lusty storm, reality tiptoed into the room. An unwanted interloper. She frowned, trying to will away the truth.

It refused to be ignored.

A heavy sigh blew through Patricio's lips, his gorgeous chest rising and falling with the weight of it. Disappointment and acceptance flitted across his face, and she moved to cup his cheek.

"We should . . . bueno, I guess, more like, we shouldn't," she said softly, regretting the words but certain they were the right ones.

"I know," he answered. He leaned his cheek into her palm. His eyes fluttered closed, as if he were basking in her touch, and a pang of despair burned in her chest.

"If it's any consolation, I'd be lying if I didn't admit that I've wanted to kiss you for a while now," she told him.

"Irresistible. That's me." A corner of his delicious mouth curved in a sexy half smirk.

"So modest, this one," she teased, giving his cheek a playful pat that turned into a lingering caress.

Aware that she was on the verge of tossing caution out the front door like another unwelcome visitor, Cat started to pull her hand away. He clasped her wrist, stopping her. She watched, heart in her throat, as Patricio slowly brought her hand to his mouth. He pressed a kiss in the center of her palm, his lips warm and wet and oh-so-tempting.

"And I'd be lying if I didn't admit to thinking about how fucking mind-blowing we'd be together," he admitted, his voice a low rumble that made her toes curl in her sandals.

He stared down at her, his gaze so intense and intimate that she felt the truth of his words deep in her core.

"Unfortunately . . ." He kissed her palm again, then released her, regret painting his handsome face. "We both know this isn't a wise move. Not with—"

"Not with the tabloids sniffing around. Already hinting that I'm sleeping my way onto your tour."

He growled low in his throat. "Hijos de puta."

"Ha!" she scoffed. "Believe me, I've called them a helluva lot worse than sons of bitches."

"Crap like this always comes with our job description. Special perk, huh?"

She scrunched her face in distaste.

"We both have good reasons for our rules against dating. Me, anyone on tour. And you, bueno—" He leaned back, a puzzled frown pinching the area between his brows. "Your no-mariachis-at-all edict. The one your sister might, at present, be unhappy with."

Alarmed by his reference to their earlier conversation, Cat sat up and slid down the supple leather away from him. "I have my reasons. Solid ones. Ironclad, really."

"Forged during the time before you arrived at Casa Capuleta," he said.

The fact that he remembered her slip of the tongue made her regret bringing up Luciano and Blanca in the first place. Very few knew any details about her birth father. No one other than her and her sister knew his name, since he wasn't listed on their birth certificates. To make sure it stayed that way, Cat had thrown away every paper and photograph, anything tied to him, the day her birth mom had been picked up by ICE while working at the Laundromat. They'd seen it happen to others in their neighborhood before. Cat had even heard about kids being sent to live with relatives they barely knew. No way could she let the authorities pawn her and Blanca off on the man who had already made it clear that he didn't want them.

"Catalina?" The insistence in Patricio's voice told her this wasn't the first time he had called her name while she'd been lost in painful memories she hated to dredge up.

"Look, I'd rather not talk about that," she answered. "And, we should probably forget about what just happened. Chalk it up to hormones and a release of tension after your father's not-so-friendly visit, okay?"

She smoothed her dress over her knees and stared down at her toes, avoiding Patricio's gaze. Praying he'd go along with her lame reasoning.

"If that's what you want," he finally said, drawing out the words.

"It is."

An uncomfortable tension arced between them. Unwilling to let this one brief—albeit incredible—incident ruin the progress they had made earlier, she straightened her shoulders and angled to face him.

"I think we lost track of what Papo's long-standing feud with Hugo Montero taught us," she said, aware she definitely needed the reminder. "Any business partnership will fail if truths are withheld and if emotions are allowed to get in the way."

"Easier said than done," Patricio mumbled, rubbing a hand along his nape.

"Few things worthwhile are easy. And our writing partnership, working on an album that will blow everyone away? That's worthwhile. So, writing partners, and the other . . . bueno, let's just leave it at writing partners, deal?"

She stuck out her hand to shake on it.

Patricio tilted his head, considering. But she couldn't back down. Too much was riding on her success. No way could she let sex or lust or whatever fleeting emotion this was get in her way.

They needed to put each other back in the friend zone. For their own good. Or at least for hers. So, she willed herself not to blink. To hold his gaze, steady and sure and confident. Even if inside, a small part of her yearned for more.

Finally, Patricio nodded. His big hand enveloped hers. Her heart flip-flopped at the warmth of his palm, his long fingers wrapped around her smaller ones. Resolutely, she ignored it.

"Deal," he murmured.

Her cell phone vibrated in her dress pocket, and she flinched, startled by the interruption. Slipping her hand out of his, she dug for her phone, relieved and anxious when she saw Blanca's name flashing on the screen.

"It's my sister, I-I have to take this." Excusing herself, she hurried to one of the sliding glass doors leading to the back patio. With a worried glance over her shoulder at Patricio, she stepped outside and slid her thumb across her cell screen to answer the call.

~

"Bella Blanca, it's good to hear your voice," Cat crooned, hoping her sister's childhood princess name, Beautiful Blanca, would break the wall of ice Blanca had erected between them in the days since their familia dinner last Wednesday.

"Um, yours, too. I'm . . . I'm sorry I've been, you know, out of touch. Perdóname." Blanca's stilted greeting, double apology, and subdued voice pinched Cat's conscience.

Her sandals slapped against the wooden deck as she strode toward one of the canopied areas, where a group of cushioned loungers awaited. She wanted to rail at her younger sister. Order Blanca to cut ties with the mariachi trumpeter before she wound up hurt and disappointed, her heart broken. Her face streaked with hot tears. Her dreams of a storybook happily-ever-after dashed. Just like their birth mother.

But with her eyes closed against the late-afternoon sun playing peekaboo from behind a dark cloud, Cat could easily picture Blanca's troubled expression. Hazel eyes shadowed, smooth brow puckered, lower lip caught between her teeth. Worry was her sister's best friend—a constant companion since their early years experiencing their birth mother's bouts of anguish and depression. Regular therapy helped Blanca, as it did for all the Capuleta sisters, each dealing with their own issues; however, as the familia worrywart, poor Blanca would probably always wear her emotions on her sleeve.

Her gentle soul was one of her sweetest traits. Cat didn't want that to change. She only wanted to protect it.

So, rather than berate her sister, Cat sucked in a deep, lung-filling breath her therapist would be proud of. Slowly releasing it to the count of ten, she channeled Mariana's steady ER-nurse demeanor. And Patricio's calm, contemplative nature, that had been put to the test earlier with his father's abrasiveness.

"That's okay. I know school's always busy for you this time of year," Cat said, giving her sister an out. Even though they both knew it wasn't the real reason Blanca had been screening Cat's phone calls. "After spring break, the kids start to check out. I'm sure you've had a lot on your plate."

"Yeah, I have," Blanca mumbled.

An uncomfortable silence fell across the line when Blanca didn't elaborate like usual. Cat gritted her teeth, a maelstrom of emotions thundering through her, mimicking the dark storm clouds continuing to roll in above.

"It's weird, not being home," she admitted. "Not going into your classroom on the weekend to help rearrange the bulletin boards or prep for the upcoming week."

"Sabrina's been coming with me instead."

"That's nice of her. And Las Nubes? How are rehearsals going without me?"

"Fine."

"Mamá told me she's juggling the music classes okay on her own. But I worry if it's too much for her. Has she said anything?"

"Not to me."

Cat swallowed her *what the hell* retort, her exasperation with Blanca's uncharacteristically brusque responses mounting. Normally her sister would be motor-mouthing about a funny remark one of her kindergarteners had made in class, what another had done that got them in trouble.

As for Las Nubes, with Cat's departure, her sisters had been forced to make changes to their set, and those always made Blanca nervous. The twins were taking turns filling Cat's spot for some of the lead vocals alongside Mariana, which also meant slight changes to their choreography. Knowing Blanca, she had fretted over song or choreo tweaks, afraid she'd mess up in the middle of a performance.

"Fine" wasn't Blanca's typical response when she was forced to adapt to something new.

And she hadn't been "fine" when they'd hugged goodbye after the San Antonio concert. They'd both been in tears. Squeezing each other tightly. Scared about how they'd fare during this extended time apart, when they had never been separated for more than a few days.

Guilt slammed into Cat's chest with a sledgehammer forged in the fires of their past.

Hating the distance separating them—physical and emotional since their dinner table argument—she sank onto one of the pool loungers and drove a hand through her hair.

"Blanca, talk to me," she pleaded. "I can't just drive over to your place to tickle and cajole you out of this funk."

"It's not a funk. I'm mad at you."

"Why? I'm not the one breaking our promise."

"A promise we made when we were kids," Blanca complained. "Por Dios, I was six years old! And you were only eight!"

"But still wise enough to know what was for our own good." Cat flung out an arm, emphasizing her point, even though Blanca couldn't see her. "That's all I want for you, Blanca. Good. A good life. A happy, safe, secure one. Filled with the love of a partner who deserves you. It's why I'm out here, on the road and writing songs and calling home every night."

"No, you're on the road because it's what you want to do. It's always been your dream."

Her frustration boiled over, and Cat pushed off the lounger, storming toward the infinity pool. "Bueno, yes. But part of that dream is doing it the right way. Providing for you. And Papo and Mamá and all the girls."

"I'm an adult now, Cat. I don't need you to provide for me. Or protect me."

"Eres mi hermanita. That will never change. No matter how old we are, you will always be my little sister. And I will always protect you."

Blanca's heavy sigh carried through the line.

Cat responded in kind as she paced down the length of the pool. The lush terrain creeping in along the perimeter of the back deck and extending out for acres blurred into a swath of colors as tears pooled in her eyes. "Blanca, por favor, listen to me."

172

"I have been. I am. And I understand why you feel this way, Cat. But you—" Her sweet sister's voice caught, and she broke off. Blanca cleared her throat, and Cat fully expected her to back down; she'd never been a fan of confrontation. Instead, Blanca pelted her with an unexpected accusation. "But you're not being fair."

"Fair? ¿Maldita sea—"

"Do not swear on God's name!"

"Are you fucking kidding me right now, Blanca?" Afraid her brain might explode from her outraged disbelief, Cat slapped a hand to her forehead and spun on her sandal, marching back to the deep end. "Was he fair to her? To us? Ever? Why would you want to spend time with someone who could be just like him?"

"Could be. But could also *not* be. Luciano hasn't broken any promises. I haven't asked him to make any."

"Good. Keep it that way."

Again, one of Blanca's annoyed sighs blew through the phone. "Ay, Catalina, I don't want to fight with you."

"I don't either."

"Then you need to try and understand that maybe I don't hold as big of a grudge as you do. Or I'm ready to let it go. It's *healthier* for us to let it go."

¡Qué jalada!

Only, Cat's therapist, who had given her the same advice as Blanca, didn't think it was nonsense.

But Cat *had* let it go, damn it! This effed-up argument and their pact weren't about their birth father's abandonment. It was about not repeating the past.

Annoyed, Cat kicked her toes at the pool's placid surface, sending a spray of water in the air and wetting the skirt of her pink sundress in the process.

"Ay, Dios mío," she complained to Blanca. "I just wanna reach through my phone and shake some sense into you, sabes?"

"Sí, I know."

The smile in Blanca's voice deflated Cat's ire, making room for homesickness to seep in. She swallowed the lump in her throat and stared wistfully at the bay, its waters a play of blues and grays reflecting the tumultuous clouds. "But I also wanna hug you. And tell you everything's going to be okay."

"I know that, too."

Blanca's soft chuckle should have lightened Cat's disquiet. But love warred with fear and worry in her chest, the clash of their swords clanging in her ears.

"Te quiero," Cat whispered, the words husky with unshed tears.

"I love you, too."

"No matter where my dreams take me, I will always come back home, Blanca. Te lo prometo."

A sniffle answered her promise.

They hung up seconds later, Blanca agreeing to think about Cat's cautionary plea as long as Cat gave similar consideration to her sister's Disney-inspired "let it go" advice.

She should have been relieved to have finally cleared the air with Blanca. Instead, Cat tucked the phone in her dress pocket and collapsed in a disgruntled heap on one of the loungers, worry for her sister disrupting her tropical retreat.

Chapter Seventeen

After snagging his shirt off the marble floor in the foyer, Patricio *should* have gone to his room. Given Catalina some privacy while she spoke with her sister. But the anxiety blanketing her beautiful face as she stepped outside had made him pause.

Then there was the way she had stood by him when he needed . . . bueno, not exactly rescuing—more like backup. Anyway, she'd been pretty fucking awesome. He owed her the same support if this disagreement with her sister deteriorated into something worse.

That's what kept him piddling around the kitchen. Or, at least, that was the lie he told himself as he washed the dishes from their fruit tray, wiped down the counters, checked the temperature on the small wine fridge, and surreptitiously watched Catalina through the sliding glass doors.

Eyes closed, she tilted her face toward the sun. The angle of her head exposed the length of her elegant neck, the move reminiscent of when she had arched back against the front door, a low moan escaping her lips as he kissed his way down her throat.

Despite the ten minutes or so that had passed, his body still thrummed with pent-up desire. Her sweet taste lingered on his tongue. His hands burned with the longing to cup the weight of her breasts, feel her nipples tighten at his touch. And damn if he wasn't hard again, his cock pulsing for her.

He adjusted his pants, steadfastly reminding himself that putting the brakes on their foreplay had been the right decision. Even if doing what was right had left him in need of a cold shower.

While he wiped down the counters—again—he sneaked glances at Catalina. His concern grew as the minutes passed and her hand gestures became jerkier, her scowl deepening. She sprang off the lounger, ducked under the canopy draping the wooden frame, and began pacing down the edge of the pool.

Normally he found the view through the panoramic windows lining the entire back wall relaxing. The earth tones used throughout the house blended with the property's natural vegetation, creating a communal sense of being one with nature. Sunlight typically reflected off the infinity pool and streamed through the glass, brightening the indoors. But the dark clouds warned of an approaching storm, heightening the tension crackling off Catalina.

She pivoted, her pale-pink dress swirling around her ankles as she made another sentry trip down the edge of the pool. The hand pressed to her forehead as if it pained her told him the conversation was not to her liking. This would probably call for some cheering up or distracting when she finished.

Unfortunately, there could be no repeat of what had been the perfect distraction after his father's departure. It didn't matter that Patricio craved the sweet taste of her like he craved nieve de garrafa on hot summer days when the hand-churned treat melted on his tongue. Just like she had melted at his touch.

But giving in to temptation could lead to ramifications he refused to bring down on her.

No, he'd have to come up with another way to make her feel better.

Last night, after Mother Nature's impressionistic artwork, Catalina had mentioned hoping for another museum-worthy sunset tonight. If the weather cooperated, he'd have a couple of hours to whip up a dinner they could share while enjoying the watercolor display.

Moments later, a guttural groan coming from outside drew his attention from his inspection of the freezer's contents. Head bent, Catalina sat on the end of a lounger. Defeat slumped her shoulders. The wind caught her hair in its fingers, lifting the dark tresses in the air, then releasing them to settle around her in a satiny sheath.

She buried her face in her hands, and he started to go to her, intending to offer comfort. A shoulder to lean on. A shirt she could wet with her tears, and he wouldn't care, not if it soothed her sorrow.

He was two steps away from one of the glass doors when Cat dropped her hands on her lap and, eyes closed, sat up—spine straight, shoulders stiff. Patricio halted, waiting to take his cue from her. Maybe she didn't want company, instead preferring to stay by the pool or wander down to the hut on her own. Just because he felt the need to comfort her didn't necessarily mean Catalina wanted him to.

Eyes still closed, she tipped her face to the sky. The clouds shifted and a pale ray of sunlight broke through to bathe her in a golden glow. Her chest lifted, then lowered on a weary exhalation Patricio couldn't hear but somehow felt.

And there it was again. This strange connection he shared with her. It didn't make sense. He couldn't, shouldn't, act on it. But neither could he ignore the compulsion to go to her any longer.

One hand on the cream lounger cushion, she pushed herself to stand. The skirt of her sundress, mottled with dark splotches of water from when he had seen her kick the pool's surface, flared around her as she swung toward the house. Her gaze met his and she froze. Head high. Shoulders erect. Hands fisted at her sides.

Transfixed, he watched her throat move with her swallow. His heart clenched at the play of emotions chasing each other across her beautiful face—frustration, pain, disappointment, and sadness-tinged chagrin. Always a fighter, she gifted him with a wobbly smile. He admired her all the more for her bravery.

Which made it so damn hard to resist the urge to hold his arms out wide, invite her to seek refuge from whatever had stolen the mischievous smile that ensnared him in its net. Instead, he slid one of the massive window doors open on its track and joined her outside.

"Bueno, Round Two in the Battle of Hardheaded Mariachis went to the wrong side," she said, tapping her dress pocket, where she had tucked her phone.

Her scrunched-nosed displeasure reminded him of a photo of Alberto's grandson, taken the first time they had tried feeding the baby mashed peas. Somehow the green pureed mess had wound up smeared all over the kid's pudgy face. Much like the mashup of emotions Catalina was bravely trying to cover with her joke.

"Is Blanca . . . ?" He left the question open-ended, unsure what to ask or do or avoid. If he took Catalina's side, it meant pointing out her sister's fault. And if there was one thing he knew about the Capuletas, it was that they always stood up for each other.

"Annoying? Yes. Uncharacteristically stubborn? Uh-huh. The queen of passive-aggressive maneuvers? ¡Amén!" Eyes gazing up at the heavens, Catalina raised her arms high like a parishioner in the front pew at mass, singing her praises with fervor.

Certain that her joking actually hid her pain over whatever had gone down with Blanca, Patricio focused on figuring out how he might be able to help her feel better. Without getting them both into another compromising position.

"And you?" he asked softly. "How are you doing?"

"Ahhh." The word blew from her on a rush of breath as Catalina lowered her arms, leaving them to hang listlessly at her sides. "I'm . . ." She bit her lower lip, an uncertainty he rarely associated with her stamping her face. "I'm confused."

"You need to do some thinking on your own? This isn't a bad spot for pondering the universe. There's plenty I can busy myself with inside and give you some space out here. Or I could join you. If you'd like."

"It *is* beautiful," she murmured.

Pivoting, she stared out at the open water. Her reflection in the pool's surface rippled, her dark hair and the skirt of her dress rustling in the humid breeze. She was postcard picture perfect. The epitome of "the view is beautiful, wish you were here." He would buy that Puerto Vallarta memory from the corner vendor as a keepsake if he saw it. But he was especially thankful he got the chance to experience it for himself.

"Honestly, though?" she said, her voice soft, pensive. "The ocean's endless infinity usually makes me feel like anything is possible. But right now, it feels daunting." She pressed a hand over the swell of her breasts as if to calm her pounding heart. "Like, the life I've been working my ass off to build for Blanca and me, dispelling this damn ghost from our past, is beyond the horizon, out of reach. Just when I think I'm finally about to exorcise him from our lives, she does this."

Patricio didn't know exactly what the "this" Blanca had done entailed, but he'd bet it involved Luciano. Worse, he had no idea who the "him" Catalina wanted to exorcise might be. What the man might have meant to her. What he *still* meant to her. If—and Patricio hated to even consider this—there was any chance she might get back together with the nameless, faceless cabrón who clearly had caused her intense pain. And threatened to drive a wedge between her and her sister.

Jealousy snapped at Patricio with sharp fangs. He wanted answers. For starters, the name of the man he felt like punching in the face. But he kept his questions to himself. This wasn't about him or his ego or his lust irrationally demanding he claim her as his.

This was about her, what she needed.

"Usually, when I'm tense, I pour myself some añejo to take off the edge. Want me to open a bottle of wine for you? Make another daiquiri?"

"It's probably not a good idea to loosen our inhibitions." She shot him a sly glance under her lashes. "At least, not with each other."

Images of them losing their inhibitions together flooded his mind. Her nestled on a bed of colorful pillows in the hut, ready and willing. On a lounger by the pool, their bodies brushing and bumping and seeking pleasure. Upstairs in his king-size bed, sheets tangled around them as he kissed a trail up her inner thigh, hungry for the taste of her arousal. Blood rushed to his cock. Now that he had tasted her, touched her, heard her moans of satisfaction, he wanted more.

"We could head down to the hut," he suggested. "Catch whatever sunset the clouds will allow and eat dinner." And only dinner. He would sample nothing more, he reminded the salacious devil whispering ideas in his ear.

Catalina drew back, a dubious expression raising her brows. "In your den of iniquity?"

"My qué?"

"Ay, por favor." She swatted his forearm, her husky chuckle making him long to kiss the smile on her lips. "With all those overstuffed pillows scattered across the rugs, inviting you to get comfortable. The mood-lighting lanterns casting a soft glow and long shadows over whatever's happening on those pillows. The orgy-size hammock, which you talked me into trying once already."

"You have a wicked imagination, sabes?" Apparently he did, too, seeing as how moments ago he'd been picturing her lying on those very pillows with him.

"Yeah, I know." She hitched a shoulder, a hint of her sassy smirk curving her mouth. "I've been told worse, though."

Patricio crossed his arms to keep himself from reaching for her. "You're assuming I meant that was a bad thing. Wicked can be very, very good."

With her, no doubt it would be sublime.

"How about we hang out in your studio?" A hopeful expression brightened her eyes. "Get lost in music for a while? Maybe fool around with one of our songs?"

Our songs.

Because as far as she knew, the songs they wrote were for his next album. That's what Padua thought, too. Because that's the line Patricio had fed them all.

So far, his original plan was working. Today had been a great day. Music had started playing in his head and heart again. For the first time in months, he felt confident that he'd prove his viejo wrong. Patricio hadn't sold out to pop music because he didn't have what it took to succeed long-term in the arena where Vicente reigned.

And yet . . . and yet, today had been great because of her.

The truth sideswiped him, sending him into a tailspin.

¡Qué chingada! He drove a hand through his hair as the curse pinballed around his head. That was exactly what his plan had devolved into. A fucking mess born from foolish pride. His father's *and* his.

No longer could Patricio delude himself into thinking that the media attention of being on tour with him brought Catalina or that his recommendation of her songwriting skills to other Padua artists would be enough to satisfy her determined drive. That his decision to write his entire album on his own and not use any of her songs wouldn't sting her pride. It would. It was foolish for him to continue thinking otherwise.

He had to find another way to help them both achieve what they wanted. A new plan that would catapult her career in the way she deserved. Because despite his best intentions to avoid it, Catalina had come to mean far more to him than simply an incredibly gifted talent, and he refused to risk hurting this captivating woman.

"So, you wanna go fool around in the recording studio, ha?" he asked.

"Patricio Galán, are you propositioning me?" Her mischievous grin made a special appearance that had him secretly cheering like a devoted fan. It curved her lush lips and sparkled in her bright eyes. "What kind of girl do you think I am anyway?"

"The stunning kind."

"Ay, you're such a sweet talker. Tell me more."

He chuckled. Madre de Dios, she had a smart mouth. And he'd give anything to taste it again.

"Vente." He tipped his head toward the house. "My sound system in the music room hasn't been fired up lately. Let's put it to good use."

Catalina started to loop her right arm through his left but paused, then dug both hands in her dress pockets. Wise move, though it didn't make him miss her touch any less. With a swish of her long skirt and a heavy dose of attitude, she swept by him. "That revenge song we've been working on? Brilliant idea, if I do say so myself."

At least one of them could lay claim to that feat. His brilliant idea was seeming more like a house of cards, in danger of toppling over.

Chapter Eighteen

Catalina held her breath, completely mesmerized by Patricio.

He sat on the edge of a padded barstool in his home recording studio, his right foot propped on the stool rung, a guitar cradled on his lap. The muscles along his left forearm tensed and relaxed as his fingers pressed and released the strings up and down the instrument's neck, masterfully playing the song's various chords. Eyes closed, face taut with emotion, he strummed the guitar strings and sang the final chorus of a well-known ranchera.

The epitome of the angsty, pining hit she'd teased him about writing, "No Lo Beses" was a song he regularly performed in concert. But despite the number of times she had seen his show, she had never heard him sound this beautiful. Intense, at times guttural, at others silky smooth. His voice trembled with passion, hitting notes she couldn't ever remember him reaching. Not even during sound check or private rehearsals.

Chin high, the veins in his neck straining, he repeated the refrain, ad-libbing with a powerful run, holding the final note until the guitar quieted. His rich voice softened, faded, and she melted in a swoony puddle at his feet.

"That was . . . that was . . . absolutely incredible," she breathed, in total fangirl mode and not caring in the least.

His arrogant smirk flashed. "I know. Tell me more."

"Ay, Dios mío." Rolling her eyes, she spun on her stool to face the electronic keyboard again. Of course he would parrot her words back at her. "This room is not big enough for you and your ego."

"Hola, pot." The sound of him knocking on the guitar punctuated his hello. "This is the kettle clarifying: Who's the one with the off-the-chart ego here?"

"When you got it, flaunt it."

His laughter pulled a smile from her. Something he had managed to do fairly often over the past hour or so they'd been "fooling around" in his music room. Taking turns choosing songs. Him playing on the guitar. Her occasionally taking it off his hands or accompanying him on the keyboard.

After her fight with Blanca, a rare occurrence because her sister had perfected the art of conflict avoidance, despair had grabbed Cat in a stranglehold. Not being at home, able to corner Blanca at her apartment or call a sister meeting in the back courtyard at Casa Capuleta like they all did when sister skirmishes arose . . . not being there to hold Blanca's hands, look in her eyes, and remind her of the hell that man had put their mother through. How he had deserted them all. This whole frustrating situation left her feeling bereft and uncertain. Emotions she hadn't felt since those days immediately following her birth mom's death.

Her heart heavy, Cat had hung up prepared to tough girl it out in front of Patricio until she could escape to her room. But while the man's bossy, demanding, hyperconfident traits could be annoying—mostly because they rubbed up against hers—his humorous, considerate, softer side had a way of breaking through the protective wall of snark she often barricaded herself behind.

Instead of hiding out and licking her wounds while contemplating how to get Blanca to see reason, Cat had escaped to the sanctuary of music. And him.

When she and Patricio sang together, something amazing happened. Their voices meshed in an incredible way, one easily picking up the harmony when the other took the melody. Occasionally hamming it up by adding a run. Playing around by changing a lyric here or there, only to miss a line while laughing at an ad-lib the other threw in. Making music with him reminded her of the joy of her craft. It was uplifting. Well refilling. Exactly what her battered heart had needed.

Now she danced her fingers over the keyboard, playing back the last few bars of the song he had just finished. "I've never heard you sing 'No Lo Beses' quite like that. Those notes in the final refrains with the added runs . . ."

Keeping her hands on the keys, she twisted at the waist to let her widened eyes relay her awe.

Patricio lifted a broad shoulder, then let it fall. With the top few buttons of his linen shirt undone, the move shifted the material, treating her to a little more of the pec muscles her hands had explored earlier. Squelching the tug of awareness low in her belly, she smiled her encouragement. "You sounded pretty freaking awesome."

A soft blush crept up his neck, into his cheeks. Was he . . . ? No, he couldn't possibly be . . .

Pushing the carpeted floor with her toes, she spun on the slick piano bench to face him.

"What?" He drew back with a scowl that couldn't hide what Cat had caught. He was strangely, adorably, embarrassed by her praise.

"What's this about?" She pointed at him and drew several circles in the air with her finger, indicating his face. The sharp angles of his jaw and cheekbones, the aquiline nose, all softened by a humility she hadn't expected. Not when it came to his musical talent.

The man had platinum albums framed on his wall. Grammys and other notable awards that many, herself included, coveted graced a glass case over in the corner. Praise and accolades for him and his music had been heralded since his teen years, growing louder with each successful album and tour. She'd been one of those voices. When Mamá had first taught her and her sisters about budgeting and money management after their first paid Mariachi Las Nubes gig, one of Cat's budgetary line items had been "Patricio Galán Fan Club dues."

"I have no idea what you're talking about." Rising from the bar-stool, he rolled his shoulders, then pinched his elbows behind him in a sensual stretch that nearly distracted her from her new discovery.

"That wasn't a fluke a few minutes ago," she insisted. "Nor with the Juan Gabriel song earlier. Was it?"

Ignoring her question, he crossed the room to prop his guitar on its stand.

"You've got some serious pipes, Patricio," she pressed, intrigued by what she'd heard. "Why don't you ever open the tap all the way onstage, let the notes flow at full blast?"

Again, he ignored her.

"You haven't, ever. Am I right?"

His back to her, he dug his fingers into the muscles along the juncture of his neck and shoulder. Either soothing an ache from hunching over a guitar for the past hour or avoiding her probing.

"I guess I could be wrong," she said, her tone telegraphing the unlikelihood. "I mean, me making a mistake doesn't happen often, but I will grudgingly admit it can, on a blue moon, occur."

One hand covering his eyes, he dropped his chin to his chest. Her stomach bottomed out. Crap! Had she upset him by pushing too far with her teasing?

His shoulders started to shake, and for a few heart-stopping, Madre-de-Dios-what's-going-on seconds, she feared he might actually be crying. She watched, aghast as he stumbled his way to the red velvet sofa—a total statement piece she'd love to have in her small apartment, though she doubted she could afford the imported furniture's price tag. Head in his hands, he dropped onto the sofa, then let loose a loud guffaw.

Catalina gasped. Dios mío, the jerk was laughing? Seriously? And here she was, heart in her throat, worried she had unintentionally crossed a line with her needling.

He snorted and fell back to rest his head along the edge of the cushion. "How do you do it?"

"Excuse me?"

Rolling his head to the side, he stared at her from under his long lashes. "One minute you're pushing my buttons, poking at something I don't talk about. With anyone. Ever. In the next, you're making me crack a smile with your smart-aleck humor."

Relief, sweet and warm, oozed through her chest.

Hot on its heels came the unnerving realization that she could charge him with the same offense.

Since their arrival at his beach house, everything they had faced together: their first sunset chat, two productive writing sessions, his father's unwelcome drop-by, her aggravating phone call with Blanca, this impromptu jam session . . . somehow, it had all led them to a new place in their relationship.

Of course, there had also been that one lapse in judgment, their bone-melting make-out session. Not that she wanted to take it back. Those kisses, his big hands and warm mouth on her breasts. His heated breath on her skin. As wrong as it might have been, giving in to her desire for him was not something she could regret.

"Smart-aleck humor, it's a gift I give to those who matter," she told him.

"And I matter."

It wasn't a question, but the serious timbre in his voice told her that her response carried special weight with him. And with everything they had shared, she owed him the truth. "Yes, you do."

He held her gaze. She didn't blink. Wasn't sure if she even breathed, sensing that there was something he wanted to tell her, but he struggled to do so.

Patricio threw in the towel in their staring contest with a flutter of his eyelids and a weary sigh.

He sat up, bending forward to rest his forearms on his thighs, hands clasped between his knees. He glanced at her, indecision and then inevitability darkening his eyes to black before he dropped his gaze to his hands.

"I hold back when I'm performing because of my father," he said, surprising her with his candor. "Because the first time I held a note longer than him when we were onstage together, he didn't talk to me for a week. And when he did, he made it clear: He is El Rey. And it was not, is not, my place to outshine him."

She stared at Patricio in shocked disbelief. Questions screamed in her head, so loud and piercing that she couldn't make sense of any of them, much less pluck one out of the shrieking crowd to ask. It didn't matter, though. Head still bowed, Patricio continued in a tired, browbeaten tone that had her aching for him.

"I didn't mind. Not at first. As a kid, all I wanted was his approval. To win his love. Earn his respect by making him proud. If I stayed *just* good enough, never more, that might do the trick. But he was always there with a dig, a well-placed jab, reminding me of the rightful order of things." He expelled a harsh breath that shuddered through his torso. His brow furrowed with pain, and she yearned to go to him, smooth the lines marring his handsome face with her fingertips, and tell him his piece of mierda of a father was wrong. So selfishly, hatefully wrong.

"The pop album was for me. A way to finally push myself, outside of his shadow. Show fans the real me, not the almost me they think they know. Prove to myself that I could do it. But . . ."

"You did!" She leaned forward on the piano bench, willing him to believe her. "You *did* prove it. To millions around the globe."

Patricio slowly shook his head. And for the first time, underneath the strong, commanding figure he showed the world, she saw the little boy in him, hungry for his father's love and approval.

"Not to him," Patricio said softly. "To El Rey, I sold out."

"He's wrong." The words she had kept to herself moments ago burst from her.

White-hot anger ignited inside her like a line of fire racing toward a powder keg. Anger for the child who'd been held down instead of lifted up. Anger for the man who secretly made himself less for a father who didn't deserve the courtesy.

"He thinks I jumped to pop because I'm afraid I can't make it long-term with mariachi like he has."

"Bullshit!" Confronted with this discouraged, disconsolate version of the man whose confidence often bordered on cocky, driven to this low point by his father's selfish behavior, Catalina hopped off the bench and raced to the sofa. She sidled up to Patricio, her thigh pressing against his as she leaned close to cover his clenched hands with both of hers. "That's Vicente's ego talking. Messed up as it is. For whatever reason, he can't stand the idea of you being better than him. So he tries to dull your shine. Bottle up your potential. That's not right, Patricio. It's not how a parent is supposed to treat their child."

Patricio looked up at her, a sad smile trembling on his lips, shadowing his eyes. "I'm not lucky enough to have Arturo and Berta Capuleta as role models. You and your sisters hit the jackpot with them."

"We did. But we also had to go through our own pretty painful shit before we found ourselves at Casa Capuleta's front door."

Unclasping his hands, Patricio twisted a wrist to weave the fingers of one hand with hers. "I didn't mean to disregard what happened to you. Or any of your sisters."

"I didn't take it that way." She squeezed his hand, letting him know it was okay.

"Actually, I don't really know what happened with you and Blanca. But I can imagine. And I'm thankful the details have been kept out of the tabloids."

"Most DFAS documents aren't public information. But even if something leaked to the press, there's no way anyone can find out the one piece of our history I'm determined to erase."

Catalina expected Patricio to ask what she meant. Hell, she hadn't tiptoed into his private life with her own nosiness. She had steamrolled right in, practically badgering him to spill his secret. But he didn't press her for details. Instead, he gently caressed her forearm with soft back-and-forth brushes, creating a warmth that seeped up her arm, into her heart, and the last vestige of her protective wall crumbled.

Blanca and only four other people in the entire world knew Catalina's secret—Mamá, Papo, Mariana, and Cat's therapist. Now, it felt right to add one more. Like she *needed* to share this with Patricio.

Swallowing her nervousness, she cleared her throat and pulled back the curtain hiding the monster that tormented her. "I have to succeed in this business and take care of my familia the right way because my birth father was a sinvergüenza who treated my birth mom like one of his groupies—a cheap pit stop when he passed through San Antonio on his going-nowhere tours with a no-name mariachi band."

"Cat, you don't have to—"

"He was a liar," she continued, unable to stop the flood of words now that she had released the safety valve. "Telling her he'd eventually settle down, but never sticking around long enough to even pretend to play house. Breaking her heart with each broken promise. And even when she got deported, and Blanca and I were thrown into the system, he didn't bother coming back for us. His unfulfilled pipe dream meant more than his familia did. Than I did."

She didn't realize she was crying until Patricio gently cupped her face and swiped her tears with his thumbs.

"These are tears of anger. I don't care about him. I haven't for a long time. I'm not—" She broke off on a hiccup.

Patricio ducked down to press a kiss to her forehead. "Whatever you're feeling, it's okay."

"I don't want to feel anything when it comes to him."

Tucking her head to his chest, Patricio leaned back on the sofa, bringing her with him and wrapping his arms around her. "That's not always easy. Trust me, I speak from experience."

"Tell me about it. Years of therapy and I still get pissed." She sniffled. "I still cry, even when I try not to."

"Cry, rail, punch something. A pillow is preferable, not a wall. That hurts. I've tried."

"Who punches a wall? You might break a nail or something," she muttered.

Beneath her cheek, his chest rumbled with soft laughter. She burrowed closer, breathing in the scent of sun, sweat, and the dregs of his spiced, earthy cologne that still clung to his skin.

His palm drew slow circles on her back. Soothing her pain. Stoking her awareness of him. She should scoot away, put a friendly distance between them. Instead, she slid her left arm around his waist, hugging him closer.

"Does your father's reaction to your pop album's success have anything to do with your writer's block?"

The hand on her back stilled, then resumed its comforting motion. "Probably."

"Have you talked with anyone about it? A therapist or a life coach?"

His huff of breath teased her hairline at the top of her forehead.

"I take it that's a no?" she asked.

"And risk the story getting out, twisted into sensationalist headlines and bogus articles with 'anonymous insider' comments? No gracias."

"What about Alberto or George?"

"They've been around long enough to know what Vicente's like. Alberto's been with me since before I signed with Padua. They try to intercede when they can. Pero you know how it is with many Latino men, especially in my viejo's generation."

She swatted at the shoulder he lifted and dropped in a clear *it is what it is* shrug. "Ay, deliver me from puro machismo."

But mental health and the wounds and scars those who were supposedly loved ones gave you weren't things to be swept under the rug or laughed off or ignored. That's when they festered, ate away at you. Blocked your creativity.

Thinking back on the last year or so, ever since that first interview when Vicente had mouthed off about the importance of honoring your familia roots and Mexico's gift to the music industry—mariachi—she realized that Patricio hadn't really been out in public much. Other than a few special appearances, he had stayed relatively out of the limelight. Until the Battle of the Mariachi Bands and now the tour. But even then, he often kept to himself. Not hanging out with others on the tour. Struggling with his demons alone.

Her heart ached over the realization that, behind his larger-than-life persona that wowed crowds globally, he was actually lonely. Beloved as the younger Galán superstar, longing to be loved for who he really was.

Sitting up, she stared at Patricio as if seeing him through a new lens. "Hiding out here, on your own for months at a time, as gorgeous as this place is, won't necessarily get you out of your writing funk."

"But the tequila's top quality and the view mesmerizing. Especially what I'm looking at right now." He tucked her hair behind her ear, ran a finger along her jawline, then lightly tapped her chin.

"Flattery will get you nowhere."

"What will ease this worry?" He traced the pad of a finger between her brows. "And bring back that smile that always gut punches me?"

The fact that he wanted to make her feel better told her that he deserved the same. Maybe they could do that for each other. "Let's make another deal."

He blinked in obvious surprise. Then a cagey, *what's up your sleeve* scowl descended on the handsome face that had graced the cover and pages of countless magazines. Once even as the year's sexiest musical artist. Cat grinned, pleased to realize that the smart man knew her well enough to expect the unexpected.

"We've already established that this Padua contract and working on your next album are big boosts for my career," she told him. "And now you know why this is so important to me."

"I keep telling you, the life in the limelight you seek isn't all it's cracked up to be, querida."

His use of the endearment made her chest tighten with the wish that she were, indeed, his beloved. But that was a fangirl wish, and she had real-life goals to achieve.

Hooking a finger through the slit between two of his shirt buttons, she tugged at the material. "I know, but I can make it work. I'm not like that man who disappointed my birth mother and chased the spotlight at all costs." She refused to name him. "I'm not your father, who needs it so badly he steals it from you. I want to share mine with my familia. And you're helping me."

"You're doing a good job finding it on your own." His smile gentle, Patricio smoothed his palm over her head, finger-combing through the length of her hair. This softer side of him made her want to snuggle up against him again, forget the outside world a little longer, and revel in the pleasure they could give each other.

"You don't know how hard it is for me to not say something snarky like the spotlight was actually made for me."

He laughed. Rich and warm. Unencumbered and free. Dios, she loved the sound of it. The way his wide smile made her heart swell with warmth and her lips curve with shared joy.

"So, while I still think you should consider talking to a therapist," she told him, "I can help by kicking your lonesome-dove act to the curb. Instead of hiding out in your palace on wheels when we're on the road, let's get out, have some fun. Live a little."

"No sé."

"What's not to know?" she argued. "We'll find a way to go incognito so you're not hounded by fans." She held up a hand, mortified by a sudden thought. "Only, let me handle that part porque your getup when you snuck over to my hotel room? Por favor, that will not cut it."

"Haters gonna hate, huh?" He pulled on the lock of hair he'd wrapped around an index finger.

"The truth hurts, don't it?" she teased.

Unease flashed in his eyes, and she figured he was thinking about his father again.

"Come on, humor me. Partners, remember?" She held out a hand to shake on their new agreement. "Deal?"

Patricio's eyes locked with hers. That pensive expression he often wore when troubleshooting an issue with Alberto or during sound check before a show stared back at her. His gaze dropped to her mouth, and she curbed the urge to lick her lips. Wanting him to kiss her. Desperate to kiss him. It was foolish. It was dangerous. It was—

"Deal." Patricio's larger hand enveloped hers. "But I get veto power on hiding-from-paparazzi outfits. Nothing too wild, okay?"

Cat grinned. "Ooh, papito, challenge accepted."

Chapter Nineteen

"I don't think I would ever get tired of looking out at the water like this."

At Catalina's sigh-filled announcement, Patricio took his eyes off the road long enough to enjoy a much better view than the San Diego Bay glistening below as they drove over Coronado Bridge. With the passenger window down and her braid loosened after a Sunday morning trip to the beach, the wind whipped long strands of hair about her head and face. They danced in reckless abandon, just like she had when they'd arrived at Coronado Beach in time for sunrise this morning.

Dropping her beach bag and chucking her chanclas off her feet, she had run toward the water, arms open wide like she meant to embrace the world. The same way she approached everything that interested her. Foot heavy on the gas pedal. Heart all in.

But as soon as her feet met the cold Pacific, she screeched like a howler monkey and backpedaled up the black-grain sand, frightening a group of sandpipers into flight.

Once she got over the shock of the frigid water, they spent the rest of the time relaxing on a sheet she had snagged from one of the maids at the hotel, watching the sun complete its morning routine. The sky changed from muted shades of orange, red, and dark purple to a brilliant, cloudless blue. While the world around them awoke and other beachgoers gradually ventured to their quiet paradise, Patricio and Catalina made progress on a new song. This one, his idea.

Since they'd left Puerto Vallarta on Wednesday, making it to Phoenix in time for a charity event that evening, he and Catalina had fallen into a pattern. Mornings they met on his bus, where they worked on music for a few hours. Early afternoons he tended to other business Alberto held off until then or Patricio ran the sound check. Thursday evening and last night, they brought the sellout crowd to their feet with cries for an extra encore. And, surprisingly, Friday night Catalina had convinced him to join her and several others for a game of cards at the hotel.

When he was with her, he felt alive. Excited, but also relaxed, at peace. So he found himself seeking ways to carve out extra time in her company.

Today should have been a travel day. Instead, he'd given everyone the day off to enjoy San Diego before heading to Los Angeles for the rest of the week. With Catalina still on her get-off-the-bus-and-have-some-fun kick, the two of them had taken their writing session to the beach. Where he had most definitely found some inspiration.

The moment she whipped off her billowy cover-up, revealing a deep-purple one-piece with large cutouts on the sides that exposed the curve of her waist and hips, leaving her skin bare from her bra line to the top edge of her bottoms, he'd been a goner. Then she had stretched out beside him, leaning on an elbow, her long braid draping over her shoulder to rest along the curve of her breast, her shapely legs crooked, teasing him with fantasies of them wrapped around his waist as he drove into her.

The desire to skim his hand up her thigh, over her hip, continuing to the dip at her waist and higher was a pleasure-pain of inspiration for the lonely-for-my-love ballad traipsing through his head. The lyrics coming in bits and pieces.

But they were coming. Music was finally trilling in his head again. Thanks to her.

As if Catalina felt his gaze on her, she turned to shoot him a wide grin. He caught his own smile in the reflection from her oversize sunglasses.

"¿Qué?" she asked.

"Nothing. Like you said, enjoying the view." He turned back to the road, contentment riding along with them in the rented SUV.

All too fast they arrived back at the hotel near Viejas Arena at San Diego State University, the site of last night's concert. Patricio pulled into a spot between two vans in the self-parking area so Catalina could hop out and enter the hotel from a side entrance, alone. The less often they were seen together, the less chance of a photograph being snapped.

"Gordo's supposed to be here in an hour for the final fitting, right?" One hand on the open passenger door, she ducked her head inside to look at him.

"Sí, but he's coming alone this time. Carmen had to answer an SOS from another client. Something about a wedding dress and a nail polish spill. I didn't ask for details, pero I'm sure Gordo will dish about it when he gets here with your charro."

"Which I will keep away from all nail polish. But I am sooooo excited to see it!" She happy clapped like a little girl on Christmas morning, then finger-waved goodbye.

Patricio imagined her eyes behind her sunglasses, alight with glee, turning their honey color to dark amber. He couldn't wait to see her new charro either.

Correction: he couldn't wait to see her in it!

~

"You need some help in there?" Gordo called to Catalina, who was back in the private area of Patricio's bus trying on the designer's new creation.

A spurt of uncalled-for jealousy burned Patricio's gut at the idea of another man being with her in any state of undress. Uncalled for because . . . One, it was Gordo talking. The designer was more interested in his creation and how Catalina wore it, not the smooth skin and luscious curves shimmying into the charro. And two, because Patricio had no right to lay claim on the woman he expected would look stunning in anything. Or nothing. Naked and sated and warm in his arms.

His body immediately responded to the image of him and Catalina lying on a bed of pillows in his den of iniquity, as she teasingly called it. Their bodies wrapped around each other. Hands exploring. Lips and tongues tasting. Mouths breathing sighs of satisfaction.

Gordo drummed his fingers impatiently on the booth tabletop. The sound jerked Patricio back to where he was. On his bus in San Diego. With an audience of two, who did not need to notice his erection.

Shifting uncomfortably on the leather couch cushion, Patricio folded his hands over his crotch.

Alberto unbuttoned his charcoal suit coat and joined Patricio on the longer couch. The expectant expression on the viejo's round face said he was as excited as the rest of them for Catalina to begin her fashion show.

Gordo's phone started vibrating, the sound amplified with the cell propped up in the cup holder carved into the wooden table.

"¡Mierda! It's Carmen. I have to take this outside." Snatching his phone, Gordo mumbled another "shit" as he slid out of the booth. "Tell Catalina to wait. I don't want to miss her grand entrance!"

Alberto hopped up to open the door for Gordo, then tucked a hand inside his suit coat to dig for his own trilling phone.

Moments later, the pocket door to the private area slid open a few inches. Half of Catalina's face appeared in the small gap. "Oye, can someone come help me with something real quick?"

Patricio glanced over at Alberto, who was standing at the top of the stairs, engaged in conversation with someone on his phone. The viejo's gaze darted from Catalina to Patricio. He mouthed the word "Padua" and pointed at the cell pressed to his ear, then he made a shooing motion for Patricio to handle whatever Catalina needed and turned his back on the two of them.

"Uh, sure. Coming," Patricio answered.

Catalina backed up as he approached. Her bottom lip was caught between her teeth, and a worried frown puckered her brow.

Patricio pushed the door open wider to find her wearing a fitted, white button-down shirt tucked into a pair of ass- and hip- and leg-skimming pantalones de charro in a deep blood red. Gold gala adorned the pants' side seams, while black embroidered roses with a gold metallic accent thread interwoven through the design trailed down her legs and across her trim lower belly.

Barefoot, half-dressed in her charro, hair in a messy bun on top of her head, and her face free of makeup, she was still breathtaking. Only the unease in her eyes marred what he would describe as perfection.

"What's wrong?" He started to slide the pocket door closed behind him out of habit, then realized it might be misconstrued if the two of them were alone in what was, technically, his bedroom. So, instead, he left the door partially closed to allow her some privacy.

"The zipper's caught in the material or something," she whispered, her voice tainted with panic. "I don't want to rip a hole or . . . or tear the material. *This is a freaking RS design!*" She twisted like a pretzel as she strained to see the back zipper, her fingers grabbing for the closure. "I can't see what's . . . Ay, there's no way I've gained weight since they measured me. Do you think I've gained weight? No! Don't answer that! Dios mío, what do I do?"

It took Patricio a beat to process her verbal barrage. This was as close to freak-out mode as he had ever seen Cat, and she'd been in far more stressful situations. The Battle of Mariachi Bands had pitted Las Nubes against her father's longtime nemesis, an old traditionalist like Patricio's father. Cat had gone toe-to-toe with the hardheaded patriarch and never flinched. Then there'd been the time her mic went out in the middle of their set in Irving. She hadn't missed a beat. Leaning closer to his mic, she'd hammed it up for the crowd and given him a hard time about having to learn how to share. The fans had lapped up her saucy teasing.

Him too.

"Hey, it's going to be fine," he promised. "You look gorgeous, and this—this is just a pair of pants."

"Just a pair of . . ." She gave a comical double shake of her head. Her eyes widened to silver dollar size and she gaped at him as if he had sprouted horns. "*Just a pair of . . . ?!* You did not really just say that! All my sisters *would kill* to wear anything by RS Designs. Even Mariana, and she's usually more comfortable in scrubs."

"Soooo, like your video chat from the spa at my place, this charro gives you more big-sis cred, huh?"

"Ay, Dios mío, the man thinks he's a freaking comedian," she complained as she spun to give her back to him. "Will you see if you can unjam the zipper, without tearing the material? Please. Before Gordo returns."

She twisted her neck and arched her back, her eyelashes swooping down to shadow her cheeks as she strained to see the zipper. He followed her gaze to the delectable curve of her butt in the figure-skimming pants. Sure enough, the hidden zipper had gotten stuck partially raised, leaving the bloodred material gaping at her lower back and waist.

"Can you get it undone?" she pleaded, her voice a husky whisper.

Oh, he wanted to get it undone, all right. Only, he was more inclined to lower the zipper all the way, strip the pants down her shapely legs, and fill his hands with her gorgeous curves.

Unfortunately, that was not what she had in mind. And with Gordo and Alberto on the other side of the partially closed door, it wasn't exactly smart for Patricio to be thinking about undressing her and carrying her to his hideaway bed, where they could have their wicked way with each other. No matter how fucking incredible it would be.

Truth be told, though, he doubted once would be enough to appease this craving for her that he was having more and more trouble denying.

"¡Oye! C'mon!" She reached behind her to swat at him impatiently, nearly swiping the front of his pants.

He sidestepped with a mumbled "Give me a sec," then bent to grab hold of the top of the material on either side of the zipper opening with one hand. His forehead grazed the center of her back as he dipped the fingers of his other hand inside the material, trying to locate where it had gotten snagged.

Her soft intake of breath made him freeze. The warmth of her skin beneath the thin white shirt heated the back of his hand. The scent of the musky, floral lotion he'd watched her rub onto her arms and legs one morning at his beach house teased him with the urge to bury his face in her neck.

She wiggled her hips and his hand slipped lower, his middle finger now cradled in the crack of her round butt cheeks. All that separated his skin from hers were the lacy black panties he caught a glimpse of below the hem of her shirt. His cock twitched in his black jeans.

"Stay still," he ordered, setting his free hand on her hip.

"What are you—"

"If you'd quit shaking your ass in my face, maybe I wouldn't get distracted," he grumbled.

"Distracted? Por favor." She shot him a *yeah right* glower over her shoulder, before facing forward again as she mumbled under her breath, "It *is* a great ass, if I do say so myself."

"I agree," he murmured.

"Hmm?"

"Nothing. Hold still." She obeyed—a rare occurrence—and Patricio carefully worked the material free from the zipper's teeth. It took a bit of maneuvering, but finally the pants zipped closed properly. Patricio straightened and gave her butt a playful smack. "There you go!"

"Hey! Watch it!" she complained, but she spun to face him with a smile of relief curving her lips. "Gracias, you saved my a—"

She broke off as Patricio backed her up against the closed bathroom door. Palms flattened on the thin wall on either side of her, he bent closer, stopping with his face inches from hers.

"What are you doing?" Her question was an excited whisper that had his mind veering off again into tangled sheets and her sighs of pleasure.

"Trying like hell to keep my hands off you," he growled.

Desire flared in her eyes as she stared up at him. She splayed her hands on his chest. Rather than push him away, though, her fingers crooked in the black material of his Henley, drawing him closer. Her tongue made a slow swipe of her lower lip, and he lost the ability to form coherent thoughts. All he knew was that he needed a taste of her. Now.

"Ahem."

At the sound of someone loudly clearing their throat, Patricio shoved off the wall. Catalina abruptly straightened and turned to face the back of the bus, hiding her mortified expression. On the other side of the half-open pocket door, Alberto and Gordo stood in the lounge area, watching with varying degrees of interest.

"Everything progressing okay back there?" The dramatic flare of Gordo's brow made his innuendo clear.

"Um, yeah! Just a—just a minor zipper glitch. But we're all set now," Cat answered, her tan cheeks flaming the same color as her new charro.

Scurrying behind him, she shoved Patricio toward the door, barely giving him time to open it enough for him to squeeze through. He banged his shoulder on his way out and stumbled into the kitchen.

Catalina shoved the door closed behind him, and he heard a muffled "I'll be out soon" from the other side.

Alberto's paternal evil-eyed reprimand made the back of Patricio's neck burn with embarrassment at being caught on the verge of devouring Cat's mouth with his.

"Your secret's safe with me, güey," Gordo promised, breaking the strained silence. The silver chain hooked to the designer's belt loop clinked as he slid onto the booth again.

Patricio lowered himself to his previous seat on the longer sofa. The leather groaned in protest, much like his body did over the exasperating, unsatisfying game of "almost" he and Catalina continued playing.

"There's no secret to keep," he told Gordo. A half truth at best.

"We all deserve some privacy, even in the entertainment industry."

"Amén," Alberto said, adding his two cents to Gordo's wise words, though the viejo's perturbed scowl darkened as he faced Patricio.

"Tell that to the paps lurking outside. It's never-ending," Patricio complained. "But I appreciate your loyalty, Gordo."

"Hey, you were the first to take a chance on a tattooed, pierced no-name from the barrio. Wearing my threads when others were shooting me down. Your support is what led to me connecting with Carmen. And becoming all this." Gordo spread his arms out wide in a classic *look at me now* pose, self-satisfied smirk included.

"You're talented." Patricio tipped his head in a show of respect for Gordo, who was an inspiring success story of his own making. "*That's* what led you to Carmen, güey. Not me."

Alberto patted Patricio's knee as the old man settled beside him. His parental glare had faded to a *Mona Lisa* satisfied smile that telegraphed a "muy bien." At least for now. Alberto might approve of what Patricio had told Gordo, but sooner or later the viejo would speak his concerns about what he and the designer had interrupted.

"Sin duda. You know I own it." Gordo gave a proud chin jut, proof of his "without a doubt" confidence. He pointed a finger with its black-painted nail at the pocket door. "If you ask me, she's one of a kind. I wouldn't want her to be the one that got away. ¿Me entiendes?"

Yeah, Patricio understood his friend's not-so-subtle message. But it wasn't that easy.

"You know as well as others, I won't date anyone on tour," Patricio said.

"Sí, pero el tour ends in—"

"And she has a no-dating-mariachis rule."

Gordo reared back so fast he banged his head on the window shade behind him. "¡No me digas! Wow, that's . . . ¡qué chingada!"

"Shhh!" Alberto shushed Gordo and jerked his head toward the back of the bus.

But the designer was right—Patricio's relationship with Catalina was a "you don't say, fucking mess" of a situation. And Gordo didn't even know the half of it.

The pocket door started to slide open, and Patricio swiped a hand across the front of his neck giving Gordo the *kill it* sign.

"Are you ready?" Catalina called.

For her, Patricio was starting to think his answer might be "always."

Her fingers hooked on the metallic recessed pull, set to tug the pocket door open, Cat paused. Anticipation, excitement, even a touch of nervousness buzzed inside her, like cicadas awakening after their years of slumber.

Dropping her hand back to her side, she turned to stare at herself in the full-length mirror hanging on the short hallway wall. That was her reflection. Intellectually, she knew that. Emotionally, it was hard to believe.

Hands trembling, she smoothed the lapel of the short bolero jacket and the vest beneath it, over the heart and vine of roses embroidered in black and metallic gold along the sleeves, the same embellishment that trailed across her lower belly and under the shiny gala marching down the side seams of her pantalones. Lightly she traced the embroidery with her fingertips—the roses a reminder of Las Nubes, her parents and sisters, and all they had done for her over the years. Putting up with her demanding taskmaster tendencies when it came to Las Nubes rehearsals and performances, accepting her bid for perfection as she sought her dreams of mariachi stardom.

Without her familia, she wouldn't be here.

Here. On Patricio Galán's private bus. Wearing a one-of-its-kind RS original designed and created for her. Set to debut the charro in front of a sold-out crowd at the Forum in Los Angeles.

Pride swelled in her chest. Tipping her chin, she eyed her reflection critically. Even without her makeup game face on, and with her hair tugged free from the ponytail holder to fall in a mass of beachy windblown waves and her feet bare, wearing the charro made her feel unstoppable.

So why, then, was nervousness tiptoeing across her shoulder blades and stopping her from sliding open the door to reveal herself?

"Catalina? You okay?" Patricio's deep voice carried through the door, inadvertently answering her question.

He was why.

Because as she'd gotten to know him better, spending more one-on-one time with the real Patricio over the past week—in Puerto Vallarta, then on the road in Phoenix and San Diego—his opinion had begun to matter. Beyond as a writing partner. Even beyond the role of industry mentor, offering advice and sharing insider knowledge.

Patricio the friend—*the man*—was starting to matter more than she wanted to admit.

And that . . . She drew in a shuddering breath. Bueno, it made the protein bar she had hastily inhaled in between showering and racing to meet with Gordo churn in her stomach.

Pressing a palm to her belly, Cat stared in the mirror and gave herself a pep talk. This didn't have to be a big deal. It was okay if she worried what he thought. If she took his advice and opinions under consideration. As long as she didn't allow them to supersede what she felt was right.

As long as she remained in control of herself and her future.

And in this charro—straightening her shoulders, she grabbed the hem of the short bolero jacket and gave it a strong tug—she felt like she could accomplish anything.

"Ready or not, here I come!" she singsonged.

The pocket door slid open with a light scrape, and she strutted into the living area, head high.

She was Catalina Capuleta, and nothing could stop her.

Bueno, except the sight of three men, eyes wide, speechless and slack-jawed as they stared at her.

Gordo recovered first, punching a fist in the air and letting loose a high-pitched grito that nearly pierced her eardrums. Alberto's round cheeks plumped with his wide grin. And then there was Patricio . . . Dark and smoldery, his gaze glided down her body, then slowly back up again. Desire flared in his eyes, and his sexy smirk flashed as he slowly nodded his approval.

Their appreciation fed her already hefty ego, and she lapped it up. Elbows bent, palms raised, she grinned as she spun in a slow circle for them. "Bueno, ¿qué piensan?"

"I think you look divine!" Gordo crowed. "Honestly, you were born to wear my designs, girl."

One hand on her hip, she struck a runway-model pose and winked at him.

"Work it, baby!" Gordo hooted. Sliding from the booth, he slow walked around her, eyeing his creation. He tugged here, smoothed the material there, hunkered down to check the length of the pants, hopped back to his feet, and fiddled with her necktie.

"You are absolutely stunning, Catalina," Alberto added. "Your mamá and papá are going to be even more proud when they see you in this."

His fatherly praise reminded her of Papo's unending support, and the ache of homesickness squeezed her chest. She sent Alberto a watery smile of thanks.

"And you?" she asked Patricio, who had yet to chime in with his opinion. "Cat got your tongue?"

"Cat's definitely got his something," Gordo murmured.

"¿Perdóname?" she asked, uncertain whether she'd heard him correctly.

"Hmm? Oh, no, excuse me. Or bueno, ignore me." Gordo waved away her question, then reached to brush at her shoulder. "I'm mumbling tonterías out loud while admiring my work."

Pinching his chin between a thumb and forefinger, the brazen designer stepped back to scrutinize the outfit. Patricio rose from the couch to stand next to Gordo. Two men in black, both in their early thirties, at the top of their game. One tall and lanky, tattooed and pierced, comfortable in his typical baggy concert tee—this one classic Maná. The other equally as tall, but broad shouldered, trim hipped, his Henley clinging to his muscular chest and arms, and his eyes . . . Oh, the heated affection Patricio wasn't bothering to hide stole her breath.

"What are you thinking for your hair?" Gordo asked.

"My—huh?"

"This gorgeous hair of yours." She flinched as Gordo lunged behind her to sweep her hair up in his hands as he continued brainstorming her look. "I know you usually wear it up, pero qué piensas if we leave it down? What do you think, Patricio?"

"I'm a fan of loose and wavy." His low, rumbly voice chased goose bumps up her arms. "But it should be Catalina's call. This is all her."

Dios mío, she didn't know what turned her on more: the thought of Patricio's hands in her hair, tugging her closer for a kiss, or the fact that the man who had his hands in even the most minute detail pertaining to his show was willingly standing aside and letting her make all the decisions.

"Actually, I was also thinking of wearing it down," she answered, focusing on Gordo's question and not the heat in Patricio's gaze. "Maybe adding a headband adorned with roses. You know, a nod to Las Nubes and mis hermanas."

"Oooh, I love it. Fab detail the media and fans will adore." Gordo released her hair and moved to stand in front of her again. "I'll take care of the headband. I know exactly what to do. No worries, everything will be waiting for you in your dressing room in LA. Girl, you are gonna slay them when you step onto that stage at the Forum."

She grinned.

Alberto gave a double thumbs-up from his seat on the couch.

Patricio folded his arms, his lips quirked in that sly, sexy smirk that had millions swooning, including her.

His face alight with glee, Gordo clapped his hands. "Just think, a beautiful charro and a crown of roses for our new princesa as she joins El Príncipe to bring down the house! What's not to love?"

Patricio's smirk widened. He shot Catalina a bold wink, and her heart fluttered.

Dios mío, what's not to love indeed.

Chapter Twenty

"Feel free to go, Alberto. I know it's been a long day." Patricio jutted his chin at the door leading back inside to the hotel's rooftop bar beyond the fifty-foot pool that gleamed a brilliant turquoise courtesy of the underwater lighting.

"All the more reason for him to stay," Catalina countered, as always contrary to his demands. "Alberto, you deserve to relax here for a bit. Enjoy the city skyline."

She motioned at the twinkling lights of Beverly Hills sprawled before them on all sides, visible through the tall glass wall lining the perimeter of the pool and deck area. Nearing midnight on a Friday, the hotel's amenities were closed, the heavy wooden door in the top-floor elevator lobby kept under lock and key. But at Patricio's request, and for a nominal fee, the hotel manager had reopened the rooftop access for a small private gathering. Any wandering hotel guests or visitors were met by a hulking security guard barring entry to all but the two individuals Patricio had indicated.

One had only just arrived, making herself comfortable on the padded lounger next to his.

Patricio hoped the other would, any minute now, make himself scarce.

"Vete, viejo," he urged. Alberto was still in his suit, the same one he'd been wearing since their first meeting at 8:00 a.m. "Go, I'm sure you're tired."

"Maybe he doesn't want to—"

"I know he—"

"How could you possibly—"

"¡Basta!" Alberto swiped a hand through the air, his uncharacteristic outburst silencing Catalina and surprising Patricio. "Enough already! It's like I have traveled back in time to when my kids were teenagers bickering with each other."

Patricio huffed a breath through his teeth. "Believe me, I do not have brotherly intentions."

"Which is exactly why he should stay. Or I can go." Catalina started to rise, setting her glass of rosé on the squat metal table between their lounge chairs.

"Wait!" Patricio clasped her wrist to stop her.

She raised her brows, her pointed stare moving from him to his hand, still manacling her wrist. He released her, adding a soft "por favor," relieved when she didn't stalk away.

"My day 'off' "—he finger quoted the misnomer—"between concerts started with a we-agree-to-disagree meeting with Padua execs, then on to a tiring extended photo shoot followed by a quick change for dinner with a charitable organization."

Releasing a tired sigh, he sank deeper into the cushion behind him. This had been the first morning since they had left for Puerto Vallarta that he and Catalina hadn't spent time writing together. He'd felt out of sorts all day, and it didn't take much delving to know why.

"I finally have a moment where I don't have to be 'on.' I'd like to relax with you. Hear about your day," he told her. "How your writing went. If you played tourist or lounged by the pool or heard back from Blanca."

It was as close to an "I missed you" as he would allow himself to admit. But he *had* missed her. And he didn't know what the hell to do with that realization.

Nothing about their situation had changed. They were both still fighting their demons—their birth fathers and those they had thought they could count on to always be on their side. For her, that meant Blanca. For him, George.

"What happened at the meeting?" Catalina asked, ignoring his mention of her sister and zeroing in on business. Always business. He admired her tenacity. At the same time, a petulant side of him hoped she had missed him, too.

"Nothing worthwhile," he groused. Folding his hands behind his head, he let out another sigh, this one full of resignation.

Catalina's glossy lips pursed at his nonanswer. Her sandals scraped against the concrete floor as she scooted down her cushion and turned to Alberto, who hovered in the area between their chairs and the glowing pool behind him. Not making himself comfortable. Not leaving either. In a limbo of sorts—caught between following Patricio's clear expectation for him to retire for the night or granting Catalina's request that he stick around to play chaperone.

Like they needed a pinche chaperone!

"What happened?" she repeated, directing her question to Alberto.

The viejo frowned, but when Patricio kept his lips clamped closed, Alberto gave in to her. "Padua is still pushing to surprise fans with a special Vicente y Patricio set during the Saturday night show in Vegas in two weeks."

Patricio growled low in his throat, annoyed that the concert remained a topic of discussion when he had clearly said no. Multiple times. To multiple people. Including George, who had the actual cojones to ask Patricio to reconsider.

"Contractually—"

"Contractually I don't give a damn!" Patricio roared, cutting off Alberto.

Catalina flinched. Stunned shock stamped her face.

Alberto slowly folded his hands at his waist, his expression stoic. The night's breeze rustled the older man's thinning hair, mussing it over his forehead. Self-conscious of his balding spot, normally he would have finger-combed and smoothed his hair back into place. Instead, he remained still, his posture stiff. The picture of an obedient assistant. Not the mentor, the sounding board, the voice of conscience Patricio depended on.

Remorse burned in his chest. Alberto had done nothing to deserve Patricio's anger. It was the older Padua executives . . . his father . . . even George.

"Not a simple set, the entire mariachi half of the concert," Patricio ground out, the words gritty and rough, pushed through his tightened jaw.

"Can they make you do that?" Catalina asked.

The simple answer to her question was no. But there would be ramifications if Patricio played hardball with them.

If he gave the finger to the execs' idea, meant to ramp up fan fervor for the record company's star duo, then Patricio's initial bait-and-switch plan to not use Catalina's songs on his album and write his own would be more difficult to execute.

Then again, that wasn't exactly his plan anymore. The songs he and Catalina were working on spoke to him. They spoke of the two of them. Even though he had mentioned Catalina's musical talent to several singers under Padua's umbrella, he didn't know if he could hand his and Catalina's songs off for someone else to record. No doubt she would balk at the idea, too. As it was, he worried about her reaction to him even thinking of doing so in the first place.

Did he need to write his entire album alone to prove his father wrong?

Did he *have* to prove *anything* to the old man and his ego?

The questions chased him like a hunter's prized bloodhound, sniffing out his weaknesses. Zeroing in on the doubt, confusion, and buried pain caused by his father, and his very real fear of losing her.

"Patricio, can they do that?" Catalina scooted to the edge of the cushion.

"There's a thin line between yes and no," he hedged. "Pero, and that's a big 'but,' denying them this risks them denying me something I want later."

His expression grim, Alberto swiveled his neck to stare out at the darkened landscape of the Hollywood Hills. The million-dollar homes were a smattering of lights dotting the pitch-black terrain like fireflies in the night. Alberto didn't say anything. The downward tilt of his mouth, the fact he wouldn't look at Patricio, said enough. Alberto knew the something Patricio had initially intended asking Padua to accept later, and the viejo didn't like it.

A relationship not built on a foundation of truth will crumble. Alberto's advice, shared privately after he and Gordo had interrupted Patricio and Catalina in their not-quite-but-close-enough-to-compromising position on the bus.

Patricio had assured his trusty assistant that he had it under control. After today—the fiery meeting at Padua, missing time with her, missing *her*—Patricio knew he'd been lying to Alberto. And himself.

"Okay, so then come up with a compromise you can live with," Cat said. "I-I don't know, a medley. A couple of songs at the end, like a surprise encore. Some way to give them the publicity shots and video footage they want. But when you do"—stretching toward him, she grasped Patricio's forearm, holding on to him tightly—"then you don't hold back. At all."

Alberto spun his head back around so quickly, Patricio bet the side of his neck burned. Disbelief raised his brows.

Patricio nodded at the viejo's unspoken but clear inquiry. Alberto's brown eyes widened at the admission: yes, Cat knew the cause of Patricio's currently strained relationship with his father, the weight it placed on Patricio's shoulders, and the toll it took on his psyche.

"That last part is most important," she said, shaking Patricio's forearm to get his attention.

"Like how you didn't hold back when you strutted onstage last night, resplendent in your new charro and crown of roses?" Patricio asked.

A Cheshire cat grin split Catalina's lush lips. "Bueno, it's going to be hard for you to top that. I set the bar pretty high."

A laugh-turned-cough racked Alberto, and he bent forward, covering his mouth with a fist.

Patricio winked at her. Pride bloomed in his chest like the brightly colored lantana planted along the back patio and growing wild across his property. "You were radiant. Puro badass mariachi in drop-dead-gorgeous red. Singing your heart out and making me proud. Making your familia proud. And I hope yourself, too."

Her lashes lowered and her throat moved with a swallow. A rare moment of bashfulness from the bold, determined woman who continuously awed him.

"Hey. It's the truth." Sitting up in his lounger, he combed her loose hair back to tuck behind her ear. Tracing her jawline with his fingertip, he nudged her chin up with a knuckle. "She wowed us all, right, viejo?"

Patricio glanced up to include Alberto in the Catalina praise fest, but the old man had quietly departed, leaving the two of them alone. He'd have to call his assistant to say thank you for the privacy and apologize for losing his temper.

"Bueno, I'm sure I can confidently speak for our wayward chaperone and say you looked and sounded spectacular." He cupped her jaw, giving in to his need to touch her again. "You were trending on social media today. The talk of entertainment shows. The star of my dreams last night, and more."

"Stop it," she murmured, giving his shoulder a gentle shove, then curling her fingers to snare a fistful of his shirtsleeve.

Leaning closer, he gently tipped her chin higher. She gazed up at him, moonbeams reflecting in her eyes. Her lashes fluttered closed, then open.

"We probably shouldn't . . ." she murmured.

"Just one." Still, he paused, waited for her permission. She tugged on his shirt, pulling him toward her, and his restraint fled.

He covered her mouth with his, pleased when she opened for him. Her tongue brushed against his in a languid caress. Teasing him with the need to taste more of her. All of her.

Gripping her waist, he lifted her to sit on his lap. She gasped his name and wrapped her arms around his shoulders. Their kiss grew more fervent, insistent and greedy. His fingers delved into her silky tresses, and he angled her head to deepen their kiss. It was hot, and frantic, and pushed him closer to the edge. She moaned his name, the guttural sound making his cock pulse for her. He broke the kiss to trail love bites down her neck, along her clavicle.

Her chest heaved with her breaths. And he knew, listening to her gasp as he grazed her neck with his teeth again, that one kiss wasn't going to be nearly enough.

But it's what he had promised.

Gathering her in his arms, he lay back in the lounger. She stretched out alongside him, draped an arm around his waist, and snuggled closer. He pressed a chaste kiss to her forehead, cherishing the perfect end to his day.

She'd been relaxing in her room before bed when he finally finished with the charity event and texted, inviting her to meet him up here. Rather than keep him waiting while she primped and made herself up, Catalina had arrived with her face shiny clean, dressed in a comfy oversize tee, black leggings, and a pair of house chanclas. Her natural, breathtakingly beautiful self.

He loved that she felt comfortable enough with him to be herself. Bold and brash onstage. Comfy and real in private. He loved . . . her.

The admission made his heart trip and stumble, like a foal birthed into a new world.

He loved her. Now he had to figure out exactly how to convince her that history would not repeat itself. He was a mariachi who wanted to stay by her side. One who would never break her heart.

Chapter Twenty-One

"Ay, Dios mío, I nearly peed my pants when that woman from Dallas asked if anyone had ever told you that you bear a slight resemblance to Patricio Galán!" Howling with laughter, Cat pushed open the glass door at the MGM Grand's main entrance late Thursday afternoon.

The frigid AC welcomed them as Patricio reached around her to hold the door, flashing her a sheepish grin. Ay, she loved teasing that smile from him. Right now, it was pretty much the only thing she could recognize about the international superstar underneath the disguise she had pieced together for him.

At first, he had balked at the getup, but having fun in Vegas wasn't the same as catching the sunrise at a relatively deserted Coronado Beach, where a baseball cap and his Ray-Bans were enough to conceal his identity. Or strolling down an empty Rodeo Drive after dark, when the stores were closed and Cat could window-shop to her heart's content, jokingly quoting the famous "big mistake" line from *Pretty Woman*. Patricio's husky chuckle at her antics heightening her fun.

In Vegas, people swarmed the casinos, shops, and restaurants. They rubbed elbows—and other body parts—out on the packed street. Here, going out to refill the well, as Cat liked to call it, had to involve a little subterfuge. At least for Patricio.

After vetoing her idea of a gray wig with '70s-style sideburns, he had agreed to a baseball cap with a mullet hairpiece sewn in the back.

Add a tropical-print button-down, his own black-and-red swim trunks, and a pair of sneakers, plus a fanny pack and the dark ski-goggle-size sunglasses he'd worn during his clandestine visit to her hotel room all those weeks ago, and . . . voilà! He transformed into the stereotypical tacky tourist ready to gamble, drink, and see the sights.

Of course, Patricio had decreed that if he was required to wear a disguise, so was she. Seeing his bet and raising it, Cat threw on a perky bleached-blonde bob wig; a pair of white, retro cat-eye sunglasses; and a bright-pink WHAT HAPPENS IN VEGAS STAYS IN VEGAS tee over her leopard-print leggings.

No one would recognize either of them in the selfies she had snapped in front of the Bellagio fountain, but she did. And she would always treasure those pics. Especially the one that caught her surprise when he pressed a kiss to her cheek, water cascading behind them, her mouth open in a soft "oh!"

"I don't know what that lady was thinking," Patricio said. "But if I ever tell you I'm considering a mullet, feel free to smack me upside the head. Or have Alberto give me a trim while I'm sleeping."

Cat chuckled. "You can count on me to have your back. Of your head at least."

"Oye, be nice."

Slipping her cell out of her leggings pocket, Cat checked the time. "Blanca should be here already. It took us a little longer to walk down the Strip."

His hand on her lower back, Patricio guided Cat around a large group wearing matching T-shirts announcing their family-reunion weekend and a gaggle of girls clearly several drinks into their bachelorette party already. Unfortunately, the two groups were gathering in the same place she had arranged to meet her sister.

Cat's heart raced. Excitement, trepidation, and homesickness churned in her stomach like a ball of tortilla masa being kneaded in her mamá's mixing bowl. Uncertainty of this magnitude wasn't something she had ever associated with her sister. Oh, they'd had their tiffs in the past. Mostly due to Cat's impatience and strong character; she'd own that. But they had never had a rift between them like the one over the past few weeks.

A rift that had led Blanca to tell Cat that she didn't need help getting from the airport to the hotel because Luciano had arranged for a car to pick her up.

Cat had gritted her teeth to stop her expletive-riddled response. Her anger came from a place of hurt, and wounding her sister would only make Cat feel worse. Instead, as soon as she'd hung up with Blanca, she had dialed Mariana's number for advice, in dire need of her older sister's rational, problem-solving skills and empathetic outlook.

Craning her neck to scan the MGM Grand's lobby area, Cat waited impatiently while the bachelorette party took yet another series of group shots and silly-faces pics in front of the hotel's famous gold lion. When the group finally headed off to find their next photo op in Sin City, Cat spotted Blanca across the lobby, talking with two men over by the front desk.

Blanca looked a little pale, and she'd lost some weight on her already thin frame. Her delicate brows were angled in a worried frown, her fists strangling her leather purse strap. Typical behaviors for the familia worrywart, but Cat hated that she was responsible for her sister's visible unease.

Blanca's gaze swept the lobby, passing over Cat, then darting back. Recognition slowly dawned on Blanca's face. Her eyes widened with joy, and her sweet smile split her pink lips. In a flash Cat was racing to her baby sister, sidestepping an elderly couple with a breathy "excuse me." Then she was hugging Blanca tightly.

"Ay, me hiciste tanta falta," she whispered.

"I missed you so much, too," Blanca said.

"I hate when we fight. Especially when—"

"When you think you're right."

Cat laughed at her sister's ability to finish her sentence. They knew each other so well. This fight and the chasm it had created between them couldn't last, especially now that they were together. They were each other's touchstone. Yes, there were others now, gracias a Mamá and Papo, but she and Blanca had been the first constants in each other's lives. Nothing could or would ever change that.

Stepping back, Cat clutched Blanca's shoulders to get a good look at her. There was so much she wanted to ask about home, so much she was missing. How were rehearsals, were Sabrina and Violeta comfortable filling in for Cat, how were the others and their music students, and what was going on with the loan their parents had taken out to cover structural repairs to Casa Capuleta's building?

But behind Blanca, Luciano waited, his fingers fiddling with the brim of his black Stetson, his youthful face, with its cute dimples and normally quick smile, now serious and sober. He leaned to his left and said something to a shorter gentleman, who stood with his back to the rest of them, wavy gray hair brushing the collar of his navy-and-gray plaid western shirt. The man turned, his paunch straining against his black leather belt. He dipped his head in greeting and . . . something about his eyes, the slightly crooked slant of his nose. There was *something* Cat couldn't quite . . .

Blanca twisted to look back at the stranger. He offered her a tentative smile, and a memory flashed in Cat's head.

Her stomach spasmed, nausea churning and rising with her dread. Saliva pooled in her mouth as bile bubbled up like hot lava, threatening to erupt, right there in the middle of the bustling lobby.

Stumbling back, she bumped into Patricio.

"Whoa, ¿qué pasa? ¿Estás bien?" Cupping her elbows, he peered down at her, but she couldn't take her eyes off the ghost from her past.

"Cat, let me explain!" Panic laced Blanca's cry.

"No. No-n-n-no!" Cat shook her head. Words of denial, betrayal, and rage tumbled on top of each other in a race to be voiced first. "This isn't happening. He is not. You are not."

"I know this is a shock. It was for me at first." Blanca stepped toward her, hands outstretched, but Cat drew back, plastering herself against Patricio. "Maybe we should talk in pri—"

"Uh-uh. I—I'm not—I can't. Not with . . ." Her pulse pounded in her head, her skin suddenly clammy and itchy and hot and . . . Overwhelmed, Cat pressed a hand to her mouth, stifling the scream threatening to break loose.

Around them hotel guests engaged in Vegas-style antics. Snapping pictures of the iconic lobby with its lavish decor. Sipping exotic drinks. Chatting animatedly about their next must-see as they bustled by, money for the casino burning a hole in their pocket.

But even surrounded by the boisterous cacophony, all Cat could focus on was her sister's betrayal burning a hole in her heart.

"How could you do this?" she rasped, the painful words scraping her throat. "How could you betray her like this?"

"I'm not—it's not like that," Blanca cried, her face pinched with anguish.

But Cat couldn't think about her sister's distress, not when her own consumed her with the intensity of fiery blue flames. "How could you, Blanca? How could you betray *me*?!"

Without waiting for her sister to respond, Cat spun and fled into the crowd, refusing to believe this was actually happening. That he was here. That Blanca was with him.

Numbness seeped over her, and she couldn't think. All she knew was that she needed to get away, couldn't even look at Blanca. Or their birth father.

She heard Blanca call her name, but she didn't stop. Didn't look back. She couldn't. Because *he* was there. Standing at her sister's side when he didn't deserve to.

Patricio raced after Catalina, thankful for the garish blonde wig, which made it easy for him to spot her as she sped through the hectic lobby toward the noise and flashing lights of the overcrowded casino. Her head swiveled from one side to the other as if she were searching for something. She ducked around a group of rowdy college kids and dodged a bride and groom either practicing for or reliving the kiss part of their ceremony, and for a few scary seconds, Patricio lost her in the melee.

Seconds later, her blonde bob and bright-pink tee appeared behind a tall waitress delivering cocktails to a group at a poker table. Patricio picked up his pace, anxious to reach her before Catalina disappeared again.

He caught up to her in front of a bank of slot machines, busy spinning their video graphic wheels at the push of a button from the aging chain-smokers who had parked themselves on the padded seats, empty plastic cups and overflowing ashtrays evidence of their lengthy stay.

"Hold up." He clasped Catalina's upper arm, and she gasped, starting to pull away until she realized who it was.

Dazed, scared hazel eyes stared up at him. Her chin trembled. She bit her lower lip, clearly fighting tears she refused to let fall. His determined fighter had taken a blow below the belt, and she was hurting. He pulled her into his arms, cradling her head against his chest.

"It's okay," he whispered. "I got you."

"I have to get out of here. I can't—" Her arms wrapped around his waist and she clung to him.

He tightened his hold, offering her solace and protection. "Which elevator bank goes to your room?"

She shook her head. "Not there. Blanca has a key. I left one at the front desk for her. I don't want to see her right now."

"Then you can hang out in my suite. There's plenty of space." He leaned back to peer down at her, palming her cheek and gently swiping a thumb at the tear trickling from her left eye. "If you want to be alone, you can rest in the main bedroom or relax on the sofa on the outdoor terrace. It's not the Bay, but the view of the Strip isn't too shabby. Sound good?"

Her top teeth worried her plump bottom lip as she nodded. "Gracias," she murmured, her beautiful face marred by lines of worry and pain he'd do anything to soothe.

"Bien, vámonos." Clasping her hand tightly, he cut a path through the crowd, leading her toward the elevator bank to his suite.

Unlike when she had arrived at his beach house or when they'd met to work in his hotel suite in LA, Catalina didn't wander around, marveling at the grandeur, teasing him about his Príncipe digs compared to her closet-size room as a mere peon. And the MGM's Skyline Terrace Suite did deserve marveling. Only, not in her current state of distress.

Instead, she trudged in, allowing him to guide her to the sectional sofa, where she toed off her sneakers, dropped her purse on the cream carpet along with the blonde wig, and then scrambled into the corner where the two sectional halves met. She grabbed one of the black-and-tan pillows, hugging it against her chest like a shield.

Eyeing her with wary concern, Patricio lowered himself to the sofa cushion next to hers. He swiped the baseball cap with its mullet hairpiece off his head and scratched his itchy nape. Relieved to be rid of the ridiculous disguise, he set the hat and his supersize sunglasses on the round coffee table.

Catalina stared straight ahead, her normally bright eyes dull. Her tan cheeks pale. Her expression drawn. Patricio didn't know how or if he could make things better for her, but whatever she needed, he would give.

"Do you want something to drink? Maybe some water?" he asked softly.

"Don't tell me you finished all the añejo." A corner of her mouth twitched. That sassy spark of hers trying but failing to bolster her spirit. His heart squeezed with pain for her.

"I keep a bottle stashed for emergencies. Say the word and I'll break it out for you."

"That's okay. Save it for something special."

"You're special. That's reason enough for me."

Her lashes fluttered closed, and a lone tear trailed down her cheek.

"Talk to me, querida," he whispered.

She dragged in a shuddery breath. Confusion and grief darkened her eyes when she finally gazed at him. "How did he find us? And why now? More importantly, how could she . . . How could Blanca go behind my back like this?"

The jarring buzz of their cell phones simultaneously vibrating interrupted her anguish-laced questions. She muttered a curse and jerked her head toward the expansive glass window overlooking the Strip. Pointedly ignoring the phone rattling like a snake inside her purse.

Patricio fumbled to unzip the fanny pack hidden under his gaudy tropical-print shirt to retrieve his cell. LUCIANO, 702-555-1988 flashed on the screen.

Instead of answering, he held the phone out toward her. "It's Luciano. I'm sure your sister's the one calling you."

"I don't want to talk to her."

"That's understandable. Pero you're going to have to, eventually."

The phones stilled.

Catalina released an audible breath weighty with inevitability, and her lashes drooped closed. "I know. It's just . . . Why? How?"

"Do you want me to find out? I can talk to Luciano, ask if he knows anything about—" Patricio broke off, realizing he didn't know the man's name.

"Pedro. Pedro Santos. The man who broke my mom's heart. Then abandoned Blanca and me for good after our mom was deported, despite being a model employee and caring mother. She died in a car accident in Mexico days after her arrival."

Stunned by the tragic story—horrifically worse than he had imagined, based on the snippets she had shared with him before—Patricio slid closer to cover one of her balled fists with a hand. He draped his other arm behind her along the sofa cushion, his fingers trembling as he caressed her nape.

Outrage stampeded over him like a herd of wild horses, their hooves pounding on his chest. Kicking up dust that choked with indignation over the injustice in her past. How two defenseless little girls had been stripped of their mother due to unfair policies and politics, robbed of their paternal influence by the man's selfishness.

"I told myself we were fine without him. Better off. And we have been. We are. Aren't we?" The self-doubt that hitched in her voice hit him like a gut punch.

Her eyes glistened with tears as she stared up at him. To fit her long locks under the blonde wig, she had fashioned her hair into an intricate crown braid that now made her look like a forlorn princess. Wispy flyaway strands dangled around her tearstained face. Gently, Patricio tucked a few behind her ear.

"You are a strong, talented, vibrant, often mouthy but always amazing woman, Catalina Capuleta. Whatever happens with Pedro Santos and you and Blanca, no one can take that away from you. I won't let them. *You* won't let them."

A shaky breath blew through her lips. Her fists relaxed, and she twisted her wrist to link her fingers with his. "You're going to tell me that I have to talk to Blanca. To him. Aren't you?"

"I doubt me telling you what to do will work," Patricio answered, pleasure warming his heart when a ghost of her sassy smirk momentarily curved her lips before disappearing. "But I will *suggest* that you talk to them. Or at least Blanca. For your sake, and hers. You two are the ones I'm worried about."

"I don't want to do it in public. And I don't think I want him in my room. My private space. Maybe we can find—"

"How about if we do it here? Tonight. Tomorrow and Saturday we'll be busy with preconcert prep before our final two shows at night. I wouldn't think you want this hanging over you."

Her shoulders sagged. Frustration puckered her brow, and she squeezed his hand. "I hate that this will taint the last weekend of the tour. Our last weekend—"

He placed a finger over her lips, silencing the words he wasn't ready to hear. "Not our last. We still have our album to finish."

Because that was how he saw it now: their album. A new, different ask he had in mind for the executives at Padua in exchange for him compromising with them and his father. A new, different plan he hoped Catalina would agree to as well.

Chapter Twenty-Two

"Are you sure you don't want me to order room service? You haven't eaten since we shared that slice of pizza at New York–New York for lunch."

"I'm fine, gracias." Catalina tried to offer Patricio a grateful smile, but she was pretty sure it looked more like a grimace.

He'd been handling her with kid gloves in the aftermath of the bomb her sister had dropped in the lobby a couple of hours ago. Letting her use his lifestyles-of-the-rich-and-famous suite as her sanctuary. He had even called for skin-care products to be brought from the spa when she asked if she could use his bathroom to clean up. She did not want to face Pedro Santos with tearstained cheeks, her hair in a disheveled crown braid after being squashed and sweaty and shoved under a cheap wig.

Patricio had urged her to take an extended shower or soak in the Jacuzzi tub, so she had—complete with bubbles, sweet-smelling lotions, and hair and face masks—and emerged rejuvenated of spirit and resolved to not be swayed by a slick-talking, self-centered, has-been mariachi. Then she had spotted the short-sleeved, red wrap dress waiting for her on the king mattress, a pair of tan heeled sandals on the floor beside the bed. A red rose lay across the dress's bodice, along with a note in Patricio's bold script:

For a brilliant star of her own making.

Patricio

Fresh tears had filled her eyes. These ones for a completely different reason.

To the world, Patricio Galán might be cocky, confident, and commanding. To her, the real Patricio was all that and so much more: compassionate, thoughtful, wickedly funny, and most important, supportive of her.

But he was still a mariachi. And while the more time she spent with Patricio, the more she longed—ay, *to the marrow of her bones*, how she longed—to cast aside her long-held conviction to not relive her birth mother's mistakes, she was too afraid he might . . . what if she wound up . . .

No, she couldn't do it.

She had vowed to never be like either of her birth parents. That's what she had to remember as she prepared to meet the sinvergüenza who had the audacity to show up here today.

A sharp sense of foreboding needled her stomach. One of her feet tap-tap-tapped on the metal chair rung, a release of little bursts of agitation like a pressure-cooker valve emitting steam. But she couldn't guarantee that an explosion wasn't imminent.

Releasing a shuddery breath, Cat ran a trembling hand over her slicked-back low ponytail. She straightened on the white pleather-and-metal low-back chair at the high-topped white granite breakfast table. Shoulders erect, back straight, ready for battle.

Patricio had suggested she make herself comfortable on the sectional sofa. But she didn't want to be comfortable for this meeting. She wanted to stay pissed. And she definitely didn't want Pedro Santos to feel any sense of comfort or welcome here. As for Blanca . . . bueno,

Blanca was going to worry no matter what, especially since it sounded like she and Luciano had plotted this godforsaken meet and greet.

In a cruel six-degrees-of-separation twist of fate, the baby-faced trumpet player with the adorable dimples who'd been wooing Catalina's sister over video chat also happened to be the son of a guitarrón player who had toured with Pedro in the early years of their careers. Their band had eventually split up, but the men had remained close friends. Luciano's father went on to realize moderate success; Pedro not so much, eventually settling in the Vegas area.

In talking with Luciano to set up their meeting, Patricio had learned that the young trumpet player usually visited his father's old friend when Luciano was in town for Patricio's annual Latinx-Hispanic Heritage Month concert. Pedro kept track of Luciano's career and had heard about Catalina in the press. From there, he stumbled upon the story about Arturo and Berta Capuleta and the girls they fostered, then adopted in San Antonio.

"So, I'm supposed to believe that the man who couldn't be bothered to find my sister and me when it mattered suddenly seeks a happy familia reunion out of the goodness of his heart?" Catalina hissed a breath between her teeth. "That it has absolutely nothing to do with the fact that I'm associated with the hottest ticket in town this weekend? Or that entertainment sites have started labeling me as one of Padua's up-and-coming stars?"

"It very well might," Patricio said, setting a glass of seltzer water with lime on a napkin in front of her. He bent and pressed a kiss to the top of her head. The sweet gesture soothed her ire. And her battered heart. "But it also might not. To be honest, I doubt you'll know for sure either way after only one conversation."

"I just want to get this over with." She took a swig of her drink, then plunked it back down. "What time is it? Shouldn't they be here already?"

"In about ten minutes. Here, you're all tense." Moving behind her, Patricio placed his hands at the crook of her neck. Delicious heat spread through her at his touch. Gently at first, then with increasing pressure, his thumbs and fingers kneaded the muscles along her neck and shoulders, knotted from the stress of her sister's betrayal and the resurrection of the man who, for all intents and purposes, had been dead to her since Blanca and Cat had arrived at their first foster house. Scared. Confused. And, at least for her, furious at the fates.

"Dios, that feels good," Cat moaned, her body quickly turning to putty under Patricio's ministrations. "Can we just skip the awkward meeting and stay like this for a while? You've got great hands."

Patricio's warm breath tickled the left side of her face as he leaned closer to murmur, "Querida, you haven't even begun to see the remarkable things these hands can do."

She shivered, desire arcing through her in a blazing trail. Thoughts of the "things" she wanted his hands to do to and with her made her breasts grow heavy. Her nipples strained for his attention, and the area between her thighs throbbed with need.

"Promises, promises," she teased, anxious to defuse the lust threatening to consume her. Afraid she might give in to the intense urge to bolt the door and surrender to the delectable pleasure of discovering exactly what he had in mind.

He chuckled, the sound husky and rumbly as he grazed her sensitive earlobe with his teeth.

A heavy knock sounded on the suite's door. She froze and the air backed up in her lungs.

Patricio cupped her shoulders, gave them a tight squeeze. "¿Estás lista?"

Was she ready?

There was no choice. She had to be.

Like Cat had done all those years ago when the abuela who lived next door and watched her and Blanca when their mom worked late at the dry cleaner's had gotten word that several employees had been picked up by ICE, Cat vowed to do whatever was needed to protect her younger sister. If Pedro Santos was a scammer, looking to capitalize on the sisters' recent success, he could take his battered guitar and get the hell out. He was good at leaving anyway.

Sliding off the high seat, she adjusted the wrap dress's bow at her left hip, then nodded. "I'm ready."

~

They wound up seated on the sectional sofa after all. Patricio had ushered Blanca, Pedro, and surprisingly, Luciano into the suite, and Cat had motioned at the cold, granite-topped table with seating for six.

Blanca's smile faltered, her crestfallen expression pleading for compassion, and Cat had caved.

Pedro had tentatively extended his hand to shake. Cat gave him a brisk nod but kept her arms crossed, unwilling to breach the physical distance when emotionally there were miles separating them.

Patricio had eased the awkwardness, stepping in to shake Pedro's hand, then leading the tense group to the living room area.

Now Pedro, Luciano, and Blanca sat on one side of the sectional, Cat and Patricio on the other. Outside, the late-afternoon sun peeked around the buildings of the Vegas skyline, giving the clouds and sky a muted purply-pink glow. Its intense beams streamed through the expansive glass windows overlooking the suite's terrace and the Strip beyond. Cat squinted at the brightness, stoically refusing to be the first to break the uncomfortable silence.

"Gracias por la invitación." Pedro dipped his graying head politely, first at Patricio, then at her.

"Privacy, for Cat and Blanca, is important. There's no reason for the press or fans to get wind of whatever happens here today. ¿De acuerdo?" Patricio's tone sharpened at his question, making it clear that he expected Pedro to agree.

"Sí, of course. I am only here because . . . bueno, porque . . ."

"Why *are* you here?" Cat demanded. "Why now? And not, say, twenty years ago, when our birth mom died? Or before that, when you promised to marry her but never actually stuck around. Always off to the next pit stop along the way to nowhere. Who knows, maybe Blanca and I have other siblings out there. Left behind just like us."

"Catalina!" Blanca's scandalized whisper cut off her tirade.

"What?" Cat scoffed, chin jutted at a haughty angle. She was a pro at pretending all was fine when inside she was a jumbled mess of fucked-up emotions. "It's the truth."

"No, mija," Pedro said. "There was—"

"I am *not* your daughter," Cat said, biting out the words of denial. "I have a father, and his name is Arturo Capuleta. He raised me and Blanca. And all our sisters. *He's* the one who stayed home with me when I got the flu and missed the fifth-grade trip to Austin. *He* took me for ice cream when my teeth ached after my orthodontist appointments. *He* was there yelling a grito when Blanca, Mariana, Violeta, Sabrina, and I first performed as Mariachi Las Nubes. He's still here, checking in by text or a quick phone call. Because that's what *real* familia does."

She finished on a shaky breath, blinking back the tears she refused to cry. Beside her, Patricio laid a hand in the center of her back. She sent him a shaky smile, thankful for his steady presence.

Blanca sniffled, then swiped at the corner of one eye. Luciano handed her a bandanna, and she murmured a soft "gracias."

Pedro hung his head. "Perdón. I mean no disrespect to Arturo y Berta Capuleta. They have my undying thanks for the life they have given you. Both of you. A life I could not have."

The truth of his words couldn't be denied by any of them. A single man who didn't know how to parent and craved life on the road was no match for two devoted parents who provided a secure, loving home.

"There was never another woman," Pedro told them, shifting his contrite gaze from Blanca to Cat. "Not one of flesh and blood. Yo era joven—too young, really—with stars in my eyes. Music became my mistress. The chase for a bigger stage, a bigger audience. It was there, around the next corner. In the next city. I thought I could eventually come back a success and make up for lost time. Pero one year became two, then three. Y cuando regresé . . . when I came back . . ." He ran a shaking hand through his hair, sadness and regret shadowing his dark-bronze face. "By then, your mother was gone. I asked the neighbors about you girls, put out some private feelers. When I finally found you, you had just arrived at Casa Capuleta."

Cat closed her eyes, memories of those eighteen months after her birth mom's deportation and death flooding her mind with a horrible slideshow she couldn't stop. Shuffling from one foster home to another, some rougher than others. Holding Blanca when she cried in the middle of the night. Squelching her own fear over the looming threat that she and Blanca might be split up.

Until Arturo and Berta had opened their door, and Mariana had peeked out from behind them. They had all sat down to familia dinner that first night, and almost every night since. Papo had played the guitar, encouraging Cat to get hers out of the case and join him while Mamá's fingers flew over the keyboard.

For the first time in months, Cat had smiled. A real, honest-to-Dios smile. Not a fake one trying to impress the DFAS counselor or a prospective foster parent, so they'd keep her and Blanca together.

For the first time in months, she'd felt hope.

Casa Capuleta became their home. Their sanctuary. How different would their lives have been if Pedro had swooped in to take them on the road with him? Or worse, to leave them behind with another stranger while he chased after his muse again?

"Wait, you found us, but you just left us there? Without even trying to see Cat and me?" Blanca's agonized voice cut into Cat's memories and the painful, scary truth of what could have been if Pedro had done what Blanca obviously wanted him to have done—contact them. Claim them as his daughters.

Pedro shifted to face Blanca on the sofa. "You barely knew me. But *I* knew me well enough to understand that I could not give you the life you deserved." He reached for Blanca's hand, and Cat's heart squeezed with anguish when her gentle, softhearted sister took his. "The life I saw you living with Arturo and Berta—that's what you deserved, mija. Did it hurt me to walk away? Sí, more than you can know. But if I have done anything good as a parent who did not have the right to be one, it was letting you go to have a better future."

"Then why seek us out now?" Cat eyed him warily, searching for even the smallest tell that might give him away. His tale of woe and self-sacrifice when it came to her and Blanca might sound believable to some, but she wasn't ready to trust him. Not yet. Maybe not ever.

"Sí, I get it." He motioned around the lavish suite, with its granite countertops and table, multiple flat-screen TVs and priceless artwork, well-stocked wet bar, and marble steps leading to the roomy main bedroom. "You probably think I'm here for a handout."

"Ha!" Cat threw back her head with a harsh laugh. "Don't get any ideas—this is Patricio's, not mine. I couldn't afford half a night's stay here."

"If I may," Luciano cut in, gesturing politely with his Stetson at Cat and Patricio. He reached his other arm behind Blanca to clasp Pedro's shoulder. "I've known this viejo for practically my whole life. I'm not condoning what happened when you were kids. But he's not looking to scam you. He's not like that, te lo juro."

Cat wasn't sure about accepting Luciano's "I swear" point-blank. Blanca, on the other hand, sent the young mariachi a besotted smile.

Pedro nodded solemnly. Eyes similar to Cat's in color and shape gazed back at her, sincerity and sorrow clouding their hazel irises. "I'm not here for money or . . . or anything like that. I read about you joining the tour and took it as a sign. That maybe this viejo could meet his daughters on their terms. As adults with a shared love of our música. And maybe, if possible, in time, you might find a way to forgive me."

Once again, a confusing mix of emotions welled inside Cat, pressing against the walls of her chest. Long-held pain and anger for the abandoned child left feeling unworthy of her father's love. Disillusion at facing Pedro, living proof of the harsh reality of the personal sacrifices many paid while chasing a dream few realized. And now, a new one: a dawning, uncomfortable sense of understanding that perhaps the monster in her memory had actually played an instrumental role in one of the biggest blessings of her life, becoming a Capuleta.

Closing her eyes, Cat allowed herself to feel all of it. No tamping down to get through or ignoring with a joke. The pain, the anger, the disillusion, the understanding . . . they were all a part of her, and she had to accept them, deal with them. Find a way to move forward.

"¿Estás bien?" Patricio murmured, smoothing a hand over her head.

She leaned into him, reassured by his presence and the knowledge that, because of the confidences they had shared, he empathized with how difficult this situation was for her.

"Yeah, I'm okay," she answered softly.

Maybe she wasn't ready to invite Pedro to a Capuleta familia dinner. And how—or even *if*—he fit into her personal life remained to be seen. But, like it or not, she had to accept that Blanca may want him in hers. Cat had no right to make her sister choose sides or hold Blanca's desire to connect with an important part of her past against her.

On some level, hearing the man's version of their history did bring a measure of closure. Pedro Santos had done his girls a favor by staying away. And with this knowledge, Catalina realized he was no longer an evil specter haunting her.

Like Patricio had claimed, she was a rising star of her own making. Her history might be troubled, with issues still needing to be worked through, but her future, which hopefully included the incredible man beside her, looked pretty freaking amazing.

Chapter Twenty-Three

"¡Otra! ¡Otra!"

Patricio stood under the bright spotlights, grinning out at the crowd standing on their feet, their chants for one more song filling the MGM Grand Garden Arena.

The last concert on the tour never failed to be his best. Oh, he gave a great show for every performance. Pero había algo . . . sí, there was something about the last one. The crowd's energy always seemed more intense, a palpable force shimmering throughout the arena. Knowing he wouldn't be in front of a crowd for a while heightened his awareness of every minute onstage. It revved him up even higher, which also meant working a little harder to hold back.

Not tonight, though. Tonight, he'd taken a page out of Cat's instruction manual and given his all. Adding runs and stretching his vocals—letting instinct guide him. It felt so damn good, and hearing his fans' show of appreciation filled him with pride.

Like always, Cat had charmed and dazzled during their set. Now she waited in the wings for tonight's special encore with the show's secret guest. Patricio's compromise with Padua.

Striding to the front of the stage, he stopped in a wide-legged stance, a foot shy of the edge. One fist planted on his hips, he jutted his chin at the precise angle that would have him eyeing the fans in the front rows under his lashes, reenacting the cover pose that had sold millions of copies of his second album, spawning T-shirts and posters and more creative fan paraphernalia. As expected, the arena erupted with screams and gritos and high-pitched whistles. Somewhere in the front few rows, a woman yelled, "Marry me, Patricio!"

He blew the woman a kiss, then motioned for the cries to quiet as he raised the microphone to his lips. Lowering his voice to a deeper, sexier octave, he asked, "I'm not ready to go home, are you?" The audience went wild. "How would you feel if I invited a secret guest for a special end-of-tour encore. ¿Les gustaría?"

The fans showed just how much they would like it, responding with more earsplitting cries of "¡Sí!"

"Por favor, welcome mi papá, El Rey, Vicente Galán!"

Camera lights flickered throughout the arena as Vicente strode out onto the raised platform at center stage. He stopped at the top of the stairs, lifting his arms wide, his lips split in a huge grin as he lapped up the adulation. Dressed in his trademark black-and-silver charro, Vicente cut a commanding figure. With age had come a slight widening of his jowls and a thickening of his waistline, but he maintained himself well, and his admirers were vociferous with their approval.

Patricio played up the crowd, jerking his head and thumb at his viejo, waggling his brows suggestively, encouraging catcalls and whistles of appreciation.

As rehearsed, before Vicente started down the steps, the band struck the opening notes of the first of two songs Patricio had agreed to sing. Cheers erupted as the audience recognized "Perdón," a classic ballad beloved by fans and a favorite of his father's. The irony of El Rey begging for forgiveness for past transgressions through the lyrics he sang was never lost on Patricio. Still, he played his part, harmonizing with his father, only this time, with this performance, he didn't hold back.

To his father's credit, the only evidence of Vicente's surprise at the few runs Patricio added was a raised brow or questioning tilt of his head. A lover of the spotlight, Vicente encouraged the crowd's cheers, calling out an "Este es mi hijo" and patting Patricio heartily on the back as he held a long note.

The song drew to a close and Vicente gestured toward him. "Mi hijo, singing better than ever, much like his viejo!" His father pounded his chest with pride, then he made a grabbing motion at his chest before pretending to toss something at the crowd, as if he were gifting them his heart. The fans ate it up. Once again, gritos and whistles and cries of joy bounced off the arena rafters.

Patricio nodded at the leader of his mariachi band, indicating he was ready for them to start the second song. One more, and then Cat would join them for the finale. Their last song of the tour. But, if everything went as planned, certainly not his and Cat's last time singing together.

Luciano and the rest of the trumpet section kicked off the second number, their notes sharp and crisp. Vicente angled toward Patricio. Rapturous joy and . . . and, unexpectantly, love . . . shimmered in the viejo's dark eyes as he sang the opening lyrics.

A camera flashed over his father's shoulder, and suddenly Patricio was transported to their first performance together when he was only five. A montage of shared moments on the stage over the years flitted through his memory. Moments when they'd connected in a way they hadn't or couldn't offstage, made possible through their shared love of music and pride in their culture. Moments like now.

Moments he deserved to want to remember, not bury because of disappointment over limiting himself. No more.

Cat's strength of character and ability to face her demons, accepting Pedro's story as his lived version of their brief familia history. Witnessing her cautiously allowing the man into her life, if still at arm's length, was eye-opening. It showed Patricio that a loved one's flaws didn't have to translate into shortcomings of your own.

Now, he gave himself up to the lyrics and notes, singing like he never had before with his father—with abandon.

By the end, they stood side by side at center stage, arms looped around each other's backs, facing the standing ovation. His father's palm pounded Patricio's shoulder blade, and through the raucous cheers, Patricio swore his viejo told him, "Fantástico, mijo."

The adulation for them continued, but soon the excitement shifted as cries of "Catalina!" alerted him that she had taken her spot at the top of the stairs. He turned to face her and his heart hiccuped in his chest when he saw her.

Vibrant and beautiful. With an air of confidence in who she was and what she brought to the stage. She tipped her head at the crowd and sent him a cheeky wink that had him wanting to storm up the stairs and kiss her smiling lips.

"Gracias for the warm welcome! Before we close, let's give it up for the original, one and only, El Rey, Vicente!" she cried into her mic. The audience responded with gusto.

"And for the next Galán generation, Patricio, brilliantly combining tradición and pop to give us sounds and songs that, if you're like me, make your heart pound, your cheeks heat, and your knees get weak, verdad?"

"¡Sí!" the crowd answered in unison.

Catalina paraded down the stairs, the gold thread in the embroidery of her red charro and the gala trailing down the sides of her pantalones catching the stage lights, glinting like the excitement shining in her expressive eyes. He held out his hand for her to take as she joined him and his father. She linked her fingers with his, giving them a tight squeeze.

Despite his initial reservations about Vicente participating in the show at all, Catalina had been right—a compromise, with him not worrying about his father's ego and being true to himself, had been the perfect way to end the tour.

Mostly, though, everything was perfect because of her.

Later tonight, he planned to do his absolute best to convince her that rules—especially theirs about dating—were meant to be broken.

~

"I love you, Vegas!" Standing at the terrace railing of his suite, arms outstretched like the actress standing on the ship's bow in that *Titanic* movie, Catalina shouted her love for the city lit up around them.

"I'm sure there were plenty at the concert who return the sentiment to you," Patricio said. Himself included.

Glancing at him over her shoulder, she sent him an impish grin. "Gracias." She spun around and leaned her elbows on the railing to face him. "You were great. Especially during the encore with your dad and in the meet and greets after. I'm so proud of you."

Her praise washed over him like refreshing rain on a parched flower bed, bringing new life to what had been withered and dull.

"And you, inviting Pedro to join Blanca in the VIP box. That was a big step."

She hitched a shoulder, tilting her head toward it like the invite was no big deal, but he knew better. He knew *her* better.

"Why'd you do it?" he pressed, awed by her generosity and ability to at least try and see her harrowing past from a different perspective.

"The same reason you compromised." Crossing the tile, she sat on the end of the gray outdoor sectional where Patricio reclined, enjoying the view of the Strip. But mostly of her. Tucked in a corner where a partial wall and several tall potted plants provided added privacy, the extra-wide sofa had enough room for two people to lie down and relax, or do something more active, together.

Barefoot and wearing a yellow-and-white-striped maxi dress with a fitted bodice, Cat looked bright and summery and enticing. All of which had him considering several "something more active" ideas he'd willingly engage in with her if she were so inclined.

"Talk about an exhilarating night," she said, reaching for her Tito's and soda with lime. "The band was on fire!"

"Are you sure you don't want to hang out with some of them a little longer? I can text a few, see if they wound up anywhere you want to go," Patricio suggested.

Not exactly his preference, but this was her first tour. He understood if she was still on the final-performance high.

The entire team had toasted the end of the tour backstage, then broken off in smaller groups to enjoy the revelry and mayhem of Vegas.

At that point, Alberto had bidden them all good night, claiming his viejito bones were tired. George—who had been instrumental in convincing the other executives that a surprise encore was a win-win for everyone—had blamed an early flight for his need to head back to his room. He'd given Patricio the finger after being reminded of the times George had partied all night, then caught the first morning flight without his head even hitting the pillow.

Catalina sipped her drink, then shook her head. "Not really. Blanca and Luciano weren't going out either. Sounded like they wanted some alone time before she leaves at noon tomorrow. We still have some feelings to work through, but I'll see her later this week when I head home."

"Speaking of which." Patricio set his glass of añejo on the metal side table, then scooted down to the end of the sofa, his legs stretched out behind her. "Are you still good with sticking around here to keep working on some music for a few days? Then, in a few weeks, you can fly out to Puerto Vallarta?"

"Mmh-hmm. That'll give me time to share some of my new ideas for Las Nubes with the girls. And it'll be nice to give my mom a break from music classes before I leave town again."

"I'm sure they'll be happy to have you home." Needing to touch her, he toyed with the ends of her hair, running his fingers through their silky waves. He knew he shouldn't, but he couldn't help feeling jealous of the familia who would get time with her while he'd be at his beach house alone.

"Plus, I'm not sure what Padua might have in mind for me now that the tour is over," she added.

"Bueno, I have a few ideas."

"You do?" She twisted to face him. "Like what?"

He shook his head, not ready to share yet. Only George knew what Patricio wanted to finagle.

As a friend and record executive, George had offered to get a read on some of the older executives and how they might react. What Patricio intended to propose would be a significant change to his contract. Something the old guard might be wary of. Contractually, he owed Padua two more solo albums. Patricio wanted to put the songs he and Cat had written on hold, allowing him to release his next album completely on his own. Then, before his second, he'd give them another—a combined Patricio Galán and Catalina Capuleta album. Duets and singles written and performed by the two of them.

While he was concentrating on his solo work, Catalina could write for other Padua talent, start making a name for herself and gaining recognition separate from him. Proving that her success was of her own making, on her own merit.

Legally, he couldn't release the combined album before his second solo one unless Padua agreed. Until they gave his plan the green light, Patricio didn't want to build up Cat's hope by saying anything to her.

"Ay, por favor, you can't drop some vague 'I might have a few ideas'"—she pitched her voice low, mimicking his deep timbre as she repeated his words—"and not expect me to want to hear them. When have I ever been known for my patience?"

He let his arched brow answer her question.

"Whatever," she mumbled, stretching forward to set her glass next to his. Before she could settle back onto the cushion beside him, Patricio grasped her waist, lifting her onto his lap.

"¡Oye! What's with the manhandling?" she complained on a laugh, grabbing his shoulders to steady herself.

But she skimmed her hands along his shoulders to cup his neck. Her thumbs brushed underneath his jawbone. A whisper-soft caress that created a flash fire of lust that blazed down his chest, into his torso, and straight to his crotch. Behind his jeans zipper, he throbbed for her.

"Tonight was our last show," he reminded her, "so that means my 'no dating anyone involved with the tour' rule is now moot."

"Mm-hmm," she hummed, her attention apparently trained on his jawline and the erotic brush of her thumbs back and forth rather than on his words.

By some silent, mutual agreement, they had stayed away from any discussion of their deepening relationship. How or if it might change after the tour. He knew what he wanted: more time getting to know each other, exclusivity, commitment. Words he worried she might not be ready to hear.

Gently he brushed her hair off her forehead and dropped a chaste peck on her smooth brow. Straightening, he trailed a finger down the length of her neck, traced her clavicle from one side to the other. Her shoulders shimmied with a shiver, and her lids grew heavy. Desire flared in her eyes in the seconds before they fluttered closed.

Bathed in moonlight and the soft glow from a recessed light in the partial wall, her face and figure were a shady sketch drawing of seduction and beauty. Perfection and charm.

Unable to resist her pull any longer, he ducked down to press a kiss on the sensitive skin behind her ear. Another on the side of her neck. Yet another on the center of her chest, where a gold crucifix dangled on a thin gold chain. Aching to taste her, he licked the curve of her cleavage at the top of her bodice, and she sucked in a sharp breath.

"I know what I want, Catalina. You." He drew back to look at her, to let her see the truth on his face and in his eyes. In his heart. "I'm not

Pedro, or my father. You know the real me. I'm a safe bet when it comes to breaking or bending that rule of yours."

She cupped his face with one hand. Traced the edge of his bottom lip with her thumb, her gaze tracking the motion. "How do you manage to do this to me?" she murmured.

"Do what?"

"Excite, sway, unnerve. Make me feel alive and scared and horny and . . ."

He kissed her. Tenderly at first. Then her hand slid from his cheek to his nape. Her tongue licked the seam of his mouth, and he opened for her, deepening their kiss. She moaned, pressing closer, her soft curves molding with his hard ones in a perfect fit. Their tongues darted and teased, twisting and coaxing the other in a sensuous dance.

She surprised him by nudging his shoulders, and they fell back onto the wide cushions. Her long tresses fanned over them, and she broke the kiss to push them out of her face. Reaching up, he wove his fingers through her hair, gathering it in one fist while he tugged the stretchy band from her wrist to tie the locks back in a wobbly rendition of a ponytail. But it did the trick and she grinned, giggling as she wound her arms around his neck. Her teeth grazed his lower lip, then she drew it into her warm mouth.

He moaned and slid his hands down her back to grab her ass. She shifted to straddle him, hiking up her dress to make it easier. That gave him the perfect opportunity to run his hands over her legs and marvel at the softness of her tanned skin. His thumbs brushed the lacy material of her panties at her hips, and she rolled her pelvis into his.

Beneath his zipper, he strained for release, and he groaned at the pleasure-pain her hip thrusts elicited. Her hands dipped under his Henley to skim up his abs, her light touch trailing over his pecs, stoking the fire of his need for her.

While their hands explored, their mouths mated—lips and tongues caressing, exciting, pleasuring. She tasted like lime and vodka, and he was soon drunk from their passionate kisses.

His fingers traced the edge of her panties at the juncture of her thighs, seeking her luscious folds. Waiting for permission, he slowly dragged his hand away.

"Touch me, por favor," she breathed into his mouth.

He delved a finger under her panty seam and brushed the short curls. She gasped when he swept across her entrance. Bucked as he found her clit, then buried his finger deep inside her. She moaned her satisfaction, grabbing on to his biceps and breaking their kiss, her plea for "more" a heated breath against his neck.

Adding a second finger, he dipped inside her again. Drawing in, then out while his thumb rubbed her clit and she writhed against his palm.

"I want you. In me," she murmured, her hips meeting his hand thrust for thrust.

A light flickered in a building across the Strip, reminding him where they were. Out on the terrace, mostly hidden by the plants, but not completely. A paparazzo with a telephoto lens and no sense of decency might still be able to snap a picture neither he nor Catalina wanted plastered on the cover of a tabloid or going viral online. He especially didn't want that for her.

"Not out here, querida. It's not private enough." He withdrew his hand from her, kissed her deeply, and then sat up, bringing her with him. He rose from the sofa and scooped her into his arms.

"Ay! ¿Qué haces?" Her arms wrapped around his shoulders as he hefted her more securely.

"I'm taking you to bed, that's what I'm doing," he answered, striding to the sliding glass door.

"I can walk, you know," she teased.

He tightened his hold on her, unwilling to let her go. Tonight. Or ever.

Chapter Twenty-Four

Cat woke to a darkened room she didn't recognize. As she wiped the sleep from her eyes, realization slowly dawned, like the sun that was trying way too hard to peek around the edges of the blackout curtains in Patricio's bedroom suite.

Reaching out, she patted the bed for him but encountered only cold sheets. She rolled over and squinted open an eye to find his side of the king mattress empty. Disappointment was not a welcome bedmate.

Last night had been amazing. Multiple condoms and orgasms amazing. She smiled, remembering the many sides of Patricio the lover—commanding, gentle, teasing, and oh so satisfying. Stretching under the covers, she noted muscles that hadn't been used much lately achingly letting her know they'd definitely gotten a delicious workout.

She didn't exactly know what this irrevocable step in her and Patricio's relationship meant, but she trusted him. And herself. They'd proven that they were good together. In multiple ways, some more deliciously seductive than others. She simply had to ensure—

No! She halted the negative thoughts from her past before they could form.

Trust, she reminded herself. Patricio had earned hers.

Before doubt could worm its way in from an empty bottle of mezcal, Cat kicked off the sheets, snagged Patricio's shirt and her panties off the floor and slipped them on, and then went in search of coffee and un *beso de buenos días*. The first would bring clarity to her mind. The good-morning kiss would be a welcome taste of what she hoped lay ahead in their day—more incredible sex.

Everything about last night had been incredible. Even now, her sore body thrummed for his again. He had a way of making her feel absolutely adored as he cherished every single inch of her. At times he took control, driving her to the edge of release, then flinging them both over it in an erotic, pleasure-filled free fall. Yet he also willingly succumbed when she grabbed the reins, telling him, showing him, what she needed to reach her climax, leaving her sated and wanting more.

But it was more than the sex; it was Patricio himself.

He was a generous lover. A compassionate friend and partner. A good man who—

Her bare feet hit the cold marble floor in the short hallway outside the bedroom, and she flinched. Tiptoeing to the stairs, she paused when she heard Patricio talking to someone. Alberto's voice rose sharply, and she cringed, realizing the older man was downstairs.

¡Madre de Dios! Her morning-after glow of satisfaction dimmed as she pictured the parental scowl of disapproval on Alberto's round face. She was about to turn tail and race back to the bedroom and hide until Patricio let her know the coast was all clear, when she heard her name.

"Does Catalina know about your plan to *not* use her songs on your album?" Alberto asked, censure coloring his words an ugly shade that made her stomach churn. "That you've been writing songs of your own instead?"

Wait . . . What?

Stunned by Alberto's revelation, Cat ducked below the stair railing, praying she hadn't been seen. Scrambling backward, she smacked her elbow against the bathroom's doorjamb. Painful pinpricks marched up her arm. Disbelief fogged her brain. Alberto must be wrong. Rubbing the injured elbow, she shook her head in denial. He had to be wrong. Or . . . or maybe she'd misunderstood him.

"It's not that I don't plan for the songs we've written together to be used. Just . . . not on this next album," Patricio answered.

Catalina crawled closer to the railing, straining to hear.

"She has said herself that some of her songs aren't a good fit for me," he continued. "That she'd pass them to Padua for another artist. I've bulldozed my creativity block, thanks to Catalina's help. If the record execs approve my plans, we'll both wind up with what we want, and more. Maybe not as she originally intended, but the wording in her contract binds her to Padua's decisions. And she'll understand that my idea is a smart business move."

Dios mío, he wasn't planning on putting their songs, the ones they'd written together, on his album? Horrified, she slumped to a seat on the floor. So, what had all their efforts been for? Nothing? Had he been stringing her along? Using her to reawaken his muse like he had just said, and then he'd cast her aside?

And what about last night? Where did *that* fit into his heinous plan?

Bitter betrayal pierced her heart, and she pressed a hand to her mouth to silence her cry of pain. Shame filled her, heating her cheeks and leaving an acrid taste on her tongue. Her pulse pounded in her ears, drowning out the two men's conversation. It didn't matter. She had heard enough.

In the end, she'd gotten caught in the same trap as her birth mom, falling for a mariachi's besotted act only to be played for a fool. Thinking she had found a partner who respected her, maybe even loved her. One who understood and championed her dreams, instead of putting his own first.

Indignation and disgust sparked, each fueling the other, until they morphed into a fiery fury that pushed her to her feet and down the marble steps, past the statement pieces of artwork in the foyer and the fully stocked wet bar, where an empty bottle of bubbly they had shared nestled in the sink. A superstar's domain, soon to be the site of a supernova explosion.

Alberto spit out his coffee when she barreled into the living room.

Patricio's cup clattered onto the round table in front of the black-and-tan sectional. He rose, smile wide, arms outstretched in welcome—his surprise at her appearance that of a sinvergüenza caught behaving in his despicably shameless ways. "Cat, you're awake!"

"How could you?" She threw the accusation at him.

His gaze shot to the stairs, his shrewd mind obviously putting two and two together and figuring out that she had overheard his conversation. "Let me explain."

"Explain what? That the cagey vibe I got from you from our very first meeting with Padua was right? I called you on it during that first rehearsal in San Antonio. Remember? But you brushed it aside." She flung an arm through the air, indignation making room for outrage as the memory coalesced in her mind. Hands fisted at her sides, she glared at Patricio, hating him for making her realize her foolishness. "I ignored my gut instinct. And you *played* me." She threw back her head with a harsh scoff that scraped her throat raw. "You played me like that old guitar propped in its stand at the beach house, counting on the fact that you had the upper hand. Padua will do whatever you want. Even if it means screwing me over. Just like Pedro did with my birth mom."

"It's not like that. Por favor, hear me out." He took a step toward her, and she recoiled.

"Don't you dare try to touch me," she sneered, palms raised to ward him off.

"Catalina, please."

"Have you been making deals and machinations with George and Padua that involve me—and my career—without my knowledge?"

He rubbed the back of his neck, the answer to her question stamped in the discomfort on his face.

She flicked a quick glance at Alberto. The older man stood by the wall of windows, looking dapper in his usual suit. Head bowed, hands clasped at his waist, his round face clouded with remorse. He opened his mouth as if to answer her question, but she shook her head and turned back to the real perpetrator of her pain.

"Answer me!" she demanded.

His mouth a grim line, Patricio nodded.

He might as well have karate kicked her in the stomach. She sucked in a sharp breath that lodged in her chest. The truth ricocheted through her, leaving tiny pings of pain with every hit. Turns out, despite her staunchest efforts, she was indeed her birth mother's daughter. In the worst possible way.

"It's not exactly what you think," Patricio said. "And yes, I have made moves, but hear me out and you'll see that—"

"No. I've heard enough. It's exactly what I think. You've been making your own plans behind my back. You took control away from me. You silenced me, the same way your father has silenced you all these years. And I can't—I won't—" A sob threatened to bubble up and out of her, and she broke off. She would not cry in front of him.

"Catalina—"

"No. We're done here." Straightening her shoulders with a regal head toss, she faced him with all the wrath of a woman scorned. Belittled and disrespected. "Don't call me. Don't text me. Don't . . . anything. We're through."

Turning on her heel, she fled up the stairs. Heartbroken, humiliated.

Tearing his Henley off her body, she threw it across the bedroom suite and quickly pulled her sundress over her head, not caring that it was inside out. She wasted precious seconds searching the carpeted floor for her sandals before remembering she had slipped them off by the granite high-topped table when she arrived last night.

In the doorway, she paused to suck in a deep breath, holding it in, then slowly releasing it through her lips. Patricio would not see her cry. He wasn't worthy of her tears.

Head high, she pranced down the stairs. Alberto waited for her at the bottom, holding her purse and cell phone.

"Gracias, Alberto. Cuídate," she murmured.

"You take care of yourself, too, mija." Sadness filling his dark eyes, Alberto clasped one of her hands in both of his. "Padua will expect to hear from you. You know that, right? Your contract is ironclad. But if you need my help . . ."

She nodded slowly, touched by his offer. Though she wouldn't take him up on it. "Sí, I know I'm contractually bound to compose for their talent. But it doesn't have to be him. My work deserves better."

Over by the sliding glass door, Patricio stood with his hands in the pockets of his gray sweatpants, his handsome face a contortion of regret and disbelief. Probably only because he'd been caught, or told no. She'd bet that didn't happen often to El Príncipe.

Cat spared him a cold glance, then hugged Alberto goodbye and strode through the foyer. Jerking the door open, she halted, a stunned "Oh" slipping from her lips when she found Vicente Galán on the other side.

"Buenos días, Catalina. This is an early-morning surprise," he greeted her, all toothy smiles and charm. Exactly like his sneaky, self-centered son. "It is wonderful to see you."

Annoyed at her misfortune in having to face two Galáns before she'd had any coffee, she grimaced. "Sí, bueno, I wish I could say the same. I'm obviously leaving, so I'm sure you can see yourself in. Adiós."

She caught a quick glimpse of El Rey's affronted displeasure at her rudeness, but she didn't stick around for his inevitable lecture. Her morning—her day, her dreams—had been ruined by enough of the Galán machismo. And her heart, bueno, it ached too much for her to be around anyone except her familia.

∼

"¡Felicidades, mijo!"

His father's booming voice coming from the suite's foyer jolted Patricio out of the spinning pit of desperation and incredulity he'd been thrown into by Catalina's scorching fury.

"I don't have time for you right now, viejo," he told his father, crossing the living room to the bottom of the steps. He needed to grab his shoes and go after her. Explain things.

"¿Pero qué es esto?" his father blustered.

"This is me telling you I can't deal with whatever it is you're cooking up or whatever complaint about me you're intent on relaying."

"Oye, respeto." Vicente jabbed his gray Stetson at Patricio in a clear warning.

Even Alberto was giving Patricio a shocked *what's with the disrespect* brow raise. He patted the air with a hand in a "take it easy" motion.

"Fine, what's up?" Patricio asked on a weary sigh.

Maybe he should give Cat a little time to cool down anyway. When they had bickered in the past, once her initial ire blew over, she was more amenable to hearing him out. Hopefully it would be the same now. Nothing he'd done had been with malicious intent. He honestly hadn't wanted to get her hopes up about their potential album. Still, her angry, agonizing words pelted him once more.

You silenced me.

It was the last thing he meant to do. But, even though he didn't want to believe it, maybe the way he'd handled things did paint him with the same self-centered brush as her father. And his.

Maldita sea . . . He had to figure out how to fix this. How to—

"The reviews are in!" Vicente announced. He set his Stetson on the high-top breakfast table with a flourish, then crooked a knee to rest one of his boots on a chair rung. A huge grin pulled his jowls wider as he slapped a beefy palm on the tabletop. "Social media and the entertainment magazines are buzzing. Our encore—like we all knew it would be—was a hit. And the trio to close the show, fantástico!"

Patricio had been so caught up in his night with Cat, what it meant for them moving forward, he hadn't even thought about the concert and the media's reaction to his father's unannounced appearance. But he wasn't surprised to hear that the compromise Cat had encouraged him to find had been a resounding success. She was, in a word, brilliant.

"And," Vicente continued, "Oscar told me about what you had George pitch to the team. Adding a duet compilation in between your next two solo albums. Magnífica idea, mijo. She is talented, that one." He waggled a finger in the direction of the door Catalina had stormed out of, her "we're through" a bull's-eye dart to Patricio's chest.

"Yes, she is," he agreed, wondering where his father was going with this. Because the viejo always seemed to have an ulterior motive when he was throwing out compliments. If he had Oscar's ear, no doubt the longtime executive had already heard whatever angle Vicente was working.

"Bueno, after the triumphant trio of last night, I think, and Oscar agrees, that the compilation album would be stronger if it included a few trios, possibly some duets with Catalina and me."

"Ex-excuse me?" Patricio sputtered.

Certain he had misheard, he looked to Alberto for confirmation. His longtime confidant's slack-jawed shock mirrored Patricio's, but Alberto remained respectfully quiet, ever the professional in front of El Rey.

But Patricio was done with being quiet. Done with stepping back to let his father have his way. "That's not going to happen, viejo."

"¿Y por qué no?"

"Because that's not what I think is best."

Vicente swatted away Patricio's reasoning, his mouth tilting downward with an irritated frown. "Ahh, you are not thinking straight. This will be a huge boost to that girl's career. And besides, how do you know she would not want to record with me anyway? Of course, she would. Not everyone is given the opportunity to sing with both Galáns!"

Patricio *didn't* know that Catalina wouldn't be interested in his father's idea. But he *did* know she wouldn't put up with any of his father's patronizing machismo bullshit. Album or no album. She wouldn't do it just to boost her career, because she knew she deserved better. So did Patricio.

"Oye, last night, you were magnificent, mijo." Vicente jabbed his Stetson at Patricio, surprising him with the exuberant praise. "Of course, you had to show off a little, ad-libbing with those runs, pero you have the pipes for it. Y los fanáticos, they love it. So, what can I say? Pero when it comes to making albums that go platinum, that is my domain. You have to listen and trust me, mijo."

And there he went. A backhanded compliment with a swipe at Patricio's talent and skill. Based on his father's triumphant grin, the viejo didn't even realize the way his ego-driven words landed like a belly flop off the high dive—humiliating and painful.

"I have listened. And my answer is still no. It's not what I want for Catalina. It's not what she would want."

"¿Y qué?" Vicente pushed the high-backed chair rung with his boot, sending it careening into the one beside it with a metal clang. His patience over having his wishes, his *demand,* ignored reached its end, and he stood, hands on his hips, nostrils flaring. "Who are you to decide what is best for that young woman? She does not strike me as one to stay quiet, content on the sidelines, while you choose for her, no?"

Patricio's scathing response shriveled on his tongue as the bald truth of his father's accusations hit him like a slap to the face. Catalina had been right. Patricio had silenced her. The humbling realization nearly brought Patricio to his knees.

Without his even being aware of it, his behavior had been as Machiavellian as his father's. Pushing his agenda. It didn't matter that he believed everything was for her benefit. It wasn't his decision to make. A true partner should have known better.

Ultimately, he had disrespected the woman he loved. The person who had listened to him bare his soul, then generously helped him to finally be his true self in every sense of the word. While he—he had wounded her in the worst way possible. And in the process, he had also broken his promise to her parents.

The reality of what he had done, what he risked losing, was like a heavyweight champ's punch. Patricio slapped a hand to his forehead in disbelief and stumbled back, his heart pounding a death knell.

"Vicente, you should go." Alberto approached them, motioning politely but purposefully toward the foyer and the suite's front door. "You and Patricio can discuss this later."

Patricio heard his father's blustering complaints about being dismissed, but they didn't register. He didn't care. Not when he was petrified that he might have ruined things with Cat, the best gift he'd been given in his life. Shell-shocked, he staggered to the living room.

An hour ago, he'd been high on life. On possibilities. On love!

Last night, he and Catalina had taken and given, freely, wantonly, beautifully, with each other. Maybe they hadn't said those precise three little words out loud. But they had shown one another with their actions and soft sighs. With intense gazes and fingers tightly intertwined. With an early-morning, chaste kiss on the forehead, wrapped in each other's arms, and his murmured "I could stay like this forever."

Now, he recognized, too late, that their happily-ever-after storybooks differed. Hers was missing several key passages. Most notably, an admission and apology from him for not being completely up front with her from the very beginning. Making matters worse, his conceit in thinking he not only knew best but that he didn't need to include her in important conversations placed him in the role of the villain in her book. Rightly so.

Shame sliced through his chest with a double-edged sword, and he buried his face in his hands with a tormented groan. How had he let himself become his father? Arrogant and pushy, his ego driving him with single-minded, selfish intent.

"Mijo, are you okay?"

Alberto's footsteps drew closer, and Patricio glanced up, storm-tossed and floundering in a turbulent sea of regret. Worry puckered the viejo's face as his fingers fiddled with one of the buttons on his suit coat. Sunday, and still the old man dressed for the office. He should be home with his familia. Spending time with those he cherished. Not here, picking up the pieces of a heart left broken and lonely, like Alberto had often done for Patricio in the past after an altercation or tumultu-ous visit with his father. Only this time, the damage had been done by Patricio's own hand.

Disgusted with himself, Patricio hung his head, unable to look Alberto in the eye.

The cushion next to his shifted, giving way to Alberto's stocky frame. His assistant, more his mentor and guiding conscience, clasped Patricio's shoulder tightly.

"La chingaste, mijo," Alberto told him.

The old man's blunt "you fucked up, son" should have stung. Instead, the mix of concerned fondness in Alberto's tone actually had Patricio huffing out a laugh. "Tell me what you really think, viejo."

Alberto shook Patricio's shoulder. "It all comes back to the advice I gave you weeks ago, the same advice mi papá gave to me when Magdalena and I were young: a relationship not built on a foundation of truth will crumble."

"'I told you so'? That's what you have for me right now? Ehhhh!" Patricio held up a hand to stall the argument he saw coming. "I get it. You did try to warn me." He shook his head, knowing Alberto was correct, about the advice and the fact that Patricio had, indeed, screwed things up. "Cat was right—making plans behind her back, expecting her to accept them, was a bullshit move my father would try. I was wrong. I can, and should, admit that. But she's wrong about something, too. We're not done. We can't be through. At least, I fucking hope not."

"Bueno, pues, what are you going to do? And how can I help?"

Such a different response than his father would have given him. The man rarely admitted his mistakes or chased after someone who pointed them out. Although he *had* tipped his Stetson to Patricio's performance last night. And if there was one thing Patricio had learned from the mature way Cat was handling Pedro Santos's reappearance, it was that Patricio could accept his father's strong personality, while still holding his own.

Vicente would never be the loving voice of counsel Patricio had craved for so long. And yet, if he needed fatherly advice, Alberto had always been there. As he was now.

"I owe Cat an explanation. An apology. And knowing her, she'll expect a decent amount of groveling." Alberto chuckled and Patricio flashed a wry smile. "For her, I will. Pero I should probably give her some time today. Catalina acts on her emotions. Some people call it rash; I call it brave because she doesn't hesitate, doesn't let fear or doubt get in her way. And sometimes, after the heat of the moment, she reassesses. I can only hope that's the case with this."

"Hmmmm." One hand cupping his elbow, the other clasping his chin, Alberto frowned, his face pensive. "I don't know, mijo. She was pretty furious. You will have to work hard to convince her."

"You're right. And I will. She's worth everything and more, viejo. I'll do whatever it takes to win back her trust. La amo."

Alberto clapped him on the shoulder, a huge grin on his face. "I knew you loved her, mijo. I've been waiting for you to realize the gift she is, and the amazing love I believe you two can share."

"I sure hope so, viejo. That's my plan. And tonight, the groveling begins."

In the end, though, it didn't matter what Patricio had intended for him and Catalina that evening. Because when he called the front desk to have flowers delivered to her room, he learned that she had checked out with her sister and caught a flight home to San Antonio—leaving him behind like that bright-pink WHAT HAPPENS IN VEGAS STAYS IN VEGAS tee she'd worn when they had played tourist together.

Desolate, but not down for the count, Patricio got busy devising his plan B.

Chapter Twenty-Five

"*Ugh!* I hate men!" Catalina snatched a bottle of Shiner Bock from the fridge at Casa Capuleta, then pushed the door closed with her hip. She pivoted to face Mariana and their mamá seated on the worn olive sofa in the sala. "Are you sure neither of you wants a beer?"

"Pobrecita," her mom commiserated, shaking her head at the drink offer and repeating her "poor thing" as she opened her arms for a hug. "Come sit with me, I miss you."

"Mamá, I've been home for two weeks now. How can you still miss me?" Cat teased. But she wormed her way in between Mariana and their mom, shoving her sister over to the next cushion with a solid hip check.

"Hey! I don't have to stick around for this abuse," Mariana complained. "I passed up a nap by our apartment complex pool with Angelo. A rare date opportunity for us since our schedules are so freaking busy lately."

"Gracias for coming to cheer me up, querida hermana." Cat patted her sister's thigh, teasing her because she couldn't help doing so but also extremely thankful for Mariana's unique mix of sensibility and compassion during these past couple of weeks of heartache and indecision.

Today was a rare occasion with the three of them alone at the apartment. The living room was home base for all eleven Capuletas, even the five older girls, who lived on their own. Usually any mix of them—if not all—could be found hanging out here in the sala or in the back courtyard. But a Sunday afternoon at the end of June meant the four teens were off enjoying the sunny weather with friends. Blanca, Violeta, and Sabrina were off getting their nails done, and Papo was busy making a run to the hardware store to finish repairing one of the toilets in the downstairs community center.

Wrapped in her mother's embrace, her older sister clasping her hand in solidarity, Cat stared at the collection of vases scattered around the sala. Gifts Patricio had sent since her return, each filled with long-stem roses and colorful lantana—the orange, red, and yellow lantana buds aching reminders of their time at his beach house. He had also made a donation in her name to the community center's music program; another to her familia's church, Little Flower Basilica; and a third to an organization here on San Antonio's West Side working to ensure the area's cultural heritage wasn't erased in the course of ongoing gentrification efforts.

The roses were beautiful, the lantana a sentimental touch that brought the sting of tears to her eyes. But the donations to her familia, her comunidad, her sanctuaries . . . Those spoke of how much Patricio understood what and who was important to her.

And yet, if that were true, how could he have lied and misled her so grossly? How could she ever trust him again after that? How could she trust herself, when she'd done the one thing she had promised she never would: put herself in a position that allowed a man to hold all the cards.

She sighed, her heart heavy, her mind confused.

"Ay, mija, when are you going to talk to him?" her mamá asked.

"Never."

Mariana squeezed Cat's hand and glowered at her at the same time Mamá softly swatted Cat's head, still resting on her shoulder. "No seas mala," Mamá chided.

"I'm not being mean. I'm protecting myself."

"Protecting or hiding?" Mariana pointed out, her perception spot-on, as usual. "I'm not going to tell you what to do—"

"Famous last words," Cat muttered.

"Oye, ingrata, watch it," her sister growled, mussing Cat's hair playfully. "Stop being ungrateful, you little brat. My point is, you said yourself you overheard him talking. Sí, he shouldn't have gone behind your back. That was uncalled for."

"Pero . . ." Cat nudged when Mariana didn't continue.

"But you didn't give him a chance to fully explain. Which could still be a load of crap, who knows." Mariana shrugged, a *beats me* expression scrunching her hawklike nose and high cheekbones. "You didn't stick around to find out. And the guy's putting in some serious effort trying to get through to you. I mean, it's a freaking floral shop in here. And I'm not taking any more vases to the ER break room."

"Mija, you care about him. This, I know. Porque si no, you would have taken his calls already and told him vete pa'l carajo, verdad?"

Cat exchanged knowing smirks with her sister. Yeah, any other guy and she would have definitely told him to go to hell days ago.

But her heart and her head couldn't let go of him. Not yet. Maybe not ever.

"I do," she admitted. "That's why his betrayal hurts so much. Worse, if I was so wrong about him, how can I trust my judgment about anything anymore?"

"Ay, mija, you are too hard on yourself," Mamá told her. "You have a good head on your shoulders, Catalina. Without your business smarts, our music school wouldn't have taken off like it did. Our classes wouldn't be full, with people on a waiting list. Las Nubes would not have been so sought-after even before you girls were crowned Battle Champs. Sí, all of us work hard, pero tú, you are sharp and shrewd and bold in the best ways."

"¡Oye!" Mariana nudged Cat's knee with her own. "You know how much I despise feeding your ego." The three of them shared a laugh; then her sister continued, Mariana's tone her special brand of pep-talk positive and ER-room serious. "But your gut instincts have rarely failed you, Cat. Even when we were kids. And I'm not so sure they totally have now. I mean, you even said, in the beginning, something felt off. There's no need to doubt yourself. I really think you should just talk to him about it."

Ay, how she wanted to believe that they were right. Praying for wisdom, Cat fingered the crucifix on her gold chain and let out a soul-weary sigh. "Maybe I will, at some point. But I also need to figure out my future with Padua."

"Attagirl," Mariana cheered.

"Así es," Mamá agreed.

Cat sat up, their words of encouragement the final nudge she needed to flip a mental light switch on, signaling an end to her dreary self-pity party. She was Catalina freaking Capuleta. If Padua wasn't already convinced of it, the powers that be would learn soon enough how lucky they were to have her on their roster of talent.

"You're both right. I've licked my wounds long enough. It's time for me to get back in the business of kicking ass and taking names. What is it you call these times, Mamá? Teachable moments?"

Her mom nodded, but Cat didn't miss the wary glance she exchanged with Mariana.

"Y Patricio? What do you plan to do about him?" her sister asked.

"Nothing. I'll get over it. I'll get over . . . him." Cat's voice caught as she struggled to spit out the lie.

Mamá reached for Cat's hands, her brown eyes serious, intent. "¿Lo quieres, mija? Dime la verdad."

Did she love him?

With her mom asking her to tell the truth, there was no way Cat could lie again. "Sí, Mamá, I do, pero I'm afraid. What if I—"

"Shhhh." Mamá placed a finger gently on Cat's lips. "That is all I needed to hear. Love isn't perfect, mija. We all make mistakes. Pero lo importante es how you and your partner work through it together. If you love each other, you will find a way."

Cat frowned, uncertain how exactly she was supposed to "find a way," only certain that her heart ached. And she missed Patricio. His teasing, his laughter, their ease with each other, the way their creativity flowed when they wrote together. His bear hugs and delicious kisses. Everything about him.

But he had broken her trust, and that . . . that hurt on a soul-deep level.

"Ay, can you still smell Fabiola's burned bacon from breakfast? That girl and her terrible cooking skills. She will starve when she decides to move out on her own." Mamá rose and crossed to one of the windows overlooking the back courtyard. "I'm going to open this to air out the house. Pero don't let me forget about it because the air-conditioning is on, okay?"

Cat looked at Mariana, who seemed equally confused by Mamá's sudden complaint. The burned smell hardly lingered in the air anymore. Then again, Mamá had a nose that could sniff out food starting to spoil in the fridge when nobody else noticed. So, who was Cat to argue with her mom now?

"Bueno, I should probably get going," Mariana said. "Angelo is grilling chicken for fajitas, and I agreed to make the rice and refried beans."

Hugs were shared between the three of them, and Cat was confirming the coming week's rehearsal date for Mariachi Las Nubes when the sound of a guitar strumming out in the courtyard carried through the open window.

They exchanged curious glances, Mariana adding a *who knows* shrug while Mamá shushed them. The music grew louder, and Cat recognized the opening bars of the old classic "Bésame Mucho." A rich baritone voice she regularly heard in her dreams sang the first line, a lover's lament begging his sweetheart to kiss him as if it were the last time. Her heart stuttered, her breath catching on a gasp.

She raced to the window and pulled aside the faded curtain to find Patricio, dressed in full charro, standing in the courtyard below. His favorite guitar hung from a black strap slung around one shoulder, the instrument's neck cradled in his left hand, his right strumming the strings as he serenaded her.

Above her, on the third floor, a window screeched open, and Cat heard Señora Pérez's "Ay, Dios mío" followed by her yelling for her husband to come quickly because El Príncipe was here. Patricio tipped his head at the older woman's cry of "te queremos, Príncipe," but his gaze never left Cat's.

What was the fool doing? Soon the entire neighborhood would gather in the courtyard, and with the way news traveled in their comunidad, word would get out that he was at Casa Capuleta giving an acoustic show and the paparazzi would descend.

She pressed her hands to her heated cheeks and mouthed the word for him to stop. He winked and flashed his sexy grin.

She motioned for him to come up. He sang louder, held an angsty note longer. His voice rich and strong, the lyrics pouring from him as if he had written them for her.

"Go to him," Mariana whispered from behind her.

"Sí, vete, mija," her mom agreed.

Patricio held a hand over his heart. "Forgive me," he called, forgoing the lyrics for his own sincere words. "I messed up. But I'll do everything and anything to make it up to you. Te quiero, Catalina Capuleta. Bésame. Bésame mucho."

His beautiful voice drew out the words of the love song, calling to her as she raced out of the apartment. In seconds she ran down the short hallway, then burst onto the second-floor landing overlooking the courtyard.

Patricio swung around to face her, his expression an endearing mix of hope, love, and remorse. She grabbed the metal railing, her legs suddenly weak, her heart pounding an allegrissimo tempo in her chest.

Slowly, he approached the stairs as he strummed his guitar, stopping at the bottom to gaze up at her.

"In the beginning, I was captivated by your energy and determination. Your creativity and joy for . . . for everything. And I thought maybe being around you could help me find my creativity and joy again. I figured if your songs were on a Padua label, it would still be a win for you. I was wrong. Horribly wrong. And for that, I'm sorry."

His honesty and humility humbled her. She took the first step down, her sandal heel clanking on the metal.

"The more time we spent together, the more captivated I found myself. Enthralled by your strength and sense of self. Enamored by the way you push me, tease me, challenge me, and make me laugh. I hear music in my head again, and it's all because of you. I'm writing again, because you helped me be comfortable with the real me. And for that, I am eternally grateful."

Ay, how could she not fall for this man when he wooed her with heartfelt admissions like this?

Cat took the next step, and another, her gaze never leaving his.

"It's not that I don't want to release our album right away. But I know it's important for you to succeed on your own merit. We both have something we want to prove. And I figured, you writing Grammy-winning songs for others, working with different talent and gaining industry recognition in your own right, separate from me, while I finished my album, would give you the kind of street cred you deserve, I don't want to give our songs away to anyone. *They're ours.* Our first of many, I hope. That's why I've asked Padua to let me add a third album to my contract. A Patricio y Catalina album, filled with duets and solos, written by us, sung by us, together."

She was so shocked by his idea that she missed the next step and nearly did a head dive the rest of the way down. Somehow, Patricio managed to sling his guitar around to his back, take the bottom four steps in one huge leap, and dive in to catch her before she face-planted at his feet.

Holding her tightly in his embrace, he buried his head in her neck. "I'm so sorry, Catalina. You were right. It was a dickish move, born out of my desire to help you achieve your dreams, but executed in the wrong way. Please tell me you'll forgive me. Please say you'll come make beautiful music with me. Now and always."

She clung to him, her heart racing. Love for him filled every part of her until she felt like she might burst.

"I'm sorry I didn't give you a chance to explain," she said, pulling back to cup his handsome face. "I automatically went into self-protective mode. Let old fears take hold, and that wasn't exactly fair to you. I want to believe in us. And while my trust is a bit shaky right now, I do believe you had my best interests at heart. But we're supposed to be partners, and remember one of the rules I learned from Papo's feud? So, no more secrets. No more 'fixing things' on your own. Deal?"

He nodded, hope filling his beautiful coffee eyes.

"There's one more problem, though," she told him.

"What? Why?" His arms tightened around her as if he refused to let her go. "Tell me and I can fix it!"

Touched by his frantic determination, she stretched up on her toes to drop a quick peck on his lips. "I think we're gonna have to forget about the other rule. It's obvious that you are emotionally attached to me. I mean, was there ever any doubt that would happen? So, we'll have to find a way to deal with that."

His sexy grin made a heart-stopping, pulse-thrumming appearance. "I can think of a lot of ways—wicked, delectable ways—to deal with how I feel about you, Catalina Capuleta."

"Promises, promises," she murmured. Tucking her head against his neck, she breathed in his earthy-ginger cologne and snuggled into his warmth. "Ay, I've been miserable without you."

"Good," he teased. "Because I've been miserable, too. Alberto is tired of my moaning and groaning. He kicked me out of my own house yesterday!"

Leaning back, Cat slid her hands up his chest, wrapping them around his nape to hug him close. "About that album. I'd say 'Catalina y Patricio' has a much better ring to it, don't you think?"

Laughter shook his strong body, the vibrations carrying deliciously into hers.

Patricio reached up to gently tuck her hair behind her ears. He caressed their tender shells, then leaned down to press his forehead against hers. "We can draw straws, okay, querida? Now, put me out of my misery already. Kiss me, Catalina. Bésame, bésame mucho . . ."

He crooned the words until her lips touched his. Then the song, the courtyard, the neighbors and familia watching from their windows faded away, and it was only the two of them and the *I burn, I pine, I perish for you* love they shared.

ACKNOWLEDGMENTS

Sí, my name is on the cover of this book, and I am extremely proud of that accomplishment. But I know that I didn't—couldn't—write Cat and Patricio's novel without the help of so many others along the way.

Sending heartfelt gracias to . . .

Farrah and Kwana . . . Our daily texts and pick-me-up messages have been lifesavers during these pandemic times; my writing cave would have been super lonely without you.

The incomparable #LatinxRom amigas, whose business savvy, laughter, and "juntas podemos" attitude mean the world to me: Alexis, Mia, Sabrina, Adriana, Zoraida, Diana, Liana, Angelina, and Natalie. Our Zoom meetups and conversations are always the vitamin B shot in the arm I need to fight the good fight alongside you. Abrazos, mis queridas amigas.

Sonali, Barbara, Jamie, and Liz . . . Cat and Patricio's story finally started coming to life during our retreat, and your cheers along the way—with Virginia, Sally, and Falguni, too—helped me silence the impostor syndrome doubts when they raised their pesky voices.

Randy, a dear high school friend with some pretty cool entertainment-industry experience . . . thanks for your patience with my random texts about tour buses, hotel parking lots, and life on the road.

Becca Syme and the Better Faster Academy coaches and community . . . learning about my Strengths thanks to your insight, guidance, and willingness to share has been truly enlightening—professionally and personally—and also a huge help while I crawled inside the heads of Patricio and Catalina, two people with totally different Top Ten Strengths from me. ☺

Rebecca Strauss, agent extraordinaire . . . whether it's coffee and croissants in NYC, phone calls in Florida, or emails at all times of the day, your guidance and Team Pris go-get-'em spirit are often just what I need!

My fabulous editors, Maria Gomez and Lindsey Faber . . . your feedback and suggestions really helped make Cat and Patricio shine; it's such a joy to work with you both!

My assistant, Melissa . . . you help make the business side of this author life fun; I'd be floundering without your stellar graphics, organizational skills, and positive personality! ☺

Mami and Papi . . . for the times you whoop-whooped my daily word count, cooked me food so I ate something other than dark chocolate–covered coffee beans and popcorn when a deadline loomed, gently reminded me to not get sucked into a K-drama because I had to get words on the page, and for being my *biggest* cheerleaders and the inspiration for all my characters' HEAs. ¡Los quiero con toda mi alma!

Jackie, my big sis, main beta reader and scene-brainstorming partner, and #1 YOLO buddy . . . we were down to the wire with the first draft, finishing just in time for a familia reunion happy hour in San Antonio, and I couldn't have done it without you!

Alexa, Gabby, and Belle . . . for the "it's your time, Mom" cheers, the out-of-town writing spots that refilled my well, the reminders to get more sleep, and your unwavering confidence in me. You three are my most prized blessings . . . "I'll love you forever!"

ABOUT THE AUTHOR

Photo © 2015 Michael A. Eaddy

Priscilla Oliveras is a *USA Today* bestselling author and 2018 RWA RITA double finalist who writes contemporary romance with a Latinx flavor. Proud of her Puerto Rican–Mexican heritage, she strives to bring authenticity to her novels by sharing her culture with readers. Her books have earned starred reviews from *Publishers Weekly*, *Kirkus Reviews*, and *Booklist* along with praise from *O, The Oprah Magazine*, the *Washington Post*, the *New York Times*, *Entertainment Weekly*, Frolic, and more. She earned her MFA in Writing Popular Fiction from Seton Hill University, where she currently serves as adjunct faculty while also teaching the online class "Romance Writing" for ed2go. A longtime romance-genre enthusiast, Priscilla is also a sports fan, beach lover, and Zumba aficionado who often practices the art of napping in her backyard hammock. For more information, visit www.prisoliveras.com.